SPELLBOUND

Praise for Jean Copeland

The Ashford Place

"[A] charming story that I can recommend to anyone who likes a well-written mystery with a good dose of romance."—*Rainbow Reflections*

The Revelation of Beatrice Darby

"Debut author Jean Copeland has come out with a novel that is abnormally superb. The pace whirls like a hula-hoop; the plot is as textured as the fabric in a touch-and-feel board book. And, with more dimension than a stereoscopic flick, the girls in 3-D incite much pulp friction as they defy the torrid, florid, horrid outcomes to which they were formerly fated."—*Curve*

"This story of Bea and her struggle to accept her homosexuality and find a place in the world is absolutely wonderful...Bea was such an interesting character and her life was that of many gay people of the time—hiding, shame, rejection. In the end, though, it was uplifting and an amazing first novel for Jean Copeland."—*Inked Rainbow Reads*

The Second Wave

"This is a must-read for anyone who enjoys romances and for those who like stories with a bit of a nostalgic or historic theme."—*Lesbian Review*

"Copeland shines a light on characters rarely depicted in romance, or in pop culture in general."—*The Lesbrary*

"The characters felt so real and I just couldn't stop reading. This is one of those books that will stay with me a long time."—*2017 Rainbow Awards Honorable Mention*

Summer Fling

"The love story between Kate and Jordan was one they make movies about, it was complex but you knew from the beginning these women had found their soul mates in each other."—*Les Rêveur*

Praise for Jackie D

The Rise of the Resistance

"I was really impressed by Jackie D's story and felt it had a truth and reality to it. She brought to life an America where things had gone badly wrong, but she gave me hope that all was not lost. The world she has imagined was compelling and the characters were so well developed."—*Kitty Kat's Book Review Blog*

"Jackie D explores how racist, homophobic, xenophobic leaders manage to seize, manipulate, and maintain power."—*Celestial Books*

Lambda Literary Award Finalist *Infiltration*

"Quick question, where has this author been my entire life?…If you are looking for a romantic book that has mystery and thriller qualities, then this is your book."—*Fantastic Book Reviews*

Lands End

"This is a great summer holiday read—likeable characters, great chemistry between the leads, interesting and unusual premise, well written dialogue, an excellent romance without any unnecessary angst. I really connected with both leads, and enjoyed the secondary characters. The attraction between Amy and Lena was palpable and the romantic storyline was paced really well."—*Melina Bickard, Librarian, Waterloo Library (London)*

Lucy's Chance

"Add a bit of conflict, add a bit of angst, a deranged killer, and you have a really good read. What this book is a great escape. You have a few hours to decompress from real-life's craziness, and enjoy a quality story with interesting characters. Well, minus the psychopath murderer, but you know what I mean."—*Romantic Reader Blog*

Pursuit

"This book is a dynamic fast-moving adventure that keeps you on the edge of your seat the whole time…enough romance for you to swoon and enough action to keep you fully engaged. Great read, you don't want to miss this one."—*Romantic Reader Blog*

By the Authors

Jean Copeland

The Revelation of Beatrice Darby

The Second Wave

Summer Fling

The Ashford Place

Jackie D.

Infiltration: Book I of the After Dark Series

Pursuit: Book II of the After Dark Series

Lands End

Lucy's Chance

The Rise of the Resistance: Phoenix One

Visit us at www.boldstrokesbooks.com

SPELLBOUND

by

Jean Copeland and Jackie D.

2020

SPELLBOUND

ISBN 13: 978-1-63555-564-6

This Trade Paperback Original Is Published By
Bold Strokes Books, Inc.
P.O. Box 249
Valley Falls, NY 12185

First Edition: January 2020

CREDITS
EDITOR: BARBARA ANN WRIGHT
PRODUCTION DESIGN: STACIA SEAMAN
COVER DESIGN BY TAMMY SEIDICK

Acknowledgments

Thank you to our editor, Barbara Ann Wright, for helping us craft our words with the most witchy intent. Thank you to Bold Strokes Books for always being so supportive of our wild ideas. To the women at Fierce Femm Media for listening to our ideas, and your endless support. To our family and friends who endure our long absences while we dive into the worlds spinning in our minds. And, finally, to the readers who are always willing to take these journeys with us.

"We are the granddaughters of the witches they weren't able to burn."—Tish Thawer

We dedicate this story to the memory of the women who suffered and died during the Salem Witch Trials of 1692 at the hands of men with unchecked political power and very little common sense.

CHAPTER ONE

Raven Dare gripped the Banshee by the throat and pushed her against a wall in the dank alley. She held the tip of the gold knife specially crafted for Banshee-slaying over the spirit's heart. "You made me chase you. I don't like chasing anyone in my personal or professional life. Now, you're going to tell me where the demon is hiding."

The creature opened her mouth, revealing rows of jagged, rotten teeth encircling a black hole. She screamed with such ferocity that Raven had to fight the urge to move away and cover her ears.

"Holy hell, your voice is as terrible as the first round of castoffs from *American Idol*." She tightened her grip around the creature's neck and squeezed. The glove she wore with gold strands woven throughout made the entity wince in pain. "Where is he? Tell me, and I won't drag out the process of sending you back to hell."

Raven recoiled from the blood-red eyes starting to ooze a black substance reeking of sulfur and soil. Raven imagined this was the smell of hatred and fear. When she opened her mouth to scream again, Raven plunged the gold knife into her heart. The beast dissolved into vapor, leaving no trace of its existence.

Raven put the knife back in its sheath and stuck the glove in her back pocket. She pulled a cigarette box from a cargo pocket, shook one out of the pack, and placed the filter between her lips. She flicked her lighter, but the end started to burn on its own.

She looked up into the air. "You can light a cigarette for me but won't lift a finger to help with a Banshee? Thanks, you're the best." She took a deep drag and shook her head. She leaned against the wall behind her and wiped the sweat from her face with her forearm. "No smart-ass comment? No comeback? Are you losing your mojo or something?"

Morgan emerged from the darkness. As she sauntered toward Raven, her white gown flowed around her, encircling her in luminescence. "You annoy me."

Raven let out a slight laugh as she took another drag. "I've been accused of much worse."

Morgan approached Raven and used her body to pin her against the wall. The soft curve of her neck and the way her blond hair brushed against Raven's cheek was intoxicating. Raven also knew this was intentional, a side effect from being near the Queen Witch. Morgan removed the glove from Raven's pocket, and it disappeared into thin air.

"I should've trusted this to someone else. You clearly weren't up for the task." Morgan placed the tip of her finger on Raven's cheek and traced down the side of her face and over her breasts.

Raven knew better than to rebuff her. Morgan was fueled by these games. Having been alive, or existing, for thousands of years, she found very little entertainment left to enjoy. Making subtle and sometimes not-so-subtle sexual advances was one of her predilections, and hell hath no fury like a witch denied her pleasure.

"She wouldn't stop screaming," Raven said. "I was getting a migraine."

"Your lack of innovation is infuriating," Morgan said, turning away from her.

Raven crushed the cigarette out on the brick wall. "Yeah, well, the same can be said about your unwillingness to assist on these little missions you send me on."

"I can't interfere. I can only keep the balance. You know that." She waved her hand. "I'll send one of the others to find the demon."

Raven's throat burned with anger. "I can do it. Banshees are impossibly unpredictable. I'll track down something else. Ghouls are always willing to trade for information." She dared to double down with a semi-defiant glare. "I'm not going back on our deal."

Morgan smiled at her and ran her fingertips over Raven's lips. "Don't worry. I'm not breaking or letting you out of our deal. Your uncle remains in suspended animation, unharmed. Magic is keeping his heart pumping and his lungs working. That said, I need you for a new mission."

Raven pulled her sunglasses out of her pocket and put them on, a shield of sorts. She knew Morgan could read her emotions without seeing her eyes, but this was as much a fight as she could bolster without infuriating the witch. "Where now?"

"Salem, Massachusetts," Morgan purred in her ear.

Raven stifled a groan. "You can't be serious. Salem's a cliché, a tourist trap. Nothing's there for me to do."

"It wasn't always a tourist trap. The energy there is heavy, and the history is violent. A shift is getting ready to happen, a disturbance of some kind, and I need you there when it comes to fruition." Morgan backed away toward the dark corner of the building.

"That's all you're going to tell me? I don't even know what gear I need or what I could be up against," Raven called after her. "Morgan."

Morgan had already disappeared, but Raven heard her faintly reply, "That's all I know."

Raven gathered herself and headed back to her car. If she left now, she could be in Salem the following night. She checked her trunk. She had enough weapons to take on almost any creature she knew existed, but that didn't mean she was prepared for all the possibilities. Several times in the past she'd encountered a new being, some entity she'd never heard of, and narrowly survived to tell the tale. She hoped Salem wouldn't be that kind of adventure.

She only owed Morgan one more favor, and when it was accomplished, her uncle would recover. Then they could figure out what to do next. She knew they'd never be fully free from Morgan because that wasn't how her family's curse worked. But she'd have her uncle back, and maybe that would alleviate some of her loneliness.

Hazel Abbot heard her dress tear right before she dropped her purse on the steps of her shop. She put a hand over her eyes and groaned with embarrassment when she looked behind her and saw the hem caught in the door. She tugged on it carefully, not wanting to tear it more or give away her mistake to the early morning tourists in the vicinity. When the cloth wouldn't budge, she reached for her keys now a foot away as if they were trying to escape her klutzy behavior, too.

After a few delicate maneuvers that allowed her to capture her keys without flashing her backside to the entire street, she undid the lock and yanked her dress from the door. Tossing items back into her purse, Hazel cursed herself for forgetting to buy coffee beans the day before, thus forcing her to venture into town for her morning caffeine fix and into this whole mess.

As she reached for her favorite lip gloss, a passerby absently kicked it out into the street. *You've got to be kidding me.* Hazel stood, took a deep breath, and pushed her glasses up her nose. *Okay, you're off to a rough start this morning, but things can only improve from here.* She still looked up and down the street several times before retrieving her lip gloss, convinced that if she was going to get hit by a car, this would be the morning.

With her gloss back inside her purse, she silently thanked the Goddess and inspected her dress: a minor tear that she could fix later. She wasn't turning back to go inside now, not until she had her large coconut roast with a shot of espresso. She moved quickly toward Front Street, wanting to beat the tourists to her favorite coffee house.

Salem, Massachusetts, had been her family's home for generations, and although there was almost always an influx of tourists, October drew more people than any other time. Some of the residents found their half a million, temporary neighbors to be nothing but a headache. But Hazel always considered it to be a bit of a rush. Business would boom this time of year. Last year, she sold more books in October than she had throughout the entire year. People would visit from all over the world to take part in the festivities. Dressed in fantastic costumes, they'd dance in the streets and seek out Salem's famed psychics for readings and guidance.

Today was the first day of October, and she could already smell the change in the air. The aroma of rain mixed with the changing leaves and burning wood. It was her favorite time of year. The morning's mishaps began to glide out of her memory as she turned in to the coffee shop. The owner had changed the artwork from the previous week, apparently preparing for the season as well. She paused to appreciate the diversity and individuality of the chosen pieces—a painting of black cats with halos, skeletons made out of papier-mâché, and a lamp that looked like a pug.

She had turned her head almost completely sideways while examining the pug lamp when the barista got her attention. "The usual this morning, Hazel?"

She tore herself away from the unusual lamp and walked to the counter. "Yes, thank you, Tim." He handed her the steaming cup, and her mouth watered in anticipation of the first sip. "You're my absolute favorite person of the day."

He smiled. "It's only seven thirty. How many other people have you had to interact with?"

She breathed in the wonderful fullness of the coffee and took another sip. "Only one, and they kicked my lip gloss into the street. But that was after I ripped my dress and dropped my purse."

He cleaned the steam wand attached to the espresso machine. "Then that one is on the house."

She shook her head. "You don't have to do that."

He tossed the rag onto the counter. "I'm going for your favorite person of the week." He winked at her and moved to the other side of the counter where a line was starting to form.

"I'll square with you later. Thanks, Tim."

She turned toward the door with a bit more bounce in her step. Maybe today wouldn't be so bad after all. She walked back out into the street, retracing her steps to her bookstore and apartment. She eyed the cobblestone sidewalks, not wanting to make a misstep while running through the things on her to-do list. She needed to unpack a few boxes in the storeroom, finish dusting, and she needed to create a Facebook invite for a reading she had set up with a local author.

Hazel inhaled deeply, allowing the crisp air to chill her throat. Despite the morning's poor start, everything seemed to be on track; she had a plan for the day. She loved plans. Anything out of the ordinary could lead to impulsivity, and impulsivity could lead to poor decisions. Hazel didn't subscribe to such behavior.

She unlocked the door to her store, flipped the sign on her window, telling the world she was open for business, and turned on the stereo behind her counter. She sipped her coffee as she checked her store's email account and smiled when she saw one from a regular customer inquiring about a specific occult collection he was interested in purchasing in its entirety. She scanned her computer inventory list and hit "select." Today was definitely going to be a good day.

CHAPTER TWO

Salem, Massachusetts, 1692

The carriage transporting the latest sweep of accused witches into custody ground to a halt outside Salem Village jail. After being jostled about in the dark of night, Sarah Hutchinson Cooper was grateful for the abrupt stop even though it meant her immediate imprisonment. Woozy and trembling, Sarah clutched her frock through her shackles and lifted it slightly to allow her to descend the back of the carriage. The two marshals seized her under her arms on either side and dragged her down and toward the jail, knocking her bonnet over her eyes. She stumbled as she tried to regain her footing.

Using her shoulder to shift the bonnet back into place, she implored her captors. "Please, good sirs. My husband, Thomas Cooper, knows not of this charge against me. He hath been several days gone, venturing to Beverly to purchase a heifer. 'Tis a false charge of witchery upon me. He shall bear witness to my goodness."

"Silence, Goody Cooper," replied one of the marshals, a young man Sarah recognized as a former hand on her farm. "Your pleas mean little as we are but dutiful servants of the law."

The less polite marshal reeking of cider bent toward her ear. "Aye, with a husband 'several days gone' you and your sisters in abomination had many a night to gather in the wood to conjure and compact with the devil."

"I beg, sir," Sarah insisted. "I have done nothing of the sort."

"Speak not your lies, Goody Cooper," he replied. "Like the

pretenses of all you night-flyers, they will soon be made plain before the wise and venerable tribunal assembled at Salem."

They ushered her into the dank cellar that had been fitted with irons to accommodate the growing number of accused. Sarah shuddered at the raw, chill air and fetid stench of prisoners crowded into cells meant to house no more than three or four at a time. She started at the clank of the key ring against the bars as the first marshal unlocked the heavy, foreboding cell door. After a forceful palm pushed her inside, the other marshal completed their appointed task with a slam of the door.

Sarah shielded her nose against the odor of unclean bodies and sickness with the back of her hand as she moved in the darkness among the dull moans and sobs of a dozen or more women and girls. She came to stop when she kicked a lump on the ground, a lump whose groan was unrecognizable as human. She lifted her shackled hands to the wall torch and bent it toward the ground to see what she'd nearly fallen over.

"No, please, no." The beseeching voice emanated from under a protective arm.

Sarah reached down to touch the dark-skinned woman's shoulder. "Pray, calm yourself, woman. I mean not to hurt you."

The woman lowered her arm. "Praise be to God," she whispered, never looking up to see who was addressing her.

The accent, the voice, although thick with sorrow and fatigue, sounded familiar. After the figure lowered her arm, Sarah froze. Once able, she parted her dry lips and blurted, "Ayotunde?"

The woman opened her eyes and raised her head from the strewn pile of hay on which she curled as tightly as a mouser sleeping before a hearth. "Miss Sarah?" she asked, rubbing her eyes. "My Lord, my Lord. That be you, Miss Sarah?"

Sarah's heart fluttered as she stared at the beautiful face she had missed so dearly over the years. Even surrounded by such sadness and inhumanity, she could not deny the pure joy at seeing her beloved childhood and adolescent companion and caretaker again. "Yes, it is I, my friend. I thought my eyes were deceived when I looked upon your face. How do you fare within these vile walls?" She crouched and helped her as she struggled into an upright position.

"Your visage do fill me with hope," she said, struggling to smile. "But wherefore you be taken in, Miss Sarah?"

Sarah sat beside her on the makeshift bed of hay. "The town has lost its sense, Ayotunde. I be named to witchcraft by the Parris children."

"Aye. Reverend Parris's girls do accuse many, but you?"

"I give their unholy vengeance good reason when I run them off the property as the troublesome imps they are. Then betimes the marshals come to me with a warrant and shackles."

"How do they come to charge you, Miss Sarah? You are no base woman in town, no beggar...or slave."

Sarah's heart grew somber at Ayotunde's awareness of her own lot. "It matters not in these times. And my husband be yet in Beverly on his errand. He will not learn of this till he return to our empty home."

"Oh, Miss Sarah," Ayotunde said. "It grieve my heart to see you so wretched. God's grace surely will shine on you."

Sarah took her hand. "If there be a God, He must surely shine on you, too, Ayotunde. I will implore the magistrates as to your innocence as strenuously as I shall my own."

"Aye. Bless you, Miss Sarah." Ayotunde stared at her with dark, weary eyes, her once beautiful brown skin now ashen, her hands spotted with sores. "'Tis heartening to see you again. It be a fair work of Providence."

Sarah forced a smile. "It is a blessed providence indeed to see your face, but the circumstance in which we meet again must needs be the work of some other, darker force running loose among the village."

"I am yet warmed by your smile." Ayotunde managed to lift the corners of her mouth as she leaned her head against the wall, clearly depleted of physical strength.

"Hath my brother made efforts to free you?"

Ayotunde laughed herself mirthlessly into a cough. After wiping her mouth, she said, "He make none, Miss Sarah. He be the one to summon the authorities for me."

Sarah's mouth dropped. "I do not understand, Ayotunde. How may he come to that when you be the caretaker of his children?"

"I be tellin' Noah and Joseph and Anna stories of my girlhood in Africa, how the children dance to drum songs and sing with merry hearts. Like I done with you as a child."

Recalling her own childhood with Ayotunde as her keeper, Sarah's horror was not lessened by the explanation. She whispered, "Did you make the poppets dance like you done with me when I was a child?"

Ayotunde swallowed with difficulty. "Aye."

Sarah tried to remain calm. "Had you been holding them in your hands as they danced?"

She lowered her eyes and shook her head.

"Oh, Ayotunde. You enchanted the poppets to do the magic dance before my brother's children? Were they aghast? Had they run to their father in terror?"

"No, no. They didn't fear the dance, Miss Sarah. Mistress Elizabeth hear the children laugh and see them flit about dancing with the poppets. When she come in, she be struck with terror."

Sarah was silent for a brief period. How could Ayotunde be so careless with the secret craft she'd only ever previously shared with her?

As if reading the full import of Sarah's expression, Ayotunde added, "I thought my mistress be out in the fields gathering flowers."

"My brother's wife out in a field gathering anything?" Sarah shook her head in despair. "She lay about the house as if Satan himself were waiting in the fields to claim her soul if she venture outside and dirty her hems."

"She scream as though Satan be in the children's room dancing, too. Then she grip the children, held them to her skirt, and demand Master Joseph lash me and turn me over for cursing the children's poppets."

Sarah's face grew hot with rage. "God forgive me for such thoughts, but I should like to curse my dear father's soul for willing you to Joseph instead of me while upon his deathbed."

"Property of the father be bequeathed only to sons."

"Aye, but you are not property to me, Ayotunde."

"Bless you, Miss Sarah, but I am yet. Who will put me to auction when I make my confession?"

Sarah was horrified at the implication. "To what will you confess?"

"To their cries of witchcraft. I must confess or they be marchin' me to the gallows. Like they be doin' to Goody Bishop at daybreak."

"Bridget? She be hangin' the morrow?" Sarah gulped as she imagined the unimaginable fate about to befall her sometime friend. "Ayotunde, you must not confess. It is but a pretense. A plot is afoot in Salem Village, a cloud of evil hath rolled in purporting itself to the fearful multitudes as the cleansing of evil. But it is trickery. Something else be upon us."

Ayotunde shifted, seeming to struggle to keep herself upright. "They beat me, Miss Sarah. They beat me and say they hang me for a witch if I deny it more."

"Oh, this be a bitter chill that hath blown into Salem Village," Sarah said, seething. "There have long been factions meant to disrupt our harmony. I have known it. I have seen the widow Bishop driven from her husband's tavern by broken Christians claiming they be in service to God to redeem her soul. She be a good woman. She need no redemption from men of many acreage seeking to claim yet more on the land left her by her late husband." Her hands shook with indignation, not for herself but for her friends. "You and Bridget and these children clinging to their mothers' aprons," she said pointing all around the cell, "be not the evil that we must fear."

Ayotunde chuckled softly. "You speak as a proper lawyer in the court."

Sarah sighed. "I am naught but a proper wife and servant of God."

"You be so much more," Ayotunde said, a twinkle returning to her pallid eyes.

Sarah gripped Ayotunde's hand as she swallowed against her sadness. Then she was taken by a new idea. She bent to the floor and whispered, "Can you not make the jailers dance as you do poppets? Perhaps conjure a spell to send them into a slumber?"

"I try many time till I have fallen over in a near faint. I fear I know not how to conjure against living things. I never learn of no other powers since they take me from my mother as a child."

Despair began creeping into Sarah's heart. "Have you no powers at all to remedy our dire affliction? What of the yarns you spun for me when I was a girl, stories of spells, incantations, magical herbs?"

"They be just stories, Miss Sarah," Ayotunde whispered. "I have no familiarity with the black arts."

Sarah glanced from side to side to ascertain no one was overhearing them and moved closer. "But it be possible you do possess other powers."

Ayotunde gave a lethargic shrug.

Sarah crouched down and whispered in her ear. "Ayotunde, I

know poppets dance not without the touch of a human hand. But I have witnessed you make them do it. I saw you compel sparrows land on my arm when I'm but a little girl. Birds such as they have a natural fear of man, yet they flitted about me like I am their kindred. You possessed that power. I have forgotten it not."

Ayotunde clutched Sarah by the shoulder with a remarkable burst of strength. "I enchant the poppets to dance, but it were not I with the power to make the birds come. It was you."

❖

When Sarah woke on the cell floor, she shook her head, gathering her wits enough to realize her reunion with her former house servant, whom she had loved so deeply, was no blissful dream framed within a nightmare.

"Miss Sarah," Ayotunde said as she gently tapped her face. "Do you hear me?"

"Yes, yes." Sarah rose to her knees as she pressed her palms against her burning cheeks. "I fear this ordeal hath weakened me. Strange words now find their way to my ears in my affliction."

"'Tis not an affliction. The words I spake you be true, Miss Sarah. I were wont to keep the secret of your charms from your girlish heart so long that when you blossomed into womanhood, I spared you the knowledge for your own good. But the time finally come for you to know."

"How knoweth you of these charms I possess?"

"I watch you grow up, Miss Sarah. I believe you have the power to transcend."

"How mean you to transcend?"

"There be incantations that can move you in body from here to there."

Sarah was stunned into silence. She'd always felt herself different from her fellow Puritan sisters in that she had often taken walks along the forest edge to gather herbs for healing and commune with furry and feathered wood dwellers, two practices forbidden by her religion and marked as enticements of the devil. Although she knew she was not nor had ever been in allegiance with the devil, she sensed the necessity to keep her activities hidden from others throughout her life.

"What you speak of confounds me greatly, Ayotunde," Sarah said. "In your knowledge, I am capable to move mine own self, soul and body, from within these walls to yonder yard outside?"

"Aye, Miss Sarah."

"Ayotunde, have you not gone daft in your ordeal? I am no witch as the warrant binding me here thus charges."

"Aye, you are not a witch as the warrant charges, a dark spirit meant to harm others. Yet you be a witch none the less."

Sarah's mind was tempest-tossed as she struggled to reconcile Ayotunde's words. Were it possible that she spoke the truth? Were Sarah indeed a witch? If witches existed in the service of good as well as evil, then perhaps it could be true. This, however, was neither the time nor the place to contemplate the moral implications.

"Ayotunde, if thou speakest true, teach me now how to transcend so that I may free us of our confinement."

Her countenance seemed more forlorn in the flickering torchlight. "You cannot free me," she said, holding back tears. "Only you can transcend."

"Then I cannot go," Sarah replied without faltering. "How might I leave my beloved Ayotunde here to rot in chains as I fly free? I shall stay and leave myself to the fate to which I have been dispatched."

"No, Miss Sarah, no. You will die. They be hangin' witches that don't confess."

"I have hurt no one, Ayotunde. I have done no crime against my neighbors. I will give a false confession of bewitchin' to no one. Methinks my eternal life be worth more than this earthly one."

"Surely mine be, too, Miss Sarah. Please. Please don't forsake yours for mine. 'Tis but a wretched one I been born into."

Sarah's emotions finally let go in a torrent. She collapsed on the floor into Ayotunde's arms, her cries joining the chorus of guttural moans filling the darkness. "My heart doth ache for you, Ayotunde. It hath yearned to be joined with yours again since I took Thomas Cooper's hand many a year ago. I begged Father include you in my dowry when I marry, but he wanted not to part with you."

Ayotunde stared longingly into Sarah's eyes. "You fill my heart with joy, Miss Sarah, since you be a child, then yet more as a young woman. That be why you must take your leave of this jail. I cannot watch you wither here."

"I like not this idea of yours, Ayotunde. I must stay with you now. When Thomas return from Beverly, it may be he can save you, too."

Ayotunde looked up at her gravely. "The time for saving be long past, Miss Sarah. You must go. Now let me think on the incantation for your transcendence." She closed her eyes and exhaled deeply.

"But, Ayotunde…"

"Hush." She pressed two fingers against Sarah's lips. After another breath, she pinched her eyes closed, and raised her hand before Sarah's face.

Sarah bit her lip against a sob as she watched Ayotunde mouthing indecipherable words. "I'll come back for you, Ayotunde. I'll find a way."

Ayotunde opened her eyes. "Aye, Miss Sarah. Find a way back to me."

Chapter Three

Raven checked into her hotel on the outskirts of town and headed into Salem on foot. It wasn't quite dark yet, and she wanted to get the lay of the land before Morgan divulged the purpose for sending her here. The shop windows were blanketed in images of witches, psychics, tarot cards, and other ghoulish descriptors. People wandered the streets, taking pictures, and pointing to different locations they intended to visit with their companions, completely unaware of the thin veil of the supernatural they were bumping up against.

Raven had been exposed to this world since she was a child. She knew that things went bump in the night. She understood that the inconsistencies most people shrugged off to coincidence, circumstance, or a weird feeling were the hands of another side trying to latch on to a small piece of the lives they'd had before. Dead or alive were not the only two existences. No, that would be too easy. There were beings and entities that roamed about, each having a purpose that they were convinced was the most crucial in any realm. Some were good, some evil, and some, like Morgan, occupied the space in between. Most people were comfortable living with the concept that things were simply black or white. Raven knew the world was made up of a spectrum of gray, the extent of which would cause most people to go insane if it were revealed.

Raven felt the hair on the back of her neck stand up, and a shiver passed through her. She looked around, trying to locate the source of this small disturbance. Unlike other people who chalked this feeling up to a strange occurrence and forgot it instantly, Raven knew it indicated something was nearby. She noticed a bookstore across the street. The lights glowing inside illuminated a young woman moving books from a box to the shelves.

Raven could tell, even from fifty feet away, this woman was different. The vibe was unlike anything she had felt before. She crossed the street to get a closer look, wanting to make sure nothing was lying in wait, preying on the woman in the store. She didn't sense anything but couldn't stop herself from opening the door either. She felt as if she *needed* to be inside.

"Hello. Welcome to A Witch in Time," said the young woman with a warm smile.

Raven took a step farther inside. "A Witch in Time? That's clever." She shoved her hands in her pockets, unsure what to do next. Now that she was inside, she felt no evil presence, only warmth and tenderness.

The woman smiled, pushing her black-framed glasses up her nose. She tucked her shoulder-length, burnt umber colored hair behind her ear and went back to unpacking boxes. "Thank you for saying that, but I had nothing to do with it. This bookstore has been in my family for generations."

Raven walked to one of the shelves and picked up the *Complete Book of Witchcraft.* "Do you believe in this stuff?"

The woman came over and touched the cover. "Do you?"

Raven was ready to tell her that she didn't, her standard answer whenever anyone spoke on these topics. But the way the woman was looking up at her, seemingly transfixed, made Raven want to tell the truth. "I do."

The woman smiled and took the book, placing it back on the shelf. "Were you looking for something specific? I have a feeling you're already familiar with that one."

"I don't know what I'm looking for." Raven didn't understand where this small streak of honesty was emanating from, but she was strangely enjoying it.

The woman crossed her arms and put her finger to her mouth. "Hmm...well, is there a particular subject you're interested in? *The Three Books of Occult Philosophy* is one of our best sellers."

Raven watched her as she spoke. Her eyes were the color of sapphires. She had never seen anything as blue or as striking in a living person. She had a small dimple on her left cheek that only seemed to appear when she smiled fully. She seemed to have a habit of biting her lower lip when she was thinking, which Raven found both sexy and adorable.

"Do any of those sound interesting?"

Raven blinked, bringing herself back into the moment. She flashed back through the last several seconds, trying to remember the question. "I'm sorry, what?"

She lifted one eyebrow and tilted her head. "I named five or six books that people with a passing curiosity seem to like. Did you not hear me?"

"I'm Raven, Raven Dare." She stuck out her hand.

The woman hesitated but shook her hand anyway. "I'm Hazel Abbot." She squinted. "Dare? That's an interesting last name. Where is your family from?"

"Virginia."

Hazel walked to the other wall of shelves and selected a book from the top. "Are you familiar with Virginia Dare, the first English child of Roanoke?"

Raven was more than familiar. That was the source of her family curse, the very reason her bloodline was tied to the supernatural. Virginia had made a bargain with Morgan le Fay, the Queen of the Witches, centuries earlier to spare her life. In exchange, her bloodline would be compelled to traverse the globe for all time, driven to send evil entities back to their realm. That was why she was here and why the curse must end with her.

Raven was about to explain that she was vaguely familiar with the story when the door opened, and four young women entered, loudly proclaiming that they needed a book of Wiccan spells. Hazel held Raven's eyes for a breath. They were filled with questions and a bit of concern. But the girls were too loud to ignore, and Hazel finally turned her attention to them.

Raven took the opportunity to leave, refusing to look back. She didn't want to know if Hazel was watching her as questions still loomed in those bright sapphire eyes. She didn't know what feelings had just been exchanged between them, but they felt all too comfortable, too much like home.

Raven needed to get away before she accidently let her guard down and put herself and an unsuspecting Hazel in danger.

❖

Hazel wanted to tell Raven to stop. She didn't want her to leave. She wanted to talk to her, discover what caused the flash of pain in her dark eyes when she asked about her last name. Nevertheless, the flurry of giggles and questions from the young women kept her rooted in her spot. She handed them book after book and did her best to answer their obscure questions. This was a regular occurrence in Salem. People came from all over to dip their toe into the unknown, if only for a weekend. Moreover, it was her job to oblige as her livelihood depended on it.

When it was all said and done, they had purchased an array of texts and a few candles, and asked if the famed graveyard was open after the sun went down. Hazel told them that it was not and that they should stay clear, leaving the dead to rest. However, as they spilled out onto the street and into the darkness, Hazel knew where they were going, and no amount of rational warning would prevent it.

She walked to the window and flipped the sign to Closed. Still, she took the time to linger after turning off the main lights, hoping to see Raven somewhere on the street. She tamped down her disappointment after searching for a few moments and headed upstairs to her apartment. She was hungry and still needed to hem her torn dress.

She put some leftovers into the microwave and went to her closet to retrieve her sewing machine. When she opened the closet door, she noticed a book she'd never seen before lying against the shelves. It was wrapped in an old, worn cloth. Her heart jumped into her throat, and she ran to the kitchen for her cell phone to call the police. Someone had been in her apartment. She was ready to dial when reasoning started to weave through her thoughts. The only entrance was through her front door unless someone wanted to scale the side of the building, and that would have been noticed by all the people milling about the city all day. Her door had been locked, and there was no other sign that anyone had been there. Maybe she had left the book in her closet, and it had merely fallen. She received shipments of books from all over the world. Perhaps this one had caught her interest, and she had brought it upstairs and forgotten about it.

Hesitantly, she walked back to her closet and peeked around the corner as if she was a secret agent. The book had fallen open, asking to be inspected. She took a deep breath and rubbed her arms, which had abruptly covered in goose bumps. She dipped her head back around the corner, eyeing the text again. *It's just a book. It's not like it can hurt you.* She took a step closer and stopped. Then another step. The book was there, begging to be read. Finally, she sat down on the floor legs crossed and flipped it open.

When she ran her fingers down the leather binding, they began to tingle as if she'd just run them over a candle. Warmth spread through her body. The pages were old and discolored, some torn, and the ink had all but disappeared from a few. She flipped it shut to see the cover. The emblem that stared back at her looked precisely like a necklace her grandmother had worn. She rushed to her jewelry box and retrieved it. She sat back down with the book and examined the intricacies of each. They were an exact match: a large knotted oak tree with a cross designed from an infinity symbol on the trunk.

She opened the book, and her head began to swim. This was a family history of some kind, a history she'd never been privy to and that her mother had never bothered to divulge. She opened her phone and called her mother. It went straight to voice mail, which was no surprise. Her mother was on a trip with her best friend that she'd waited and saved a lifetime to take. They were exploring the world, visiting places like Africa, Australia, Greece, and Japan. She was three weeks into the three-month voyage, and Hazel had only heard from her once. They were very close, but her mother had warned that her cell reception was spotty, and she would call when she was able.

Hazel felt a bit betrayed by her mother but then realized that she might not have any knowledge of the book either. After all, the book matched her grandmother's jewelry, nothing she'd ever seen on her mother. She flipped it open and started from the beginning. The names of women she had never heard of filled the pages. She focused on one, Sarah Hutchinson Cooper, a great-aunt several times over, who had been a part of the Salem Witch Trials. Her fingers lingered over the name, feeling as if she owed her an apology for what she had been forced to endure.

Hazel had walked the streets of Salem her entire life. She knew the stories, the history, the gory details, but she never knew that her flesh and blood had been part of the tragedy. She'd been told that her family didn't settle here until ten years after the famed event, but she knew now this hadn't been the truth. A bit of anger rumbled inside her stomach as she traced the words. As she touched each one, it illuminated slightly. Surprise and fear caused her to shut the book and shove it away.

Her heart was pounding in her throat, and she felt a severe headache creeping toward her eyes. She wrapped the book back in the cloth and brought it to her kitchen table. She'd have to look at it later; it was all too much for one night. She needed to sit with this new information. After a long day, her mind was clearly playing tricks on her. She needed to eat, shower, and go to bed. She assured herself that this was all happenstance. The light playing tricks on her eyes, probably a symptom from an extraordinary headache she was experiencing. A perfectly reasonable explanation existed for all of this, and she'd figure it out in the morning. Things always looked better in the morning after a good night's sleep.

She lay in bed, doing her best to ignore everything that happened that day, feeling as if the book was calling to her. A small hum rang through every inch of her body, willing her to return to the book. She did the only thing any reasonable person would do: she put her earbuds in and listened to her favorite audiobook, waiting for the familiarity of the words to lull her to sleep.

"Yo, what are you doing napping in front of everyone?" Sarah felt a tap on her calf.

When she opened her eyes, she had to shield them from the blinding midday sun. She barely made out the backlit figure of a Puritan girl chomping like a cow on its cud, holding a strange device between her hands.

"Wherefore am I not jailed?" Sarah's voice was gravelly, as though she'd been asleep for a hundred years.

"Britany and Ashley are working at the jail." The girl rolled her eyes and scratched at her pink hair stashed under her crooked white bonnet. "We're supposed to be walking around greeting tourists. Are you drunk or something?"

Sarah gasped at the suggestion. "Not a drop of draught hath ever passed my lip." She sat up slowly, still light-headed and unsteady. "But I am a bit bewildered."

"Why are you talking like that? We're on break."

"I am Sarah Hutchinson Cooper. It pleases to make your acquaintance." She held out her hand as she gingerly got to her feet, but the girl hadn't noticed as her attention was fixed on the peculiar device. "That charm doth bewitch you."

"Sorry," the girl said as she chewed. "I just switched over to a Samsung from an iPhone, and it's a bitch getting used to it."

Sarah smiled, thoroughly confused at the explanation. "I feel as though I have waked but am yet in a dream," she said, glancing at the parked cars lining the street. "Art thou real?" She reached out to touch the young woman's sleeve.

The girl eyed her with apparent judgment. "Look, I'm gonna get back to work before they fire my ass. My mom's making me pay my spring tuition, so I need this corny-ass job. Be at the Meetinghouse by three forty-five. The trial starts at four."

Sarah was mortified. "Aye. 'Tis no dream then," she whispered to herself. "They mean to clap me in shackles and send me to the gallows, yet. I must find Ayotunde."

She glanced around again, troubled by the unaccountable changes in the village. The people walking about were dressed in garish colors, children were loudly laughing as though possessed, and women's hair hung free and flapped about in the early autumn breeze. How long had she been asleep? And how had she arrived outside on the bench from her jail cell?

As she stepped off the curb, a strident wail startled her back toward the bench.

"Get in the crosswalk before you get clipped, idiot," shouted the man passing by.

"So many shiny, horseless carriages. Heavenly Father," she said, placing her hand over her heart pounding beneath her dress. "The devil hath indeed arrived in Salem."

She grasped fistfuls of her garment and lifted it so she could hurry off down the road. She wasn't sure where she should go. Surely, the marshals would be at her homestead awaiting her return. She thought to run to Bridget Bishop's house, but last she knew, Bridget was also jailed and marked for hanging. Had she been able to escape, too?

As she wandered the streets, she searched the crowds for Ayotunde. She began to realize her incantation had worked. Sarah had clearly transcended time, but the question was, how far had she transcended? Her heart sank when she remembered Ayotunde saying she hadn't the power to physically transcend with her.

Seeing Ayotunde again had brought about memories of the most joyous time in her life, when she and her family's house servant would work together on the homestead baking breads, sweeping the floors, and preparing meals for her father and older brothers. On summer mornings, she and Ayotunde would steal away into the fields to gather wildflowers. Sarah's heart warmed at the memory of her fifteenth summer when she and Ayotunde, who was somewhere in her twenties, had wandered to the outskirts of her father's land, talking about young Thomas Cooper's interest in Sarah.

"The boy want to marry you, Miss Sarah," Ayotunde teased.

Sarah giggled. "He hath not asked for my hand. And I would give it not even if he had."

"His father bring him around when he have business with yours," Ayotunde said. "The boy surely be smitten with you."

The teasing made Sarah uncomfortable. She hadn't liked to think of leaving her father's home or Ayotunde. Times like those when they could enjoy a respite from the drudgery of domestic work and Bible study alone together near the woods were the happiest she could remember.

Ayotunde had torn up a handful of purple-petal wildflowers and approached her. "Miss Sarah Hutchinson," she began, mimicking a man's voice. "I give these to you and ask you be my wife."

Sarah giggled again at Ayotunde's sporting. She curtsied and sniffed the bouquet. "Their fragrance doth make my heart happy."

"And you be the fragrance of my heart, Miss Sarah."

It was not the first time they had exchanged such playful banter. As springtime had brought warmth to the colony, so had it warmed Sarah's heart for her childhood companion. As the sun lowered in the afternoon sky in the summer of 1677, they had held each other in a lingering glance, Sarah studying Ayotunde's bright smile rarely seen in the company of others, and her deep, black eyes full of the same taboo yearning Sarah had recently recognized in herself. Without regard for or fear of custom, piety, or social regulation, Sarah allowed her body to tilt forward ever so slightly until her lips met Ayotunde's.

Now, standing on the bustling streets of Salem, Sarah licked her lips as if she were experiencing the kiss again just as she'd felt it more than fifteen years ago.

She opened her eyes, startled by the intensity of the feeling. With her senses on overload, she scanned her surroundings, trying to regain her composure. Effigies and emblems of witches were scattered about all over town. She looked down where she stood on the hardened ground and discovered the image of a white witch on a broomstick beneath her feet.

Had Reverend Hale failed in his efforts to root out the evil they'd feared had taken a foothold in the village? Was she in danger of being apprehended to sign her name to his book by Old Scratch himself?

Paralyzed by the thought, she stopped walking and picked up her head. The weathered old building before her housed a store called A Witch in Time. "What in God's name…" After glancing around her to ensure the minister hadn't been meandering, she approached the brown wooden door adorned with an herbal pentagram wreath. Afraid of what she might encounter when she knocked, she wondered if Ayotunde's spell had mistakenly sent her to the nether regions of Hell where witches walked freely by day and soared through the air by night.

Perhaps this was her fate after all, given what Ayotunde had revealed about her before casting the spell.

When she raised her hand to knock, a teenage couple breezed past. "'Scuse us," the boy said as they opened the door and went inside.

Sarah scrunched her eyes shut, anticipating the shrieks of terror about to issue forth from within once the children were captured and forced to capitulate to whatever horrid end the hags inside had in store for them.

After a long moment without screams, she opened her eyes and rallied her courage to enter. The jingle of a bell above her head heralded her entrance.

"Hi," the woman said from behind the register. "Let me know if you need help finding anything."

Sarah approached the counter. "Good morrow, Miss," she said, keeping her voice small. "Pray, how comes it there be witches abounding? Have they stopped the hangings?"

Hazel cracked up laughing. "You are *the* best actor I've ever seen." She stepped out from behind the counter and surveyed Sarah from head to toe. "Your look is perfect. You're all ratty and ragged looking, and your style of speech is top-notch. Did you take a class or something?"

"Pray pardon?"

"I hope you're at the top of the pay scale, because if you told me you stepped right out of a time machine, I'd almost believe you."

"Time machine? What is a machine?"

Hazel laughed again. "C'mon, you're killing me."

"Killing?" Sarah's heart sank. "Have you too been condemned to the gallows?"

Hazel's smile shriveled. "You're starting to freak me out a little. Can I help you find something in here?"

"Miss, I am quite bewildered. Last night I was jailed on suspicion of witchcraft and saw my father's house servant, my dear Ayotunde, after many a year. And I wake today free, knowing not where I am."

"You're in Salem, Massachusetts," Hazel said.

"Aye, but the village appears not as it had before I took my slumber. How am I freed? Where is Ayotunde? And what are those shiny carriages that require not a horse for pulling?"

"Cars?" Hazel said, hanging on the "s."

"Cars?"

"The shiny carriages that move without horses."

"Aye," Sarah said pensively. "'Tis a black art indeed." Her thoughts suddenly shifted. "Reverend Hale. What hath become of him? Have the witches run him back to Beverly? I tremble to think on what else they would do to him."

❖

Hazel wasn't sure if she should call the authorities and have this poor woman committed for overnight observation. Clearly, she was not acting.

"Let's start with names. I'm Hazel Abbot." She extended her hand.

"Sarah Hutchinson Cooper," she said with a curtsy.

Hazel choked on her own saliva. She glanced around at the other customers, unsure if someone was trying to punk her. She leaned closer, not wanting anyone to hear her. "Sarah Hutchinson? As in the accused witch who was mysteriously able to escape her fate during the 1692 Salem Witch Trials?"

"It would appear that is I."

Hazel's body flushed, and her hands grew clammy. She recognized the name from the book she had discovered. But there was no possible way they were one and the same. The Sarah Hutchinson in her book, her great-aunt, lived over three hundred years ago. It had to be a coincidence, but everything in her body told her that wasn't at all the case.

Hazel saw no logical reason to believe Sarah. She had to be confused, possibly off her meds, but even as she thought it, something in her subconscious railed against the thought.

"I'd like to help you," Hazel said calmly, not wanting to scare her. "Will you come upstairs with me? Maybe we can figure this out together."

Sarah looked as if she was going to protest, but only for a minute. She studied Hazel's face as though searching for signs of danger. She must not have found any because she indicated her agreement with a nod.

Hazel turned and told the customers they needed to go, that she was closing for the day for a...family emergency. They huffed but walked out of the store. Hazel locked the door and walked Sarah up the stairs to her apartment.

She couldn't make sense of her feelings, but she knew she was doing the right thing. She felt a connection to Sarah, a need to help her, if not protect her. Hazel just needed to figure out why.

CHAPTER FOUR

Raven could feel the shift in the realms. Morgan had been right. Something was happening in Salem. She twirled her lighter on the bar top, watching the blurred reflection in her pint glass. The family curse bestowed upon her when she accepted her uncle's place from Morgan wasn't anything she'd ever wanted, but she accepted her reality all the same.

This shift was unlike anything she'd ever felt. She could sense when a demon was close or when an entity was out of place, but it was nothing like this. It left her more unsettled than she could ever remember being. Her subconscious was drawing her to the bookstore again, but she was trying to sit with the inclination, wanting to make sure it wasn't merely the connection she'd felt to the owner manipulating her senses.

"Another beer?" The bartender stared at her, towel in hand.

"No, thank you," she said, thankful for the break in her thoughts. She threw her money on the bar and walked into the street, unsure where she was headed. As if impelled by an unknown force, she started for A Witch in Time.

She maneuvered down the streets, slightly paying attention to the people who passed: women in heels trying to navigate the cobblestones, people laughing at jokes she couldn't hear, and others deciding on where to eat dinner. It only took her a few minutes until she was once again standing on the other side of the street, looking at the shop.

She glanced down at her watch, surprised to see a Closed sign hanging in the window so early in the evening. She thought about turning around and heading back to the bar, but something told her to stay. The feeling pushed its way up from her stomach and into her throat like an invisible hand, squeezing the air out of her body. She started toward the store, and with each step, the vise around her throat lessened, indicating she was heading in the right direction.

She looked around the side of the building and saw a stairway. With each step, the intensity of the shifting realms filled her body. Her shirt began to stick to her back with sweat seeping from every pore, heightening the effects of the changing night air.

She knocked on the door and waited. When no one came, she tried again, but still no answer. The tightness in her chest started again. She pounded on the door with much more ferocity, and the bolt unlatched.

Hazel looked perplexed as she swung the door open. "What are you doing here?"

Raven hadn't thought about this part. She'd been so focused on following her intuition that she wasn't sure how to explain what was happening. "Are you okay?"

Hazel crossed her arms and looked down the staircase. "Why wouldn't I be okay?"

Raven was trying to figure out what to say next when she saw a woman behind Hazel. She was dressed in Puritan costume, her face scrunched with angst as she stepped lightly across the creaky floor, but Raven had a strong sense that this was no actor.

She drew her seraph blade from its holster. The blade, forged in the other realm, was infused with white light and the only weapon strong enough to kill a demon.

Hazel touched her arm. Raven's body warmed, and a sense of calm came over her. "She's not dangerous. Her name is Sarah."

Raven recoiled, recognizing the sensation from her time with Morgan. "You're a witch?"

Hazel looked confused, as if she'd taken the remark as an accusation. "What? No." She paused and led Raven inside. "At least, that would've been my answer as of yesterday. Now, I'm not so sure."

Raven was overwhelmed with the intensity in the room. The energy enveloping her was undoubtedly from white magic. She looked back and forth between the two women. "You're both witches."

The other woman's face relaxed slightly. "You know of witchcraft?"

Hazel shook her head and stepped closer to Raven. "Who are you exactly?"

She seemed genuinely confused. Her face radiated questions and a great deal of concern. She had no reason to lie. If Hazel's powers were just now emerging, she would gain control of them soon and then would be privy to the realms. She'd be able to see Raven's identity even if she tried to hide it.

"I'm a shadowhunter. I track and banish demons, evil entities, or whatever Morgan le Fay decides." She took off her leather jacket and exposed a tattoo on her right arm, a pentagram with a pair of knives through the emblem, a brand she received once she accepted the curse.

Sarah ran her hands over her face. "Pray, hath Ayotunde sent thee to save me from the gallows?"

"Gallows?" Raven darted her eyes from Sarah to Hazel. "She's serious?"

Hazel stepped in front of Sarah, seeming to block or protect her from Raven. "Who is this Morgan le Fay person? Did she send you?"

Raven struggled to understand what was happening. If Hazel's powers were developing, why had Morgan sent her? Surely Morgan would want to be the one to explain her existence. Plus, who was this odd witch with her?

Raven put her hands up in a sign of acceptance. "I'll answer your questions, but you're going to have to answer some of mine as well." She pointed at Sarah. "For starters, who's the Puritan?"

Sarah stepped forward as if eager to share her story. Her face brightened as she moved around Hazel, who looked less than thrilled. "My name is Sarah Hutchison Cooper, wife of Thomas Cooper. I come from the year sixteen hundred and ninety-two. The Salem magistrates have summoned me after accusations of witchcraft. When jailed, I found my dear friend, Ayotunde, who freed me from my shackles with her chants. She says I possess magical powers, but of witchcraft I know not." Her face turned grave again. "Please...I am much bewildered."

Raven looked at Hazel for her confirmation.

Hazel rubbed her forehead, and Raven couldn't tell if it was out of annoyance or frustration. "Let me show you this book I found."

Hazel disappeared for a few moments and returned carrying a large object covered in cloth. "My mother went to pretty significant lengths to hide this from me, and I'm not sure why. She's on a trip with her friend right now, but when she's finally back in cell range, I have quite a few questions for her."

Raven took the book and placed it on the table. She carefully opened the cloth to reveal the intricate family crest and felt the power vibrating from it. It was warm and peaceful, no dark magic present. She flipped open the cover and started scouring the pages.

"Do you know what this is?" Hazel's mouth was next to Raven's ear, reading over her shoulder.

"It's your family grimoire," Raven said with a glance at her. She tingled at the feel of Hazel's breath on her cheek.

Raven continued to flip through until she reached a section of blank pages. She kept flipping, not understanding why it had stopped so abruptly.

Sarah sat on her heels on the floor, folding her dress under her, and reached for the book. "Allow me." She dragged her hand across the page, and the words started to appear. "Ayotunde once told me that the hands of a Hutchinson have the power to reveal secrets." She looked up at Raven and Hazel. "She spun many childhood tales to me that I thought were only to make me smile."

Hazel gasped. "I can't believe this is real." She sank back against the couch. "I've studied the occult my entire life and have never seen anything like this."

Raven faced her. "You really had no inclination?"

Hazel chewed on her fingernail. "I thought I was just intuitive, maybe extra sensitive. But this? No, I had no idea." She motioned to the book.

Raven smiled with empathy. "I don't know as much as I'd like, but I can offer you some answers."

Hazel and Sarah looked at each other with a twin air of vulnerability that Raven found adorable.

"I'm sure we'd both love that," Hazel said.

After helping Sarah to her feet, Raven leaned back on the couch. "I don't know all the secrets of the witches; only your kind are privy to that type of information, but I'll tell you what I know." She looked between Hazel and Sarah, who offered their rapt attention. "Witches have been around since the beginning of time. Witches have been tasked with keeping the balance between the realms. For many of you, this means making sure that demons and other creatures aren't able to overrun this world. Each of you has distinct powers, which, from what I understand, take a lifetime to develop. However, it may happen a bit faster for you two. Witches' powers always increase when they're around family members who embrace and share their connections."

"So, she and I really are related?" Hazel gave Sarah a tentative smile.

"That's the vibe I'm getting," Raven said. "Aunt Sarah, meet your great-niece Hazel."

Sarah gently squeezed Hazel's hand as though relieved at the connection.

"You know what we are," Hazel said, "but we know very little about you."

Raven wasn't comfortable sharing personal information, but she tried to push through those feelings. She wanted these women to trust her. "I'm a descendant of Virginia Dare, the first English child born on this continent. Morgan le Fay, the Queen of the Witches, made a bargain with the king of the other realm in exchange for Virginia. I'm not sure what the deal entailed, but I do know the cost for my family was a curse. One person from my family has always worked for Morgan. We do her bidding, helping her to rid this realm of evil."

"Sounds very noble," Hazel said.

Raven suppressed a laugh. "Maybe, but it doesn't feel that way. My life doesn't belong to me. It belongs to Morgan."

"Per chance this Morgan can help me? Pray, may I speak with her?" Sarah said.

Raven stood. "You're going to get your chance. I'm going to take you to her. But we need to go to New Orleans."

Hazel matched Raven's movement, standing to speak. "I can't just leave my shop. It's October. I make almost the entirety of my living this month. No, it will have to wait."

Raven felt the vise sensation at her throat again. It choked her, pushing out words she didn't form in her mind. "You don't have a choice. You come with me, or I'll be forced to take you." Raven pressed a hand against her throat once the sentence was out in the open, unsure of where it came from.

Hazel held her hand to her chest. "Are you threatening me?"

Raven shook her head, hating herself for making Hazel feel that way. "No, Morgan is; that was her talking through me. Before you argue, Morgan doesn't make requests. If you don't come with me, she'll come and get you herself. Believe me when I tell you, you don't want that. Pack a bag. I'll be back in the morning."

Raven walked out of the apartment before Hazel could protest. When the door shut behind her, she felt Hazel's absence. She told herself it was just Hazel's power combined with Sarah's that left her feeling this overwhelming emptiness.

She let the cool air chill her skin, not bothering to put on her jacket. She wanted to feel her skin prickle and her body shiver, a reminder that her body was still her own and not beholden to any witch, at least for the time being.

❖

Sarah rubbed her arms at the chill caused by Raven's swift departure and Morgan's ominous words. She glanced at Hazel, who still seemed unsettled by the events.

"'Tis providence indeed that we have not to endure this alone. I fear that even the most zealous of my Christian brethren in Salem have failed lamentably in ridding this village of evil."

Hazel smiled and sat down beside her. "I'm still trying to wrap my head around all this. I cannot believe you're sitting here in my apartment, a living, breathing historical figure I read about as a kid. Not to mention the fact that I now know time travel is possible. Mind blown." She flicked both sets of fingers at each of her temples.

"You hast read my life's story betimes our meeting? Do I bear children one day?"

Hazel frowned and shook her head. "It doesn't appear that way; at least, nothing was documented in my family's history. I'm a direct descendant of your sister, Mary."

"Ah yes, my dear sister hath birthed six healthy children," Sarah said, drifting off. "I have wondered, to my chagrin, wherefore God blessed her with such a bounty and give me none. Perhaps today I have my answer."

"What do you mean?" Hazel said.

"If I be a witch, God shall grant no such blessing upon me."

"If you're a witch, your sister must've been, too. Weren't all the Hutchinson women?"

Sarah shrugged. "Our mother perished hours after she birthed me. Were it possible that I am the original Hutchinson witch, and death be her punishment for bringing me forth into the world?"

"Sarah, you're a white witch. You're not evil."

"Puritan law deems all witchcraft evil. There be no mention of good witches in the Scriptures."

"Well, maybe whoever wrote the Scriptures didn't know everything they should've known. There are other schools of thought besides Puritanism. Today, that's not even a religion anymore. Once it was acknowledged that all nineteen people hanged in Salem were really innocent, Puritanism kinda lost its bite."

Horrified, Sarah whispered, "Nineteen? Dear God."

"Oh crap," Hazel said. "You didn't know that, did you?"

"And my dear friend, Bridget Bishop?"

Hazel shook her head solemnly. "She was the first."

Overcome, Sarah buried her face in her hands and wept. Hazel patted her upper back gently as she repeated, "I'm sorry," in a whisper.

After a few minutes, Sarah lifted her head and dried her cheeks with the sleeve of her dress. "We must stop this."

"Stop what? It's already done."

"Perhaps not. We, you and Raven and I, must travel back and put an end to the persecution, to save the innocents from these wretched, unjust fates."

"Uh…"

"Hazel, we cannot let them face the gallows. They be good, honest Christians."

"Sarah, I understand your indignation, but you're suggesting we go back and rewrite American history. We can't do that…at least I don't think we can."

"Ayotunde," Sarah said, gripped by fear. She stood and began pacing the room. "Is my Ayotunde among the condemned who will hang?"

"Um, I don't remember the name Ayotunde. The only enslaved person I remember reading about was Tituba, who belonged to Reverend Parris. She was spared death because she confessed."

"Aye, Reverend Parris. It was he who hath stirred this pot of venom in Salem Village, for he not kept proper watch over his niece and daughter. I like not to speak ill of such a learned and revered man, but my soul doth shiver during his sermons. And not for his preaching of a wrathful God."

"I'm sorry to break this to you, but he wasn't the last powerful, prominent man to fall to corruption, not by a long shot."

Lightheaded, Sarah leaned against the wall and placed the back of her hand to her forehead. "I must pray. I must entreat God for forgiveness. I must find a way…"

Hazel took her by the elbow and guided her to the couch again. "Sarah, you've done nothing that needs forgiving. Whatever's going on here, we're going to figure it out. Raven's coming back tomorrow to take us to Morgan. In the meantime, I'm going to google everything I can about white witches and Salem and demon thresholds and whatever else I can think of."

"Google?" Sarah asked, somewhat dazed. "How far ahead in time have I traveled?"

"It's the twenty-first century," Hazel said. "Over three hundred years."

"Mercy," Sarah said. "And in this time, Salem Village hath begotten shiny horseless carriages and googles."

Hazel giggled, but Sarah couldn't comprehend her amusement.

"I know it's a lot to process right now," Hazel said. "Let's take a walk, order lattes, and try to catch our breath." She stood and encouraged Sarah up with her.

"Aye, but it is dark now. We cannot walk about town unaccompanied by your husband."

Hazel smirked. "Women today can go wherever they want whenever they want. We have the same rights as men. And I don't have a husband. I'm a, um, hmm, let's see," she said, tapping her index finger to her lips. "How do I put this?"

Sarah stared at her in anticipation.

"On second thought," Hazel said. "We better save that conversation for something stronger than lattes."

Sarah folded her arms as Hazel eyed her worn dress from top to bottom. "Right now," Hazel added, "we need to get you to a Gap."

❖

Hazel woke at dawn after a restless night and padded down the hall toward the kitchen. So many outrageous thoughts and visions bewitched her mind as she tossed and turned, not the least of which was the fact that her great-aunt Sarah had apparently time-hopped through three centuries and was now sitting at her kitchen table in front of a sandalwood Yankee candle.

"I probably should've explained what these things are last night," Hazel said as she pointed to the wall switch and flicked on the overhead light.

Sarah flinched as she gazed up at the magnificent beam of light shining down on them. "Good morrow, Hazel. Have you no oats for a pottage?"

"I'm going to go ahead and assume you're referring to breakfast, but we'll just swing by a drive-thru and grab coffees and croissants or something." Sarah looked perplexed. It was an expression Hazel had already grown accustomed to her wearing. "Okay, um, I think what you mean is oatmeal, and we can definitely get you a cup of it once Raven gets here, and we hit the road. Can I get you a glass of juice or something? Actually, here's the fridge," she said as she flung open the door. "Help yourself to whatever you want. I have to jump in the shower."

When Hazel closed the bathroom door, Sarah rose from her chair and tugged at the tight denim breeches Hazel had bought her in town yesterday at the trading post called Gap. Although they lacked comfort, she felt warm and protected in them. And relieving herself on top of that prodigious chamber pot, then watching it vanish beneath her was a marvel indeed. As befuddling as the experience had been thus far, Sarah woke before dawn with a sense of calm having been visited by her long-dead mother in a dream.

She confirmed for Sarah that she, Sarah, and her sister Mary were all descendants of Arcadia, a medieval witch from the Tuscany region of Italy. After numerous attempts by Roman Catholics to wipe out Paganism, it was believed that Arcadia's daughters fled to England, which was where Sarah's maternal lineage was traced. Sarah's mother also revealed that the reason she did not survive the birth of her second daughter was that Sarah's powers were so strong, more so than her sister Mary's, that a Christian demon slayer killed Sarah's mother so that she would not bring forth another, even more powerful sorceress. The explanation that her mother had died in childbirth having her was much more palatable for the time than the truth.

Sarah had wept at the notion that she was the cause of her mother's demise, but her mother had assured her in the dream that Sarah was about to fulfill a much greater purpose.

While she was engrossed in the mesmerizing task of turning the kitchen faucets on and off, a knocking sounded on the door, and Raven walked in.

"What up, witches?" Raven called out. When she got to the kitchen, her boots skidded to a stop. "Whoa, Sarah. Those jeans are fire on you."

"Fire?" Startled, Sarah twirled around, examining her pants for smoke or flames.

"Oh, sorry. Bad word choice on my part," Raven said. "What I meant to say is you look pretty in your new clothes."

Sarah curtsied in appreciation. "'Tis more comfortable than a petticoat."

"Yeah, I bet," Raven said, glancing around the kitchen. "So, are you guys ready to fly?"

"Fly?" Sarah was aghast. "We must make our journey on broomsticks?"

Raven swiped a hand across her face. "This is going to be one long road trip."

Hazel appeared in the archway holding two duffel bags. "Good morning, Raven." She extended her smile at Raven while handing one of the bags to Sarah. "Are we ready to go?"

Raven nodded and collected both of their bags. "I hope you packed a Puritan-to-English dictionary in one of these."

CHAPTER FIVE

Lucien McCoulter was on his knees in the small room, illuminated by nothing except the candles on the altar. He traced the symbol on his chest from the ashes in the dish in front of him. He made a circle with the tips of his fingers and then a triangle inside the circle. He'd lost track of how many times he'd practiced this technique.

The old him, Samuel Cranwell, would've called this heresy. The person he was before he and his children had walked in on the witches performing their spell in the jail would've shouted this atrocity from the rooftops and to anyone who'd listen. Luckily, Samuel no longer existed. No, "Lucien" had left him behind the day he'd discovered the King of the Warlocks, Blaise. If it hadn't been for Blaise, he would've never survived being thrust into this new world in 2008, over a decade ago.

Blaise had opened Samuel's eyes to all that he'd been ignorant of his entire life. Blaise showed him that people don't reach their full potential through piety and sacrifice. Those were tales spun by the disillusioned, lies whispered to children to nudge them in the direction predetermined for them by an entity they'd never be able to know.

But Blaise he could see and touch. Blaise was a tangible thing. Blaise had been there when Samuel passed through to this strange world. A world plagued by rot, rot cleverly disguised as equity, equality, and social justice. These ideas diluted the purity of his people, his race, and limited future generations to mind-numbing mediocrity.

The decision was the easiest one he'd ever made. He left "Samuel" behind and all the baggage that went along with him, embracing his new identity as Lucien. For that he was given an array of abilities, ones that would put any of the angels he'd once adulated to shame. Lucien felt those abilities growing by the day, and as more people listened to him and believed in his preaching, the more powerful he became. He'd entered into a covenant with Blaise whereby as soon as he accomplished his appointed task, he would join the ranks of Blaise's force of omnipotent evil.

Lucien clutched at the burning in the pit of his stomach, his signal that Blaise had arrived. "Master, thank you for coming."

"It looks as if time has finally caught up with us," Blaise said. "Are you ready?" His form was hidden, but Lucien could see his scarlet eyes glowing from the corner of the room.

"I'm ready." Lucien knelt in Blaise's direction and put his head down. "Tell me what to do, and I'll do it."

Blaise growled, and a wave of anger sliced through Lucien's skin. "The witches have to be dealt with, all of them. We cannot complete our mission while they exist."

Lucien felt the excitement of imminent violence prick the hairs on the back of his neck. "We'll take care of it."

Blaise entered Lucien's mind, not bothering to say the words out loud. "If you fail, I'll banish you to a region of Hell your people couldn't have conjured up in their most twisted nightmares."

Lucien felt him leave just as he'd felt him arrive. His body fell forward, the absence of his leader immediately evident.

The radio in the corner of the room crackled, and a nervous sounding voice came through the speaker. "Mr. McCoulter, we're ready for you."

Lucien stood and looked in the mirror while buttoning his shirt. He smiled at his reflection, admiring the transformation that had occurred since his arrival in this time. This wonder of bathing on a daily basis was magical for the complexion. He tucked the pocket square into his jacket, making sure the gold cross was visible.

It was time to go to work. Millions of his adoring followers waited to hear from him. He knew they were sitting in that stadium, salivating for a mere glimpse of him. They waited to be told what to do, what was right, and who was to blame for their struggles. As it turned out, people at their core hadn't changed all that much in three hundred years. They still needed someone to justify their feelings, their dissatisfaction with life, their anger, and their hatred for whoever was to blame for it. They still wanted someone to tell them it was okay to distrust those who were different and those who threatened their peace and prosperity. They did exactly as they were told because they needed to believe it was all a plan handed down from their God.

It was the easiest job he'd ever had.

He stepped onto the stage and let the applause and the screams wash over him. The sensation was invigorating. He snatched the microphone and walked to the center of the stage while images flashed on the screen behind him. He didn't need to look to know what they were. Pictures of men kissing men, women dressed as men, and black men standing over the bodies of white children.

"Are you tired of being called a bigot just because you believe in the word of God?" he shouted into the microphone.

Screams of agreement filled the arena.

"Are you tired of working your whole life to send your child to college, just to find out their spot has been taken by an illegal immigrant who received free tuition?" He paused for applause. "Are you sick and tired of men dressed as women stalking our children in public bathrooms?" He shook his head for effect. "Do I speak for all of you when I say we've had enough?" The crowd roared, sending a charge of exhilaration through Lucien's body. "It's time for a revolution, my friends. It's time to put God back into 'In God We Trust.' This is our America they're trying to take. We want our Jesus back, the *real* Jesus, not the corrupted version who allegedly accepts the gay lifestyle and wants us to welcome the droves of illegal immigrants stampeding our borders. Our Jesus would want us to protect our families and our Christian values. Our Jesus wants us to fight to protect His name, His legacy, His creations. Our Jesus wants us to resist the resistance and to destroy those who decimate His name to promote their own selfish and perverse agenda!"

He raised his arms over his head and looked out into the simmering crowd of true believers numbering in the thousands screaming back. They loved him, believed in him, and were eager to play their part.

The arena shook with their thunderous applause. He was unstoppable now, and those witches didn't stand a chance.

CHAPTER SIX

Hazel did her best to look at anything except Raven, but it was proving to be more difficult than she'd imagined. There was something magnetic about her, and Hazel wanted to understand why she felt so drawn to her. Raven had an easy and relaxed way about her that had Hazel enthralled.

"How's it going back there?" Raven shouted to Sarah through the highway noise as her Jeep bounced down Interstate 81 South.

"Methinks a broomstick would jolt me less," Sarah said.

"Atta girl," Raven said to the rearview mirror, then smiled at Hazel. "She's a good sport."

"Yes," Hazel said, and felt her lips spread into a grin. "She cleans up pretty good, too, doesn't she?"

Raven's eyebrows bobbed with approval as a grin stretched across her face. "I've had my share of complicated women, but I draw the line at time-traveling Puritan witches obsessed with auto-flushing rest stop toilets."

"Almost as bad as a new girlfriend who's still uncomfortably close friends with her ex," Hazel said.

They shared a laugh and lingering smiles.

"Look at her," Raven said, glancing in the rearview mirror. "She's like a kid seeing Disney World for the first time."

Hazel turned and smiled at Sarah, who was quietly taking in the sights. Out of nowhere, her insides began trembling. "I'm starting to feel a little weird," she said, turning to Raven. "Can we make a stop soon?"

"How do you like that?" Raven glanced up at an interstate sign.

"Roanoke. That's as good a place as any to stop." She opened her podcast app for a little background noise, intending to catch up on some episodes of *The Weekly Wine Down*.

"You've been listening to *The Right Side* with Tammi Lee Sanderson," the announcer's voice boomed. "Real talk, right talk with zero tolerance for leftist agendas."

Hazel and Raven looked at each other. Raven shrugged. "That's not what I clicked on."

"Okay, folks," the woman's husky voice said. "We're back, continuing our discussion on this week's episode: 'The War on God.' So, we've been talking about the increasing threat to Christian values ever since the liberal activist Supreme Court justices legalized gay marriage. Since then, gay rights groups have had a field day taking their grab on equality to the extreme. And what's been their favorite entitlement? Forcing us into going against our own strongly held beliefs and dictating how we should be serving God."

"What the hell is this?" Hazel said.

"I don't know." Raven tapped the app on the console screen to try to change the podcast, but it didn't respond to her command. "Of all the times for this piece of shit to freeze."

"Without further ado," Tammi said, "I'd like to introduce a guest I've been chomping at the bit to interview ever since his rise to religious stardom began during the last presidential campaign: Lucien McCoulter, pastor at True Light Ministries. Lucien, you're a best-selling author, motivational speaker, and most importantly, Christian educator and preacher. How do you manage to do it all?"

Lucien chuckled. "Well, Tammi, first of all, thank you for that humbling introduction, and I must say, I couldn't do any of it without a whole lot of divine help from above."

"Turn off the radio," Hazel said. "I can't listen to this garbage."

"Not yet," Raven said. "There's a reason this has come on."

"Beyond bad cell reception?"

Raven rolled her eyes. "For a witch, you're awfully logic oriented. You better start tuning in to your intuition. Our success, and dare I say our survival in whatever Morgan has planned, could depend on your ability to follow it."

"I am tuned in," Hazel said. "I just said I'm starting to feel weird and think we should stop."

"That's very good," Raven said. "And no coincidence you're feeling it this close to Roanoke."

Hazel closed her eyes and rubbed her temples, rattled by the onslaught of new sensations.

Raven watched in concern. "Are you okay?"

Hazel looked up and tried to give her a reassuring smile. "Yeah, yeah. I'm just a little overwhelmed by the juju around here."

"That's because Roanoke isn't what it appears to be." Raven reached toward Hazel, then retreated, gripping the wheel with both hands until her knuckles turned white.

"I don't mean to sound ignorant, but what's the significance?" Hazel said. "I thought the first colony was in North Carolina."

"It was, but Roanoke's had a long, intimate relationship with evil. It wasn't named Roanoke until the late eighteen hundreds. Before that, Native Americans used it as a transportation hub of sorts, and it later became part of the Great Wagon Road. What the history books don't tell you is that this was the area where Morgan helped Virginia Dare and her mother, Ellinor, escape to."

"Escape from what?" Hazel said.

"Native Americans who didn't want settlers encroaching on their lands. When the original settlers left and then returned from England, they found 'CROATOAN' carved into a palisade. They'd assumed the Croatoan tribe captured and massacred them with the rest of the people they'd left behind."

"And Morgan le Fay helped them escape from the Croatoans?"

Raven nodded. "For a steep price, of course. The Roanoke River runs from the lost colony of Roanoke up through here and then by Salem, Virginia. No witching influence there, huh?" She shook her head and scoffed. "Anyway, Morgan compelled the people to name this area Roanoke as a tribute to Virginia Dare and her family. That's the story she tells anyway. I always thought it was a big 'fuck you' to humans for not figuring out what was right under their noses." Raven glanced over at Hazel before she continued. "This is the birthplace, or rather rebirth, of the first shadowhunter, Virginia Dare. For that reason, this area is alive with paranormal influence. Demons in all shapes and sizes constantly scour the area looking for Virginia's remains. If they can destroy the remains, they can destroy the legacy of the shadowhunter, the people responsible for sending them back to Hell—me."

Hazel shook her head in disbelief. "So, you," she said, pointing at Raven, "have the power to send Sarah and me to Hell?" Hazel poked Raven in the arm. "You should have mentioned that before you kidnapped us."

"Kidnapped, huh?" Raven smirked. "You and Sarah are probably the world's first kidnapping victims who ever waited to be abducted at the front door with their bags packed."

That smirk of Raven's. It annoyed the hell out of Hazel while simultaneously triggering a persistent case of the warm tinglies all through her. "Would you keep your voice down?" she said, glancing over her shoulder. "I don't want Sarah to get scared. She's already been through enough."

"Relax. Ninety percent of the time she has no idea what we're saying. It's like we're road-tripping with Long Duk Dong from *Sixteen Candles*. Besides, I can't send you or Sarah anywhere. Witches weren't forged in Hell. You're out of my jurisdiction, honey," she added with a wink.

"Pray, pardon, Goody Raven," Sarah said from the back. "I am beckoned, but I know not by what. Will our carriage be stopping soon?"

Hazel grinned victoriously at Raven. "Guess who else is in touch with her intuition?"

As Raven drove into the parking lot of a traveler's motel in downtown Roanoke, Tammi Lee Sanderson's voice continued droning through the speakers.

"Can't you turn this off? It's making my headache worse." Hazel didn't want to sound as if she was whining, but this woman's voice was like nails on a chalkboard.

"I'm trying," Raven said as she threw the Jeep into park. "The volume button is literally stuck."

"Thank you so much for joining us today, Pastor McCoulter," Tammi said.

"It's been my pleasure, indeed," he replied in a velvety rich voice.

"And don't forget, *Right Side* listeners down there in Roanoke," Tammi said. "Tonight is the first of several worship services hosted by the great Lucien McCoulter at his newly renovated and expanded facility, True Light Ministries Church in downtown Roanoke. Tickets are still available for tonight's sermon, but they're going fast."

Hazel and Raven got out of the Jeep. Hazel helped Sarah out of the back as Raven gathered their duffel bags. Hazel came around to Raven's side and looked up at a huge billboard of Lucien McCoulter's wise, welcoming face and compelling smile shining down on the world with the dates of his engagement. Hazel elbowed Raven for her attention. They stared at the billboard and exchanged looks.

Raven nodded toward Sarah. "Now we know why you two got those weird vibes approaching Roanoke."

Hazel grinned as she maintained eye contact with Raven. "Hey, Aunt Sarah, feel like attending church tonight?"

"Aye," Sarah said with a sigh. "After such a lengthy sojourn, my soul doth need the nourishment of the Scripture."

Hazel gently patted Sarah's back. "Don't worry. It's going to be okay." She forced herself not to watch Raven as she walked toward the motel manager's office, but that confident swagger was impossible to ignore.

She wasn't sure what to make of her emotions over the last few days. Everything she thought she'd known revealed a different reality. She couldn't trust what she thought when her body tingled at being close to Raven. She had an overpowering desire to be near her, to touch her, but everything felt overpowering lately. Just a few days ago, her life was simple; she was a small business owner with an ordinary family history. Now she was sharing space with not only a shadowhunter, but a time-traveling witch from three hundred years ago, who, oh by the way, was also her aunt. Her head hurt, her stomach churned, her nerves were fried, and all she wanted to do was take a long bath with a glass of chilled wine. But she needed to know what was happening to understand why she was being summoned by the Queen of the Witches. She needed her life to go back to normal. But normal didn't include Raven Dare.

Raven with her talk of danger, survival, and demons. She was clearly deeply entrenched in a world that Hazel wanted nothing to do with. She didn't want to be a witch, not in this sense. She didn't want to have to contend with what used to be abstract notions of demons or Hell. She wanted everything back the way it had been before Raven and Sarah had shown up at her door. Her life was neat, planned, and predictable. But oh so boring. She glanced over at Raven, who was walking out of the motel office, keys dangling in front of her, a triumphant look on her face.

Hazel tried to push down the sensation of excitement upon seeing Raven smiling in her direction. She needed to keep her distance, and if she couldn't do it physically, she needed to do it emotionally. *Allowing her in is a mistake.* She repeated the words in her head, hoping to engrain the mantra into her psyche.

Raven's warm eyes traced the outline of Hazel's face and neck as she gathered their bags. The simple action had Hazel second-guessing everything she'd just been telling herself. Raven, it seemed, had a way of making her second-guess everything. She wasn't sure if she loved the feeling or desperately wanted it to go away.

CHAPTER SEVEN

Inside the arena, Sarah clung to the arms of Hazel and Raven as they were jostled about by the clamoring crowd rushing to get to their seats for Lucien McCoulter's sermon. Sarah felt disoriented by the lights, gaggles of people, and loud music. She tried to push through her unease and focus on the positive in the situation.

"Never have I witnessed such a prodigious horde of worshippers. My heart is warmed that piety and faith have not lost their battle with evil through the ages."

"Don't start celebrating yet," Raven said. "Yes, religious fervor still exists, but this kind is...hmm, how do I put this delicately?"

Hazel cut in. "Pretty much as insane as the religious fervor that got twenty-three people dead during the Salem Witch Trials."

"Twenty-three?" Sarah stopped short on the stairs leading to their section in the nosebleeds, causing a brief bottleneck of fans behind them.

Raven glared at Hazel. "You gotta stop with the spoilers."

"I know," she said, bowing her head. "I keep forgetting."

"Pray, how may I stop all of the murders?" Her eyes flitted between theirs, searching for hope. "Couldst thou accompany me back to Salem Village with your sorcery, so that we may spare those innocent souls?"

"Not an option," Raven said, practically dragging Sarah to their row. "That's way beyond our area of expertise."

"Um, I'm still not sure what my area of expertise is," Hazel said.

"Perhaps Miss le Fay could be of assistance?" Sarah said.

"I'm sure she can..." Raven spread her reproachful glance between them. "If we can ever get there."

"Don't look at us like that," Hazel said. "Obviously, your great-granny Virginia had something to do with us getting drawn off the highway, too."

"Fair point," Raven said.

Hazel smiled and bumped Raven's shoulder. "Then let's make the best of it."

Raven put her feet up on the chair in front of her and put her hands behind her head. "Sure. Let's just sit back and revel in the heavenly glow of Reverend Slimeball's celebrated return to Roanoke. Maybe we can figure out why we ended up here in his glorious presence."

"Goody Raven." Sarah placed a hand on her arm. "I fear the evil that dwelleth around us. 'Tis a familiar feeling of foreboding."

"That's good. You should fear it." Raven appeared stern but reassuring. "It's complacency that killed most of you over the centuries, and it's what threatens you still. But that's why we're all together."

"We are to stop the evil?"

"That's the plan I've gleaned from Morgan."

Hazel leaned forward to look at Raven. "The three of us?"

Raven nodded. "Unless Morgan plans to slap together an army to back us up."

Sarah covered her ears at the noise in the stadium, but it continued vibrating through her chest. This world that Ayotunde's incantation had sent her to as an escape was beginning to feel more like a punishment. Her head swirled in bewilderment at this strange new world. Technology, Hazel called it, the result of man's endless quest to improve upon God's ideas. If Puritan leaders thought using herbs and roots for healing means was the work of the devil, what would they make of these handheld sorcery devices that all seemed to possess? And her body felt different as well. All the talk of witches and evil had wrought troubling sensations upon her. In a matter of days, she'd been catapulted from her humble life as a farmer's wife who'd endeavored each day to be a good Christian and avoid displeasing God into what seemed like the precise realm of supernatural forces she'd been taught to fear her entire life.

Further compounding the confusion was the paradox of finding Ayotunde, the one whose presence had brought her life its greatest joy, at the most ominous hour of their lives. Would she ever see her again? Her eyes teared at the thought that they had again been ripped apart after so brief an interlude and that Ayotunde might yet be destined for the hangman's noose along with the others.

She watched Hazel and Raven huddled closely, laughing. In their younger years, she and Ayotunde would sneak off to the fields and wood for play such as theirs. Her heart yet ached for those days. And for Ayotunde.

Hazel leaned across Raven's lap. "Sarah, are you okay?"

"I'm sure she's not used to this decibel level," Raven said.

"'Tis unnerving this commotion," Sarah said.

"Yeah, it's pretty loud," said Raven. "And it's going to get even louder once the main attraction hits the stage."

"I mean not only the sound," Sarah said. "The commotion that also dwells within me."

"You're not alone there," Hazel said.

Raven consulted her watch. "The show's about to start."

The screams of adoration were deafening. Raven had never witnessed such unabashed, almost orgiastic worship in her entire life. *How have I never heard of this guy?* From the moment he stepped on the stage, his hatred was so evident, so tangible, she thought she might be able to chew on it.

"They think they're as good as you; they think they're one of you; they think they deserve what you and your families have worked so hard to create." McCoulter's words were annunciated by pictures of gay couples on a one-hundred-foot screen. The next image appeared, and Raven felt her stomach roll. Pictures of people of color dressed in gang clothing, holding guns, and standing with their foot on a white man. "The craft of the Gibeonites. Joshua maketh a league with them. For their craft they are condemned to perpetual slavery." McCoulter let the cheering settle before he continued. "You see, it's right there in the Bible. These people intentionally deceived the Israelites. They came to Joshua pretending to be in need, and when Joshua agreed to help, they destroyed the Israelites." He pointed up at the screen. "That's what they want. They want you to feel sorry for them. They want you to help them just so they can take us all down."

Raven's hands trembled. This man was despicable. She leaned over and talked against Hazel's ear. "He's insane."

Hazel's face was flushed, and Raven wasn't sure if it was from their shared anger or something else. "I've studied the Bible at length, and I don't remember this at all," Hazel said.

Sarah's brows furrowed. "Aye, it 'tis indeed in the Bible. The Book of Joshua."

Hazel put her hand on Sarah's arm. "Which Bible, Sarah?"

Sarah looked frazzled. "The only Bible." She looked up toward the large screen and turned her head slightly. "That man, he is familiar. Our paths have once crossed. I know it."

Hazel grasped Raven's knee. "We don't recognize it because the wording is from a much older version of the Bible. The Geneva Bible, it was used by the Puritans." Hazel loosened her grip, and her eyes looked worried. "What if Sarah wasn't the only person to come through? What if there were others?"

Raven wished she could tell her that such a thing would be impossible, but she couldn't. "Can you focus your energy at all? Can you sense him? I'm not close enough."

Hazel closed her eyes for a moment and then shook her head. "I have no idea what I'm doing. I wouldn't even know where to start."

Sarah stood abruptly and pawed the air for Hazel's arm. "I know who he is now. That is Samuel Cranwell. He once roamed the village an aimless drunkard until my husband hired him as a hand and preached the word of God in him. He hath since been appointed marshal in Salem and takes great pleasure in arresting the women. He means to see them hang!"

Raven sprang to her feet. She put herself between McCoulter and the witches. She knew it was a pointless act, especially from this distance, but it was something she needed to do. She leaned down between them. "We need to get out of here. Now."

Raven led them to the stairs, putting Hazel in the front and Sarah in the middle. She didn't like being several feet from Hazel in case something happened, but the likelihood of Sarah getting lost was too great a risk. She reached into her waistband and pulled the seraph from its sheath. This was the only weapon she'd been able to get past the metal detectors since it was cloaked in white magic.

They hurried down the expansive hallway toward the exit. Raven felt demons approaching from different sides. Her skin burned with the recognition of their presence, and they were getting closer by the second. She needed to get outside where the large walls wouldn't restrain her ability to maneuver between the entities. Her lungs started to burn as the darkness closed in. Finally, Hazel reached the large door and shoved it open, the cold night air swallowing them as they spilled out into the parking lot.

"Hey! Stop!" the largest of the four demons yelled. He was well over six foot and at least three hundred pounds. Like most demons she'd encountered, this one had taken on a human form, an especially formidable one. As he stalked toward them, Raven noticed the other three approaching from different sides.

Raven held Hazel by the shoulders when the demons were only about two hundred feet away. She reached into her pocket and threw Hazel her keys. "Take Sarah and get back to the hotel. There's an amulet in my bag; put it around your neck. It will keep you cloaked from the demons. At least, for the moment."

One hundred and fifty feet.

Hazel shook her head. "No. I'm not leaving you here."

One hundred feet.

Raven turned them in the direction of the car. "I'll be fine. You have to listen to me. Go. Now!"

Fifty feet.

Hazel pulled Sarah close to her. "Raven, there are four of them and only one of you."

Twenty-five feet.

Raven flipped the knife in her hand and changed her weight to the balls of her feet, readying herself for the fight. "Hazel, please."

They were out of time. Raven threw the seraph at the closest demon. It struck him in the chest, and she yanked it out before his body finished dissolving into ash. Another charged her while the other two made their way toward Hazel and Sarah. She ran toward the witches when she felt a sharp pain in her back that spread across her shoulders like paint splashed onto a canvas. She winced and willed herself not to fall forward as the demon's footsteps grew louder behind her. She stepped to the side and turned, pushing the seraph into his neck. The smell of sulfur once again filled the air.

The last two demons were on either side of Sarah and Hazel,

circling like sharks. They skulked about them but made no real movement to advance.

"Come with us, and you won't get hurt," said the one closest to Sarah.

Raven closed in, hoping to subdue the demon before it was too late. That would draw the other demon's attention, and she'd be able to save Hazel as well. It wasn't a perfect plan, but it was all she had.

She ignored the throbbing coming from her shoulder and moved closer. The air seemed to shift. Everything grew still. A blast of light erupted from Sarah as her arm rose slowly above her head. Raven felt euphoric for a flash as the smell of the deep woods and wildflowers filled her nose. Hazel's movements echoed Sarah's and intensified the pressure building in the air, a stark and startling contrast from what was just transpiring. Sarah seemed to draw the demons closer together, and in a gust of wind out of nowhere, they fell over backward. As they struggled to get to their feet, Raven was able to reach one and slide her blade into his heart as the other ran off. She wanted to go after him, but Hazel appeared next to her, keeping her from moving.

Hazel ran her hand over Raven's back. "Oh my Goddess. There's a tiny arrow sticking in your back."

Raven turned to look, but the motion made her dizzy. "It's laced with something. Can you pull it out?"

Hazel looked concerned. "I don't know if I should. We need to get you to a hospital."

Raven scoffed. "And say what exactly? 'Hey, Doc, a demon shot a magic arrow into my back. Can you do me a solid and get it out?'" She put her hand down to prevent her from falling over. "They'll throw me in the psych ward."

Sarah worked the arrow out, dug a bandana out of Raven's backpack, and applied pressure. "'Tis a mild wound. I have witnessed much worse on the farm when my Thomas first took a sickle to the crops. I'll remedy it with some goldenrod. Where is the nearest forest?"

"See?" Raven motioned to Hazel and felt as if she was going to throw up. "We just need to get out of here and back to the motel. That demon will be back, and he won't be alone." Hazel looked as if she was about to object. "Don't worry. I heal faster than most people. It's part of the curse."

Raven pushed up into the kneeling position, and Sarah and Hazel lifted her from either side, helping her stand.

"Perhaps we should bring the carriage to her," Sarah said.

"I'll be good as new in a few hours." Raven began to walk forward. "But don't think I didn't notice that witchy thing you two did back there. We need to talk about that."

Hazel's grip around her waist tightened, and Raven let herself enjoy the slight nod to their connection. "We can talk. But only when you feel better. I'm not really sure what's going on. I have no idea how I did any of that."

Raven hoped her silence was interpreted as her agreement. She let the two of them lead her back to the car, and she flopped in the back seat. Already the discomfort from her wound was abating, but she hoped the whole arrow had come out when Sarah removed it. She still had the tip of a knife in her from an altercation that happened almost two years ago.

She watched Hazel from the darkened protection of the back seat. Her skin was flushed from using magic, and the redness on her cheeks made her look younger. She chewed on her finger, a habit Raven found adorable on her when she would've found it disgusting on anyone else. Strands of dark hair had fallen from her ponytail, and she used her long, elegant fingers to move them out of the way.

Raven closed her eyes, realizing the attraction she felt toward her had nothing to do with Hazel's supernatural powers and everything to do with her. *Perfect. Just what I need.*

CHAPTER EIGHT

Despite Raven's assurances that she'd be all right, Hazel couldn't get back to the motel fast enough. She wanted to pull her inside and get a good look at the open wound on her back. The thought of Raven suffering in any way made her nauseous and angry. She should probably feel much more overwhelmed by the four demons that chased them down, the apparent magic she and Sarah had invoked, or the fact that a Puritan preacher on par with Jonathan Edwards had followed Sarah into the twenty-first century with his own dubious agenda. Yes, all of that was terrifying and important, but not more important than Raven's well-being.

Hazel glanced back at her as she slept on the bench in her back seat. She wanted to touch her, to make sure she was okay, but she kept her eyes forward in case anything else decided to ambush them.

She looked over at Sarah, whose leg was shaking up and down. Hazel shook her head, disappointed that she hadn't been more aware of how all of this was affecting her.

"Hey, are you okay?" she asked.

Sarah rubbed her arms as though chilled. "Those men dissolved into ash when Goody Raven struck them with her blade. I have witnessed the reverend preach of demons many a time but imagined not in my wildest nightmare that I should ever encounter one. I thought he hath been speaking in metaphor."

"I know how overwhelming this is for me. I can't imagine what it feels like for you. You must be—" She cut her sentence short when she noticed the black Suburban parked in front of their motel room.

It was far too fancy a car for anyone staying at this place. The man in a black suit standing with his arms crossed behind the vehicle proved her point.

Slowing the car, she reached back and shook Raven's arm, causing her to stir. "Raven, I think we may have a problem."

Raven shot straight up and reached for the blade she'd used earlier. "What's wrong?" She looked around and then peered out the window. "Shit." She put her blade back down. "Those are Morgan's guys."

Hazel wasn't sure what that meant. Were they in trouble? Or about to be the next group vaporized into ash? "What do you want me to do?"

Raven pointed to the Suburban. "Park next to them. I have a feeling we'll be riding with them anyway."

"You need to rest. You aren't going anywhere," Hazel said. She didn't know Morgan, nor did she answer to her.

Raven's voice held no agitation, only acceptance. "I go wherever Morgan tells me."

Hazel put the car in park and got out. She was about to help Raven out of the back seat when another man in a black suit beat her to it.

"Your bags are already in the car, Ms. Abbot. Please get in." He didn't bother to turn his head in her direction.

"I'm not getting in a car with you. I don't know you." Hazel hoped her voice sounded more authoritative than it felt.

The hulking man finally turned toward her, clearly unaccustomed to being questioned. "I wasn't asking. The Queen requests your presence. This particular course you three are on has become too dangerous to attempt on your own. You will come with us."

Raven placed a hand on her back. "Get in the car." She looked up at the man. "Who's taking my car down to New Orleans?"

The man nodded once and opened the door. "We'll take care of it."

Once the three of them were in the back seat, Sarah grabbed Hazel's arm. "Are we under arrest?"

Hazel put her hand over hers. "No, no. We're going to New Orleans."

The driver peered into the rearview mirror and finished answering for her. "We're taking you to the Roanoke Airport. From there, you'll fly to New Orleans. Then we'll take you directly to Madame le Fay."

Sarah looked confused. "We are to fly? As real witches do through the sky?"

Hazel and Raven exchanged smiles. Raven leaned over Hazel and addressed Sarah. "You thought cars were impressive? Wait until you see an airplane." Raven withdrew her hand, letting it rest on Hazel's leg on its way back.

A few minutes later the car drove into the airport, past a large gate, and directly onto the airstrip where a private jet awaited them.

Sarah's mouth opened in awe. "'Tis a giant metal bird."

"Yeah, it kind of is," Hazel said. "Except we'll be riding inside of it."

"Have mercy," Sarah said breathlessly. "Like Jonah inside the belly of the whale."

"Okay," Hazel said, unsure how to address that one.

Sarah shook her head adamantly. "I shall not enter the belly of that bird willfully."

Raven looked at Sarah. "Well, just like Jonah couldn't refuse God, you can't refuse Morgan."

The car stopped, and the driver opened their car door. "Ladies... and Raven."

Raven hopped out and moved her shoulder around in a large circle. "Funny, Max. You should take your show on the road." She hit him in the arm.

Hazel peeled off the cloth on Raven's back, wanting to check on the wound. She felt her breath catch. "It's almost completely healed. That's impossible."

Raven shrugged. "Still stings like a bitch." She winked. "I told you I'd be fine."

Hazel had more questions, but her attention shifted to her aunt shaking with fear next to her. "Everything okay?"

Sarah's hands gripped Hazel's arm. "If God had meant for man to soar through the sky, would he not hath given us wings?"

Raven put her arm around her and led her toward the plane. "Good thing we're women, then. Seriously, it will be fine. Besides, you've already traveled three hundred and something years through time. A few hours on a jet is nothing."

Hazel wasn't sure of a lot of the things happening around her. Just a few days ago she was preparing for tourists to infiltrate her small town, and now she was boarding a private jet, heading for New Orleans for an audience with a witch queen. Not to mention fending off a demon attack. If she hadn't experienced it, she would never have believed it.

As she was walking toward the plane, she tried another time to reach her mother, but there was still no answer. She thought about leaving a message and then changed her mind. As angry as she was with her, she didn't want to worry her either. This was a conversation that couldn't be started via voice mail.

She took the short staircase onto the jet and was blown away by the inside. It was just how she would've pictured a private jet. The smell of leather and wine, clean large seats, and television monitors along the wall. She sat down next to Raven, enjoying the familiar way her body felt. She felt safe, and even if it was only temporary, she'd take what she could get.

❖

Somewhere over Tennessee, Sarah sat mesmerized, staring out the small window at the puffy clouds that seemed close enough to run her fingers through. Until now she'd always envisioned God's kingdom above the clouds: God sitting atop his throne meting out harsh judgments of eternal damnation for the sinners or ushering the pious chosen ones through His gate toward life everlasting. Wasn't that where the expression "Heaven above" originated? She strained her neck searching the white vastness for heavenly signs but only felt the warmth of the sun on her face.

She closed her eyes and recalled the summer days of her yet blossoming womanhood helping Ayotunde harvest crops. One day, as Ayotunde gathered squash on the far end of the farm, Sarah sat in the grass with her eyes closed, the sun kissing her face as she held out her apron for Ayotunde to fill with the yield.

"Ay, *lui miesie*! Get up off your bottom and help me pick," Ayotunde had yelled playfully. "Your brother needs take this to market to sell."

At that, Sarah ran to her and knocked the bundle of squash in Ayotunde's arms to the ground. She screeched with laughter, hoping Ayotunde would chase her. And she did.

"Oh, you wicked child," she'd yelled as she pursued her. "If I get the switch from your papa for bruised squash, I give you it, too, on your bare behind."

Sarah slowed just enough so that Ayotunde could catch her, and they tumbled to the ground together in laughter. After that, the game had become a regular part of the summer harvests, always ending in the two young women entwined together under the warm New England sun.

For many years, Sarah had fretted that her husband's touch had never felt as glorious as Ayotunde's.

Hazel tapped her shoulder. "What are you smiling about?"

Sarah started. "I hadn't known I was," she said. "I am suddenly struck with homesickness, but not for my husband Thomas." She glanced around and then leaned toward Hazel's ear. "For my Ayotunde, my father's house servant."

"I remember you telling me about her." Hazel's smile grew wide across her face. "Do tell."

"'Tis a troublesome burden," she said softly. "God hath punished me for my thoughts and dreams of her." Her eyes fell to her lap. "He leave me barren these ten years of my marriage."

"Wait. You think you're childless because you were in love with Ayotunde?"

Sarah looked at her quizzically. "What mean you *in love*? That is a sacred emotion for mine husband only."

Hazel cocked an eyebrow. "Is it?"

Sarah looked down again and fiddled with the cap on the mini bottled water in her lap.

"Sarah." Hazel's voice was rich with compassion and sincerity. "In spite of what you've been told or not told, it's natural for some women to fall in love with other women. God isn't going to punish you for it. That's a myth created in religion to force people into submission. Maybe you don't have kids because your husband is shooting blanks."

"I know not what are blanks."

"Doesn't matter," Hazel said. "Look. I can totally empathize with you feeling out of place and even homesick, given how far you've come, but you were sent to the future for a reason."

"Aye. To escape false accusations—"

"I guarantee you that's not the main reason. I'm not sure exactly what it is, but I'm certain that creep Lucien McCoulter, or Samuel Cranwell, is behind it."

Sarah nodded. "I doubt it not. There be no love lost between Samuel Cranwell and me. The man lusted for power in 1692, and he yet lusts for it centuries later. I think it not well that he learn I have come to this century."

"What does he have against you? Didn't you say your husband took him out of the gutter and gave him a job?"

"Aye, and gave him the word of God. Not long after, working fields for an honest wage satisfied him not. Cranwell liked not to take orders and took to drink again. When Thomas asked him to leave our homestead, he set out to preaching on the street by the meeting house. Many a parishioner took to listening, so much fervor had he for God. When he learned of the church's need for a new reverend, he campaigned for it…fiercely."

"Did he get it?"

Sarah shook her head. "At my urging, my Thomas went to meeting and spake against his appointment. He told of Cranwell's drinking and indolence. One other farmer, Joseph Warren, claimed thievery against him. The magistrates chose Reverend Parris instead."

"I imagine that didn't sit well with Cranwell."

"Aye. Indeed not. Soon after Reverend Parris took the pulpit, my husband's barn caught fire, and Joseph Warren's sow gone missing. The marshal sought to question Cranwell, but he were gone, too. 'Twere rumored that he and his followers ventured to the wood to form their own congregation involving the black arts. They were not seen again in Salem Village."

Hazel's body visibly shivered as she listened. She turned and nudged Raven awake. "I hate to break this to you, but it appears we have more than one time traveler on our hands, and they aren't all as sweet-natured as my aunt."

"Huh?" Raven said, still groggy.

Sarah relayed the story again to Raven, who sat quietly dumbfounded.

"Goody Raven?" Sarah shook her gently. "Art thee bewitched?"

"In a manner of speaking," Raven said. "This explains why Morgan demanded we all see her immediately." Her tone turned grave. "I can't let Sarah out of my sight for even a minute until Morgan tells us exactly what we're dealing with."

Fear plummeted into Sarah's stomach worse than a sudden drop in altitude. "Good heavens. What have I done?"

Hazel whipped her head toward her. "What do you mean? You

didn't do anything except save yourself. Every one of those victims would've done the same thing if they could've."

Sarah's vision began clouding with tears. "I should have stayed behind with my Ayotunde and faced my lot as bravely as the others."

"So you could all be rotting in jail awaiting execution?" Hazel said. "No. No. That's not the answer."

"Sarah," Raven said gently. "We're landing soon. Let's stay calm until we get to Morgan."

Hazel glared at her. "Then we can panic?"

"That's not what I meant."

Sarah wrung her hands in her lap. "I must conceive of a way to bring Ayotunde here," she began chanting to herself. "My dear Ayotunde."

CHAPTER NINE

Lucien paced in his living room. After he passed the vase on the coffee table for the third time, he picked it up and threw it against the wall. The shattering glass gave his mind a nice reprieve from the demons' failure that echoed in his head.

"So, let me get this straight," he said to Amon, the demon cowering on the couch. "The four of you couldn't manage to catch one shadowhunter, a book dealer, and a Puritan?" The question was rhetorical, but that didn't matter. He wanted his disgust with the lone survivor to be palpable.

The demon dipped his head. "The book dealer and the Puritan are witches, and the shadowhunter, well, she is very fast."

Lucien grabbed the demon by the shirt and wrenched him up off the ground, his closed fists shaking with rage. "They barely know they're witches. They have no idea what they can do yet. I gave you ties to bind them. All you had to do was what you were told." He whisked the blade off the coffee table and held it to the demon's neck. "You've failed me. What's stopping me from destroying you right now?" A knock on the door lured his attention away. "Who is it?" His voice boomed throughout the small room, causing a picture on the wall to shift from the vibration.

"It's Tammi," the voice on the other side of the door answered.

Lucien put the demon and the blade down and did his best to get his breathing under control. He walked over to the door and whipped it open. The short blond in a tailored pantsuit sauntered in and deposited her purse on the table near the door.

"What's Amon doing here?" She sat down on the couch and crossed her legs.

He followed her into the living room and but couldn't stand still. There was too much raw energy pumping through him right now to sit. "He's explaining to me why I shouldn't send him back to Hell."

"This should be good," she said with a smile.

Amon fumbled over his words for the next several minutes, trying to paint himself in a positive light as he explained his failure. When he was finished, he dipped his head again. Pitiful excuse for a demon.

Tammi Lee looked at Lucien, her eyes flashing to a brighter color blue from their shared anger. "Are these witches going to be a problem for us?"

Lucien snarled at the question. "I'm not a fool. I have a hellhound tracking them. They'll be taken care of, but this time, we won't try to capture the witches. We're just going to kill them."

"And the shadowhunter, what will you do with her?" Tammi Lee stood and walked to the coffee table. She picked up the blade and turned its tip on her finger, drawing a drop of blood.

Lucien snorted. "Morgan's pet? She's the last in the family line. When she's gone, nothing will be left in our way."

Tammi Lee licked the drop of blood off her fingertip and dragged the blade down Amon's chest. She smiled when the metal scorched his skin, leaving a bubbling, fleshy boil in its wake. "The master will be pleased." When the blade reached the demon's belly button, she thrust it in, and he screamed until his form dissolved into a pile of ash around the blade.

CHAPTER TEN

After what seemed like a journey into eternity, Hazel sighed with relief when she saw the sign for New Orleans's French Quarter. She was tired, sweaty, and ravenous but was thoroughly enjoying sitting next to Raven in the back seat, close enough to smell the cinnamon of her gum and the musk of her cologne.

"I think this is it," Raven said as the car slowed on their approach to Morgan le Fay's Bourbon Street residence. She stared at the two-story town house with wrought iron bars around the windows and balcony above. "Impressive architecture. Digs suitable for witches, warlocks, and voodoo priestesses."

Hazel nodded. "The hair on the back of my neck is already standing up."

Raven reached forward for Sarah, who was fast asleep. "Sarah, wake up. We're here."

Sarah roused with a start. "Have we reached our journey's end?"

"Something tells me this is just the beginning," Hazel said as they all disembarked the black SUV.

Raven turned to face them as they gathered on the doorstep. "Ready?" She leaned in toward them. "Be cognitive of your emotions. Morgan can sense them and manipulate them if she chooses."

Hazel and Sarah clutched each other's arms in anticipation. "Sure," Hazel said dryly. "I mean, I think. Ready as I could ever be."

Raven smirked. After she announced their arrival via the gorgon door knocker, the housekeeper welcomed them into the ornately adorned French-Creole town house. Hazel wasn't sure what to expect, but she hadn't envisioned a witch queen's lair to be an American historical showplace replete with French provincial furnishings and accented with various types of pirate booty that looked recently looted from some fortune-seeking mariner.

The housekeeper, dressed in a black and white uniform, escorted them across a creaking wooden floor polished to a blinding sheen and through an arched doorway into a lavish sitting room.

Morgan le Fay lounged cross-legged on a chaise in a black chemise and sheer tulle shoulder wrap and begrudgingly poked an iPad with her long black fingernails.

"*Volez!*" Morgan spat. "*Anndan tourego!*" she added, then looked up at her visitors. "Marie Laveau." She calmly pointed at her tablet. "She always cheats in *Words with Friends*."

"Hi, Morgan," Raven said with a knowing grin.

Morgan tossed the iPad aside and leapt up from her chaise. "What took you so long?"

"You summoned me yesterday," Raven replied with an attitude as she glanced at her watch. "It's not like the broomstick thing is real." She turned to Sarah. "Is it?"

"I have heard conflicting reports," Sarah said and lowered her eyes again.

"You're looking well," Morgan said to Raven, sparking a twinge of jealousy in Hazel.

Morgan was the most beautiful woman Hazel had ever seen. Her shimmering blond hair looked as if it was spun from fine silk. Her flawless skin seemed almost to glow. Her features were delicate, but strong. Hazel was transfixed on her magnetism. If that was Raven's type, how could Hazel ever compete? Thankfully, Raven seemed unmoved by the flirtatious lilt in Morgan's voice.

"So, this is Sarah Hutchinson and her niece Hazel Abbot," Raven said as she encouraged Hazel to step forward.

Hazel curtsied to Morgan as though she were Queen Elizabeth II. "It's an honor to meet you, Your Highness." She extended her hand, but Morgan walked right past it.

"That means you're our trans-century border wall jumper," Morgan said to Sarah, then turned to Raven and Hazel. "Sorry. Couldn't resist."

"Aye," Sarah said softly. "'Tis a marvel to make your acquaintance."

"Mmm," Morgan replied absently, slowly circling Sarah as

though verifying she was an actual, three-dimensional mortal. When it appeared she was satisfied with her inspection, she stopped, faced Sarah, and waved black-taloned fingers in a circle in front of her. "You, my dear, have gravely complicated matters with your appearance." She lifted Sarah's chin with one finger. "Some enterprising little entities followed you through the wormhole you and your voodoo boo-boo inadvertently created in your effort to flee those stuffy old Puritans. They had to have emerged in a time several years before you appeared, but they managed to stay off my radar until recently, which was no easy task. They have to be getting help from someone, but I have no idea who yet."

"Entities?" Raven said, cutting in front of Sarah. "As in more than one?"

"I thought it was just that smarmy preacher," Hazel said.

Morgan shook her head. "Three. The father, the son, and the holy host...of a wildly popular conservative podcast that is soon to be part of Fox's prime time lineup."

"Tammi Lee Sanderson," Raven said in defeat.

Hazel's mind briefly flashed to the conservative talking head. Her views fell somewhere between believing women belonged barefoot and pregnant and bringing back slavery. The sound of her voice made Hazel's skin crawl.

"That's her," Morgan said. "Amazing how fast one's star rises in the partisan news wars when one's daddy knows a network programming exec and said daddy is also one of Satan's most ardent devotees."

"Sarah, did Samuel Cranwell have children?" Raven said.

"I know not of Samuel having a wife or children," she replied. "Perhaps he found a bride amid his followers after leaving Salem Village."

"Oh, he found more than one," Morgan said with a chuckle. "But Brigham Young got all the credit for polygamy. That sure put a bee in Cranwell's bonnet."

"So, what's Cranwell's deal?" Raven asked. "Why did he send his lackeys after us at the arena?"

Hazel's body shivered at the mention of the men who'd attacked them. She knew everyone was now safe, but that didn't make the memory any less terrifying.

"Cranwell, or Lucien McCoulter, as he calls himself these days, knows that as long as Sarah's here, he can be banished back to 1692, and he's having none of that. He enjoys the life of excess that comes with being a false idol worshipped by his flock way too much to go back to the days of flinging the contents of a chamber pot out the window when it's ten below outside. Besides, there's been bad blood between him and Sarah since forever."

"Aye. He harbored much ill will toward my husband."

"Why do you think he accused you of witchcraft?" Morgan said. "What better way to avenge himself than to get the wife of the guy who quashed his bid for religious supremacy set to swinging like a bedsheet on a prairie clothesline?"

"'Twas he who accused me? He hath been gone months from Salem without a word before the children commenced their devilish sport."

"Yeah, well, you give the people what they want, and they'll show up for it," Morgan said. "He informed the authorities that you sent your spirit out to try to tempt him with alcohol now that he was a reformed man of God."

"That foul drunkard," Sarah spat, more riled up than she'd ever appeared. "Liar! He needed not the temptation of others to partake of the vile swill. I detested his presence from the very moment he arrived at our home."

"Your people were horribly misguided, Sarah," Morgan said. "What they did to each other in the name of God." She shook her head and smirked to herself.

"Who's the third demon, the son you mentioned?" Raven said.

"Dirk Fowler," Morgan said. "Some white nationalist half-wit who works as a political lobbyist for one of those organizations proclaiming they protect the American family values under attack from the scourge that is the progressive movement." Sarcasm seeped even deeper into her words. "You know, all those heretics clamoring to be treated equally in the eyes of the law. However will society survive? So bourgeois."

"What exactly do you need us for, Morgan?" Raven said. "Getting rid of these three morons isn't exactly a heavy lift for you."

"Oh, you mortals. Always in such a hurry. Let's take a while to get reacquainted, Raven. It's been so long." She ran her fingers across the front of Raven's hair and down her jaw.

The sensual flirtation sent another jolt of jealousy charging through Hazel's veins. Morgan must have felt it somehow because she turned to Hazel and smiled.

Hazel tried to shake off the intensity of the situation. Unsure of Morgan's capabilities, she didn't want to give her a reason to peek into her mind. "If you have time, I'd like to talk to you. I have about a zillion questions, and I'm sure Sarah does, too."

Morgan tapped her nails against her lips and raked her eyes over Hazel. "There will be time for that." As she stepped closer, Hazel fought the urge to step backward. "Tonight, we celebrate."

Hazel felt her breath catch in her chest as the Queen moved around her. She tried to refocus. "Celebrate what, exactly?"

Morgan laughed and stepped away, sauntering back to the couch. "Everything, darling." She motioned to the staircase. "Your things should already be in your rooms. Go freshen up, and then we'll eat, drink, and..." Morgan's eyes flickered over to Raven again. "Well, we'll see where it goes from there."

Hazel headed toward the stairs, hoping she'd made her escape before any of her feelings seeped into Morgan's psyche. It was unnerving to be near someone who could experience your emotions. It was like a violation, a burglary of some kind. Hazel wanted to be as far away from her as possible. She was having a hard enough time sorting out her feelings for Raven, and she didn't need a centuries-old witch complicating matters. She'd been feeling slightly off since the moment she walked through the door. Being in Morgan's orbit was causing her senses to collide. She'd sensed power bubbling beneath her surface, but couldn't place its origin. It was confusing and enthralling all at the same time.

She checked several rooms until she found her bag sitting next to a bed. It was unlike her to be dramatic, but she was terribly overwhelmed. She flopped down on her bed face-first and propped the pillow over her. She wanted to scream into the mattress but thought that would be a bit over the top.

She rolled over and took a deep breath, needing a moment to gather her thoughts. Her entire world had been upended over the last few days. If you'd asked her three days ago if she knew demons were currently prancing around the world, she would have laughed off the idea as an ancient myth. She couldn't have dreamed up the circumstances that brought Sarah into her bookstore. Throw in a queen witch, a few evil entities trying to kill her, and a supernatural hunter whose eyes could stop a hell-bound truck of lost souls, and she would've told you to lay off the acid.

Raven. Just thinking of her made her skin tingle. But what game was she really playing? Granted, Raven had never given any indication that something was happening between them, but there were glances, small touches, and flirtatious smiles.

She sat up in bed. Maybe she didn't have control over anything else that was going on, but she could find out what was happening between her and Raven. At the very least, maybe she could get some answers as to why Morgan looked at her like she wanted to devour her…and not in a sexy way.

A soft voice that Hazel recognized as Morgan's housekeeper was on the other side of the door. "Cocktails and hors d'oeuvres will be served in ten minutes."

Hazel looked down at her jeans and shirt. "Okay. Be down in a few."

Perfect. Hazel hoisted her bag onto the bed. She wasn't sure what one was supposed to wear to dinner with *the* Morgan le Fay, but she was sure it wasn't a Wonder Woman shirt.

Raven received the glass of wine Morgan handed her, careful not to allow their fingers to touch.

"I hope you like this," Morgan said. "I had it brought up from the cellar just for you." She examined the label on the bottle. "It's a two-hundred-year-old Bordeaux, a thank-you gift from Napoleon."

Raven swirled the plum colored liquid around in her glass, sniffed, and took a sip. "This is fantastic, but I can't tell the difference between this and boxed wine."

Morgan laughed. "Oh, I do find you amusing." She leaned over and traced her finger down Raven's arm. "Tell me how much you've missed me."

Raven heard the creak on the stairs. Hazel and Sarah were coming to join them. Hazel looked beautiful but relaxed in her jeans and gray sweater falling slightly off the shoulder. Raven experienced a brief flash of what Hazel's skin might taste like. Before her thoughts could go any further, Morgan waved her hand, and two seats jetted back from the table.

"I'm so glad you could join us," Morgan said as Hazel sat next to Raven and Sarah next to Morgan. "Raven was just impressing me with her knowledge of her favorite vintage of boxed wine." Morgan waved her hand again, and the bottle floated into the air toward the glasses in front of Sarah and Hazel.

Sarah clutched Hazel's arm as their eyes followed the floating bottle. While Sarah stared with amazement, Hazel observed the bottle as it poured wine into their glasses.

"Is that a Penfolds Grange Hermitage 1951?" Hazel reached for the unopened bottle on the table, then drew back her hand. "I thought there were only twelve bottles in existence."

Morgan seemed impressed. She nodded and sat back. "When it was first made, it was given out, an experiment of sorts. I knew Max Schubert, the genius who created it. I took several cases off his hands. Now, this wine goes for upward of fifty thousand dollars a bottle. But please, don't let it overshadow General Buonaparte's favorite."

Hazel did a double take at Morgan before taking a sip and setting her glass down. "What is it that you really want from us, Morgan?"

The smile on Morgan's face disappeared into a warning. "You've felt different since you've arrived? A little more brazen, a little bolder, feeling a surge of power pumping through your veins?" Morgan got up from the table and walked over to Hazel. She stood behind her and placed her hands on Hazel's shoulders. "It's because you're in my presence. You have no idea what it means to be a witch. You have no idea the power we wield or what we're capable of when pushed." When Morgan leaned next to her ear, Hazel shuddered. "I'm the most powerful entity in this realm, and you're absorbing small amounts of my power through mere proximity. Imagine what my full strength must be. Imagine what I'm capable of doing." She kissed her cheek and walked back to her chair. "Now, let's start again. Are you enjoying your wine?"

Morgan waved her hand again, and Hazel slumped as if she had just been released from an invisible grip.

Raven saw the panic in Hazel's eyes and reached out, taking her hand under the table. She wanted to give her any strength she could, however she could. Hazel squeezed her hand, accepting her support.

"It's wonderful. Thank you." Hazel smiled at Morgan. "I'm looking forward to learning whatever you have to teach me."

Morgan stared at Hazel for a moment as if deciding whether to move on or continue this battle; she seemed to land on the former. "I'm thrilled to have you here, my dear. *Mi casa es su casa.*"

Raven let out her breath and picked up her wineglass. "To new friends."

"May God bless our bounty," Sarah said, pressing her hands together and bowing her head over her place setting. She took a sip from her glass and started coughing. "Savage fire water," she exclaimed when the coughing stopped.

Raven and Hazel exchanged covert smiles.

Morgan ran her finger over the top of her wineglass, leaning toward Sarah. "I'm terribly interested in the spell you cast that brought you here, Sarah. You're either a very powerful or very lucky witch. I haven't decided yet."

Sarah brushed her hair from her eyes and attempted to take another sip of wine before answering. "It were not I who cast a spell. Ayotunde spake incantations from our cell, and I waked outside near Goody Hazel's shop. She hath saved me from the noose, and I fear she be jailed yet. If I be a witch, then I must find a way to rescue her, too."

Morgan shot Raven a warning glance as she addressed Sarah. "Let's pipe down with this crazy talk for a moment, *oui*? Before I know it, with a poof of smoke, you'll have the Proctors, Nurses, and Coreys sitting at the table with us, and I don't have enough beef bourguignon to go around."

The room was quiet for a moment as they all waited for the awkwardness to dissipate.

Morgan studied Sarah and Hazel. "Do either of you know the genesis of your power?" She paused and clearly noted the blank expressions on both of their faces. "Of course you don't." Morgan finished her wine, and the bottle dipped back over the opening, refilling the lonely glass. "You're descendants of a witch I used to know very well, in more ways than one." She smiled, seeming to reminisce. "Mary and I met in England almost six hundred years ago. She was charming, had a wonderful wit, and a face men would go to war over. Her father intended to marry her off to a wealthy merchant. The merchant was a terrible man with a heavy hand and an affinity for prostitutes. Mary and I had become very good friends, and she came to me, begging for a way out." Morgan took a deep breath and shook her head.

Raven had never seen Morgan show any inkling of fondness for anyone from her past. Her revealing any chink in her armor was unfathomable. Raven wanted to ask questions but was worried any interruption would halt the sincere glimpse into Morgan's psyche. If that happened, she'd never be given another opportunity to peek behind the iron curtain of Morgan's secrets.

"I was willing to do anything to protect her, to keep her with me. So, I shared my blood with her, changing her forever. We were very happy together for many years. We traveled anywhere our hearts desired, met fascinating people, and had the most wonderful experiences. When we started hearing whisperings of the New World, we thought it would be our next great adventure. When those settlers came to Roanoke, Mary wanted to help them survive. They weren't doing very well on their own, and against my better judgment, I agreed. I never could say no to her. It had been so long since I was challenged, and since the humans never posed any real threat to us, I thought helping them get on their feet would be easy." Morgan looked past all of them as if she were looking directly into the past and watching it unfold again. "She took a liking to one of the settlers, a young man with broad shoulders and a toothy smile. He was nice enough, and I thought he was just a phase, another one of her crazy whims. It wasn't until she became pregnant that I realized the depth of their relationship. I'd grown comfortable in our pairing. I thought we were untouchable." She wiped a tear from the corner of her eye. "The baby girl was born two days before the attack and a day after Virginia Dare."

Raven had never heard this story and didn't know what to make of it. "The attack by the Native Americans?"

Morgan put her hand on Raven's. "No, darling. The attack by the demons and the dark magic witches. When they found out Mary had reproduced, they…well, let's just say they were less than amenable to the new course of events."

Hazel leaned forward. "But why would they care? Obviously, witches reproduce; otherwise, we wouldn't exist."

Morgan turned Raven's hand over and started tracing small circles on her palm. Raven was surprised when the shiver that usually accompanied Morgan's attention didn't come. She wasn't sure if it was Morgan manipulating her reactions or the fact that she could feel Hazel's eyes tracking their encounter. Hazel was smart, willful, and beautiful. Raven knew she was attracted to her, but was it becoming something more? She rolled her neck, hoping to displace the thought for now.

"Ordinary witches reproduce. But this child had my blood coursing through her veins. I had inadvertently created a line of heirs to my throne. This was not something that was ever supposed to be done. Unlike humans, witch DNA doesn't dilute as the generations progress. It only strengthens, adapts, evolves."

Sarah appeared shaken. "What came of Mary and her baby?"

Morgan kissed Raven's palm, then rested it against her cheek. "I cloaked the baby in an invisibility spell and told them the baby had died in childbirth. Their magic wasn't strong enough to detect the spell I had cast. But as my punishment, they burned Mary at the stake." She looked almost apologetic, a demeanor Raven hadn't ever seen on her before. In all the years they'd known each other, Raven had never felt sorry for her. This situation had clearly scarred Morgan and probably dictated a great deal of her current apathy toward people. Raven had always assumed Morgan was above human emotions, superior. But not even the great Morgan le Fay could escape this type of pain.

"They destroyed the village, killing everyone and burning everything to the ground. I made a bargain with them to spare Virginia. I convinced them she'd serve as a message to all other entities in our realm, good and evil, that they weren't to be trifled with. After all, who leaves a baby without parents and with nowhere to go? The only clause was that there would be a curse on her and her family forever. The curse they laid on her was one of solitude, perpetual loneliness. I couldn't lift that curse as it was tied to her life, so I added a second. The Virginia Dare bloodline would be saddled with ridding the world of the demons. They are the shadowhunters of our realm. They keep the peace, and every one of them is tied to me."

Raven felt Hazel squeeze her hand, and she instinctively pulled away. She hadn't been aware of the first curse, the one that would keep her alone in this world, the curse that would ensure that she never felt love, happiness, or what it felt like to be part of a family. She wanted to bolt from the desire, passion, and comfort Hazel stirred in her, but there was nowhere she could go where Morgan wouldn't find her. She belonged to Morgan…she always would.

"And the child?" Sarah asked.

"I took her to a family I knew in England, the Hutchinsons. And, well, you two know the rest." Morgan's face transformed from apology to glee almost instantly. "We need more wine." She clapped her hands.

Hazel ran her hand across her face. "Wait. Are you telling us that we're related to you?"

Morgan laughed. "More or less. There are worse things, you know. Had you been properly trained, you two would be some of the most powerful witches who've ever existed. But your talents have been squandered and ignored." The housekeeper brought out a tray of food, and Morgan popped a cube of cheese into her mouth. "I've kept an eye on your family for ages. Hazel, your grandmother was a fantastic witch. But when a rather elaborate spell accidently killed your grandfather, your mother swore off magic. It's a shame really. You could've been so much more."

Hazel shook her head. "My grandfather died in a fire at work when my mother was ten."

Morgan popped a grape in her mouth and grinned. "You sure about that?"

Hazel's face went ghostly white, and Raven fought the urge to put an arm around her. "My mother has been lying to me my whole life?"

Morgan rolled her eyes and leaned back in her chair. "You mortals, so predictable with your selective outrage. Hazel, darling, clearly, your mother was trying to protect you. You all lie. Lying is a social construct you've designed to protect yourselves from the harsh reality of this realm. You're all so fragile, and I think you underestimate how easy it is to kill one of you. Plus, you're all completely ruled by your emotions, which makes you even easier to manipulate."

Hazel snatched the bottle of wine and filled her glass. "I don't live by lies. Trust is what holds us together."

Morgan slithered out of her seat and onto Raven's lap, but Raven didn't want this kind of attention from Morgan. She wanted to check on Hazel. Morgan had just dropped a huge bomb on her, and from the look on Hazel's face, she wasn't handling it well. Instead, she did nothing. Pushing Morgan away from her now could spur a streak of anger that Raven didn't want directed toward Hazel. Morgan picked a grape off the plate and slid it into Raven's mouth. "I'm bored with this conversation now. I've told you everything you need to know about how you got here. What you do with it from this point is your decision."

❖

The evening had been littered with new information and a family history that was almost beyond comprehension. Hazel was so angry from a sense of betrayal she could scream. Her mother never should've kept this from her. She had tried calling her mom, but again, it went straight to voice mail.

However, what kept her moving around the room was the interaction between Raven and Morgan. Morgan had handled Raven like property, touching her without reservation or hesitation. Raven, for her part, seemed to tolerate the contact but made no effort to advance or rebuff the interaction. Hazel had finally reached her limit after watching Morgan nuzzle into Raven's neck on the couch. She'd said her good nights and retreated into her bedroom, but not before flinging a passive-aggressive remark in Raven's direction.

After calming down, she realized she owed Raven an apology for her behavior. She didn't want things to be awkward or weird between them. She needed to get her mind clear and her emotions back on their usual clear and steady track. Before she could change her mind, she found herself in the hall outside Raven's room, quietly knocking on the heavy wooden door.

Raven opened it a second later and motioned for her to come inside. She looked as if she'd been in bed, wearing nothing but black boxer briefs and a black tank top, her short black hair still wet from the shower. She shifted her weight back and forth, looking uncharacteristically nervous. And it was adorable.

"I'm, um…I'm sorry about Morgan," Raven said.

Hazel took a step closer, still not fully understanding why she felt so compelled to be close to this woman. She didn't understand why she felt so possessive of her. The feeling was both terrifying and wonderful. "You don't have a reason to be sorry. You're a single woman. You don't owe me an explanation."

"I may not owe you one, but I feel compelled to give you one."

Hazel wanted to touch her, to caress her well-defined shoulders, but she fought the impulse, wanting to give Raven space to say what she wanted.

"I don't know why Morgan behaves the way she does. She takes what she wants whenever she wants it. It's how it's always been."

The protectiveness she felt for Raven always bubbling beneath the surface flared. "No one is entitled to touch you. That's not how it's supposed to work."

Raven took a small step closer. "I never thought twice about it either way, not until I knew you were watching. I just don't want you to think something's going on between Morgan and me."

Raven was so close Hazel felt the heat of her breath, smelled the remnants of the shower, a bit of soap with Raven's natural earthy smell. "Why is that?"

Raven's slow smile shot a jolt to Hazel's stomach. "You know why."

That was all the confirmation Hazel needed. Before her normal brand of sensibility could take root in her response, her body reacted. She reached up, draped her arms around Raven's neck, and pulled her in. She intended the kiss to be delicate at first, but her raw instincts took over. Raven's lips pushed against hers, the warmth of them igniting a spark deep within Hazel that she'd never felt before. She moved against her, the taste of exquisitely aged wine still lingering on her lips. Raven wrapped her arms around her and tugged her closer. Hazel shuddered as the space between them completely disappeared. She wasn't sure she was making the right choice, but in that moment, she didn't care. All she wanted was more of Raven, as much as Raven would give her, as much as she could get.

When Raven finally broke contact, Hazel went cold at the loss.

"We should get some rest," Raven said. "I'm certain Morgan has big plans for everyone tomorrow. She never shows her hand ahead of time." She kissed Hazel's forehead.

Hazel let her face rest on Raven's lips. She ran her hands down Raven's bare arms and reveled in the goose bumps her touch left in its wake.

"Sleep well." She kissed Raven's cheek.

Raven held her there for a second longer and then let her go. She seemed like she wanted to say more, so Hazel lingered, waiting for an invitation to stay the night. She wanted Raven with every cell in her body but knew enough not to push. Hazel wanted this feeling etched in her mind without the persistence of "what-ifs" and "whys" clouding it.

Hazel went back to her room, her skin still electrified in all the places Raven had just visited. The information she'd received that night would alter her life and what she knew of her history forever, but those weren't her last thoughts as she let her mind drift toward sleep. The only image that occupied her mind in those passing seconds was the taste of Raven's lips and the smell of her skin.

It would be the most peaceful night of sleep Hazel had ever had.

Chapter Eleven

As the long day and evening finally drew to a close after midnight, Sarah changed into her nightgown and knelt in prayer beside the bed in one of Morgan's guestrooms. After the last few days, she felt in need of God's light more than ever. The overwhelming tumult and confusion from the wizardry of this "modern" world had left her reeling like a tempest-tossed mariner. She asked God for strength and guidance in whatever challenges lay ahead and for safety for Raven and her niece, Hazel, who at times seemed as bewildered as she.

But were her prayers spoken in vain? After learning of her witch lineage, she couldn't help pondering if God's grace had been unattainable to a woman of her bloodline all along. Had He completely forsaken her for escaping her fate in Salem Village and for using mystical arts?

And then there was Ayotunde. Despite the dire circumstances in which Sarah had landed, her thoughts continually drifted back to Ayotunde. It had been many a year since she'd seen or spoken to her only to rediscover her in a jail cell in the most wretched of conditions. And through her tribulations, a sparkle yet remained in her gloomy, soulful eyes. Sarah could not banish it from her mind. One thing was certain: No matter her fate, from this point on, Sarah would not let Ayotunde slip away again.

Instead of climbing into bed after her prayers, she found a candle and walked downstairs to find Morgan. She crept as quietly as she could across the creaking floors and found Morgan sitting pensively before a roaring hearth in her parlor.

"Madame le Fay," Sarah said in a whisper. She stood in the arched doorway waiting for Morgan's invitation.

"Oh, Sarah. I thought you'd gone to sleep," Morgan said.

"I am afraid sleep doth elude me this night, weary as I am."

"Come, come." Morgan waved her to the sofa. "Is your chamber not comfortable?"

Sarah curtsied before she sat next to her. "Heavens no. Thy accommodations are most pleasing."

Morgan glanced at the candle Sarah was holding. "You do realize you don't need to walk around with one of those, not since old Tommy Edison gave us the light bulb." She waved her fingers, and the lamp beside the sofa clicked on.

Sarah flinched at the sudden brightness. "Merciful heavens," she said, patting her chest. "Methinks I shall never grow accustomed to such marvels."

"Wait till you give a tampon a try."

"Pray pardon?"

"Never mind. I'll let that experience speak for itself. Now, tell me what's troubling you at this ungodly hour?"

"All things be ungodly these days, it would seem. I know not where to turn."

Morgan nodded as if commiserating. "Look. Try not to stress about it. You're in good hands with Raven. I only contract the best."

"It is not Goody Raven who causes me anguish. 'Tis my Ayotunde. She doth sit imprisoned, accused of bewitching children. I know it to be a false charge, and I fear for her."

"All the charges were false," Morgan said. "If any witchery was going on in Salem back then, it was of the white kind, to help the Puritans forge the new world. And it was working, too, until Lucifer wanted in on it and beckoned his dark brood. I mean, how easy must it have been to manipulate the burgeoning colonies into the realm of evil thanks to man's innate greed and lust for power? What a shit show it turned out to be," she said, shaking her head. "That's why over three hundred years later, tourists are still making pilgrimages there every Halloween. Mortals do love a good shit show, bless their ghastly hearts."

Sarah took a deep breath before suggesting what had been gnawing inside her for hours. "Madame le Fay…be it in your power to shed light on the misguided of Salem Village and help free the innocent?"

Morgan sat up and stared at her. "Do you know what you're asking?"

"Aye," Sarah said, summoning bravery. "To save my friends from their unjust peril."

Morgan leapt up. "You're asking me to rewrite American history, to send the course that destiny had previously charted into a tailspin that humanity would likely never recover from."

Sarah gulped at the thought of such impending doom.

"I adore that idea." Morgan fairly squealed with delight. "I only wish it was within my scope of power." She walked to the credenza and poured two fingers of bourbon over a glass of ice. "I gotta tell you, over the last several hundred years, you humans have worked my last nerve. No matter how many opportunities we give you to help you evolve to a higher level of consciousness, you never fail to fuck it up."

"Pray, I know not what it mean to *fuck it up.*"

Morgan rolled her eyes. "It's like…like saying a fart on all our efforts to help humanity."

"Aye. 'Tis true that mankind is flawed." Sarah sank into the sofa cushions. "No matter how pure our intentions, we do fail our God often."

From the bar Morgan raised her drink to Sarah's observation and continued eyeing her over the glass as she took a sip.

Sarah rose and approached apprehensively. "Ayotunde. Wouldst thou make it so that she may come hither with us?" She took a deep breath to temper the emotion threatening to break free. "I fear I shall never see her again if she remain in that jail."

"I knew that was coming next," Morgan said, then sighed. "I like your style, Sarah. You're clearly a woman ahead of her time and way too smart to thrive in that dreary culture of Puritan oppression, but I can't help you with that either."

Sarah's lips quivered as she blinked away tears.

"C'mon, don't cry," Morgan said. "I don't know how you managed to open that wormhole and sneak into the twenty-first century, but it never should've happened. I understand your desire to escape death, but actions have consequences, as you well know. There's no way I can open yet another portal so even more of Lucifer's dim-witted spawn can rush the gates and run amok here. Raven's hands are already full with the three that followed you."

"Aye." Sarah lowered her head.

"On the bright side, you'll have to go back eventually. You can look forward to a nice chaste reunion with your lady love in a barn or a covered wagon or something."

"If she be alive upon my return." Sarah sighed in resignation. What was the point of being a witch if she couldn't use her powers to save the person she loved the most?

Morgan frowned but offered nothing more.

Crestfallen, Sarah returned to her chamber but found she was too anxious for sleep. She changed into her day clothing and stepped like a mouse down the stairs and out into the balmy night. It was nearing one a.m. as she strolled down Rue Bourbon. Music pouring out from bars grew louder with each step as it guided her toward the bustling center.

Through the garish lights of the city and a cacophony of musical instruments, she marveled at the young people laughing as they undulated together in an obscene fashion inside the establishments and spilled out into the street delirious with intoxication. What must God think looking down on these heathens who seemed to care not of the severe consequences of their behavior in the afterlife?

Once past the chaotic debauchery of the carefree revelers, she stopped and leaned against a darkened storefront to collect herself. A light toward the back of the shop went on. Sarah looked up at the name of the business: *Salon Laveau*. As she peered in the window, past the line of swivel chairs and dryers backlit by the glow from the back room, a figure moved about the rear of the salon. The front door then opened on its own.

"*Entrez*, mademoiselle," the feminine voice said.

When Sarah did as instructed, a woman stepped from the shadows clad in a long frock, colorful head wrap, and a tapestry shawl draped over her shoulders.

"*Vous avez un probleme, no?*"

"Pray pardon?"

"Pardon me. English it is," said the woman as she extended her hand. "Marie Laveau, Voudon Queen. How do you do?"

Sarah curtsied. "I am bewildered. But it be a sentiment I'm wont to feel of late."

"What I said before was, you're here because you have a problem, no?"

"Aye. What I mean to say is that I come to find myself in a most desperate circumstance. My friends and I have been summoned by Madame le Fay to—" She stopped her explanation, wondering if Madame Laveau could or should be trusted.

Marie seemed to notice her apprehension. "Please, sit." She offered a spot next to her on the loveseat in the waiting area. "If you've been summoned by Morgan, we must have some demons in our midst. That's her territory. What is it you want of me?"

"My quandary, Madame Laveau, be not about demons," Sarah said. "My dearest friend Ayotunde sits in a jail falsely charged with witchcraft. The magistrates mean to hang her. She helped me escape my charges, but I know not how to save her."

"Let me guess…you're from Salem, Massachusetts?"

Sarah nodded.

"Puritans," Marie said, shaking her head with a look of disdain. "If only they knew half of what they thought they knew. Ayotunde isn't a witch. She's a voudon or voodoo priestess and a *magnifique* one at that, although she doesn't realize this until later in her life."

"Later? You mean she will not hang?"

"Apparently not, since she's going to become a notorious voodoo queen—almost as good as yours truly. I'm fairly confident in assuming she'll be fine because ain't no voodoo queen sits in jail for long."

Sarah clapped her hands together and looked to the ceiling in relief. "Merciful heavens. God is good. Thank you, God. Thank you."

"Here's the part you might not like," Marie said gravely. "You're probably never going to see her again."

Sarah's heart plummeted as fast as it had risen. "How could that be?"

"She's going to escape her imprisonment and likely flee Salem, *tout de suite*. When you go back—and you'll obviously want to go back once the hysteria is over, and they've stopped the hangings—Ayotunde will be long gone."

Sarah collapsed into a chair and buried her face in her hands. Through her sobs, she heard Marie offering gentle apologies and felt a comforting hand on her shoulder. She composed herself and looked up. "Can you bring Ayotunde here?"

"Say what? *Moi?* Oh, *cherie*, once again, that's Morgan le Fay's department, not mine."

"Madame Laveau, pray, please help me. I cannot bear to go on if I'll not see Ayotunde more. Conjure her forth, and she shall help my friends and me do Morgan le Fay's bidding."

"Hmm. It would be nice to pay homage to my mentor in person," Marie said pensively. "Have you run this by Morgan? She tends to get a little testy when anyone tries to usurp her domain."

"She hath refused me. She fears it may create a portal for other demons."

"Valid," Marie said, scratching at her cheek in thought. "However, we practitioners of voudon are a little more efficient at conjuring than the witches. Of course, they'll never admit it."

Sarah's heart lifted in hope. "Then you will send for her?"

"I'll try," Marie said cautiously. "I've never attempted this level of magic before, but I'll be sure to include some safeguards to ensure that nothing except Ayotunde makes it through."

Sarah dropped to her knees, held Marie's hand, and covered it with kisses. "Thank you, Madame Laveau. Thank you. I shall be forever in your debt."

Marie freed her hand from Sarah's grip and smiled. "A fact that will no doubt come in handy some century."

The unusual phrase caught Sarah off guard. "Some century?"

Marie studied her quizzically. "You do know I'm a ghost, don't you?"

Once Sarah had come to from the shocking news that the woman she'd been talking to in the salon had not actually been a flesh and blood woman, Sarah picked herself up from the floor, received Madame Laveau's instructions, and headed out on her night journey. Just before dawn, she located Marie Laveau's tomb, guided to it through the orange gloaming by a secret sense or preternatural lure of some kind. She placed a small, mangled bouquet of snapdragons and a blessed and anointed candle at the foot of the tomb as an offering; how she obtained them was a matter that would require penance, but that was to be reconciled at a later date.

Recalling Marie's incantation instructions, she faced the front of the tomb, pressed her hands flat against the cold white stone, and recited a prayer first for her own deity, the Lord's Prayer, to cleanse her spirit.

Then she removed from her jacket pocket a crudely fashioned poppet representing Ayotunde that Marie had given her before she embarked on her journey of several blocks to the cemetery. She plucked a blossom from the snapdragon bouquet and rubbed its pollen over the doll as she recited the binding spell:

"With this dust, I bind thee to me, Ayotunde.
In heart, in mind, in body, you shall transcend;
I forge this image in mind, and will it in soul;
I bewitch your body to lift, to fly, to appear,
Bound to me;
Spirit of the heavens, conjure it! Spirit of nature, conjure it!"

She closed her eyes and clutched the doll to her chest with both hands, reciting the Lord's Prayer again. She then used the anointed candle to light and burn the small poppet down to ashes. When the fire died out, she dipped her fingers in the ashes and scrawled an X on the front of the tomb near the numerous other ones around Marie Laveau's engraved name.

With hands still trembling, she glanced around the cemetery through the pinkish glow from the rising sun. Why hadn't Ayotunde materialized before her? Had she not performed the spell correctly? Overwhelmed with disappointment, she leaned against the tomb and buried her head in her hands. Marie Laveau's spell was her only hope of ever seeing Ayotunde again, she thought as her breath escaped in short whimpers.

Furthermore, she'd incurred God's wrath in seeking help from the voodoo priestess. Was there no way of turning back? Had she condemned her soul for all eternity on a fool's errand? Her tears escalated into unrestrained sobs. "God in heaven, please, do not forsake me." She wailed into the insentient dewy dawn until collapsing unconscious at the base of the tomb.

"Them be the tears of my Sarah," the voice whispered. "My ear know the music of that sweet voice."

Sarah opened her eyes, and a figure in a long bulky frock and bonnet rounded the corner and continued toward her. "Ayotunde?" Sarah whispered in awe.

"Aye, my sweet." She knelt down and caressed Sarah's chin.

Sarah struggled to her feet and cupped Ayotunde's warm face in her hands, then traced its familiar edges and contours. "Ayotunde, promise me this be not a cruel dream."

"If it be, I dream it, too." Ayotunde closed her eyes as if spirited away by Sarah's touch.

Sarah scooped her up in an embrace, lifting her off the ground. "If my eyes deceive me now, may they never see clearly again."

Ayotunde laughed as Sarah returned her to the ground. "You did it, Miss Sarah. You sent for me. You learnt of the powers you possess."

"I beseeched the voodoo queen to teach me to send for you," Sarah said, with a mix of pride and sheer delight. "And it worked."

The light of joy extinguished in Ayotunde's eyes, replaced by terror. "No, no, Miss Sarah. No voodoo."

"Yes, Ayotunde. 'Twas the only way. Madame Laveau hath instructed how to conjure you to me. Were it not for her, we should never see each other more."

"I rather never see you then you be beholden."

"Oh, my Ayotunde." Sarah stared into her troubled eyes. "And I would rather choose to be beholden."

She lifted Ayotunde's chin and kissed her gently on the lips, supple kisses that filled her heart with a light God's word had never illuminated with such brilliance.

Chapter Twelve

Just before dawn, Raven jumped from her bed and retrieved her blade from under the pillow before her feet hit the floor. She turned in circles, trying to make out whatever entity had entered the room during her fitful sleep. The only sound she heard was her own bare feet on the ground and her labored breathing. The sweat on her neck and arms started to chill her, an eerie reminder that not everything was as it seemed. She flipped on the light and allowed a moment for her eyes to adjust. The room was empty. She'd learned a long time ago to pay attention to her instincts because they were almost never wrong. Something might not have been there with her in that moment, but that didn't mean it wasn't coming. The realms hadn't calmed since she brought Hazel and Sarah to Morgan. She could feel the energy shifting more rapidly now.

She thought briefly about going to Morgan but changed her mind. Morgan's arrogance sometimes blinded her from what was happening. Her age brought with it the luxury of apathy, something Raven had never been able to settle her mind around.

She opened her door and looked down the hall. The dim lighting cast shadows against the old wooden floors, teasing Raven's reality. She watched Hazel's door for several seconds as her mind and heart battled for position. She wanted to go to her, to make sure she was okay, but she stayed rooted in her spot, the weight of Morgan's words about her eternal solitude and loneliness like cement around her feet. She'd given in to Hazel earlier, the warmth of her breath and the softness of her eyes lulling her into a sense of possibility that would never come to fruition. There was no happily ever after for Raven. She'd always sensed it; Morgan's words simply solidified the feeling of emptiness she'd felt her whole life. Entertaining any other possibility was simply the hollow musings of naiveté, and that wasn't her style. She'd entered every romantic encounter with the same gusto she brought to picking out what to eat for dinner: to satisfy a need. Whatever was happening between them had to stop before she played any part in hurting Hazel. She could send a million cursed souls back to Hell, but she didn't think she'd be able to look at herself in the mirror if she brought pain to Hazel.

Raven closed the door and got back into bed, keeping the blade in hand instead of tucking it under her pillow. She couldn't be sure of what was coming, but she'd damn sure be ready. She closed her eyes and allowed her mind to replay the look in Hazel's eyes from earlier. She remembered the way her eyes had grown darker and her hands slightly trembled the first time she'd touched Raven. She recalled with fervor the buzz of electricity that had charged through her when their lips finally met. Hazel's body emitted a literal pulse when her emotions were teetering on the edge. The power that coursed through Hazel was palpable; once she finally learned to harness it, she'd be unstoppable. That was where she could safely keep Hazel, in her mind without the possibility of hurting her. Hazel didn't need the distraction, and Raven couldn't bear the inevitability of losing her.

A few hours later, Raven woke to the smell of lilacs and the feel of summer warming her body. It was a pleasant, almost giddy sensation that could only mean one thing: witchcraft. She opened her eyes to see Morgan sitting in a chair across the room. Her legs were crossed, and she was dragging her finger around the top of a coffee cup, a soft hum coming from the ceramic mug.

"I thought only crystal made that noise." Raven rubbed her eyes and sat up, leaning against the headboard.

Morgan raised an eyebrow and sipped from the mug. "It does. That was simply for you."

Raven got out of bed and threw on her jeans and shirt. "Thanks? So, what's up? You never wake me up personally."

Morgan stood and walked to the window, her white nightgown flowing tantalizingly across her body. "Despite what you might think, it doesn't bring me any pleasure to keep you in my service."

Raven walked over and took the mug from Morgan's hands, taking a sip. "It brings you a little pleasure."

Morgan smirked and glanced at her. "I do enjoy you, yes."

Raven focused on the large weeping willow tree in the backyard. "I know you have bad news, so I'd prefer if you just say it. I don't like idle chitchat as camouflage."

Morgan cupped Raven's face. "If only we had met in a different lifetime." She kissed Raven's cheek and ran her thumb over the area. "Come downstairs." She kissed her other cheek and let her face linger next to Raven's. "Hmm…your witch is waiting."

Morgan had been suffocating Raven with the sensation of euphoria, but the thought of Hazel being nearby cut through the haze. "She's not *my* witch."

Morgan took a step away and gave her a sad smile, an obvious attempt to hide whatever else she was feeling. "Some things are true whether you believe them or not."

❖

Hazel had gone to get Raven before coming down for breakfast but changed her mind when she saw her at the window with Morgan. She hadn't expected to find them in such an intimate encounter, and now, as she waited for them to come down, she wasn't sure how she felt or how she should feel. Her skin was prickling, almost vibrating. She looked at her fingertips glowing white. She shook her hands, wanting the sensation and the change to go away as she paced around the living room.

"You can't stop it. You can only learn to control it," Morgan said from the stairs.

"What's happening to me?" Hazel closed and opened her fist repeatedly, hoping it was an illusion.

Morgan was in front of her instantly. She took Hazel's hands and stared at them. "Your powers are growing stronger. You don't know how to control them yet, so they're seeping out of you whenever your temperament is altered."

Hazel jerked her hands away. "I want it to stop."

Morgan laughed as she led Hazel to the dining room table, the sound seeming to rise up from deep in her belly. "Oh, sweetheart. Denying who you are, trying to ignore it or push it down, will only end in self-destruction." She waved her hand. "You're a witch. It's time to embrace what you are and what you're meant to be."

Raven came downstairs and briefly made eye contact. She made her way to the table and put several pieces of fruit on her plate. "Where's Sarah?"

Morgan looked between them. "She's not upstairs?"

Raven shook her head.

"I thought she woke up early and came down," Hazel said.

"Then where is she?" Raven said.

Two sets of footsteps came down the hallway, heading toward the staircase outside the dining room.

Morgan closed her eyes and then opened them again, a look of rage igniting on her face. "Not so fast, Hutchinson," she roared. "I'd like a word."

Hazel moved away, the intensity of Morgan's emotions pushing her backward like heat from an oven. "What's wrong?" She wasn't sure what her aunt had done to incite this type of anger, but it couldn't have been good.

Morgan lifted both hands and flung them downward. Every plate and serving dish on the table floated up and then fell back down to the table. A few pieces shattered while others teetered before regaining their balance.

"She defied me," Morgan said through clenched teeth. She waved her hand again, and every door in the room opened and slammed shut.

Sarah appeared in the archway to the dining room, flitting her hand at something behind her. "Good morrow, all. 'Tis is a glorious gift from God the weather be."

"I know what you're up to, Sarah," Morgan said. "I can see her poofy skirt behind you." She ran her hand through her hair in apparent frustration. "Fucking Marie Laveau. I'll have her catfish-eating, voodoo-loving ass for this."

"I'm not sure what's happening right now," Hazel said.

Morgan poured a glass of orange juice, took a sip, and then shook her head. A bottle of vodka floated toward her hand. She dumped the contents into the juice before turning to Hazel. "Your darling aunt has failed to see the import of obeying my strict orders about ushering anyone else through from Salem. It seems she's taken it upon herself to visit the Voodoo Queen to have her girlfriend summoned into the present." She whipped her head toward Sarah. "Didn't you, Sarah?"

"What?" Hazel and Raven said the same time.

"Ayotunde is here, hiding behind Sarah." Morgan drank the contents of her glass in one gulp. "Because we don't have enough shit to worry about. Well, come on, show yourself, Ayotunde. Now that the cat's out of the bag."

Ayotunde crept around from behind Sarah. "How do you do?" she said timidly and followed her greeting with a cautious smile and a curtsey.

"Un-fucking-real," Raven muttered in astonishment.

"Madame le Fay," Sarah said, her hands clasped over heart as if in prayer. "Pray, do forgive my grievous transgression. I shall commit to whatever penance thou wouldst demand of me. I just…I just couldn't let Ayotunde…"

Hazel made a move toward Sarah to comfort her, but Morgan apparently had other plans as an invisible force pitched her into her seat. To struggle against it, she knew, would be in vain.

"Look, Sarah," Morgan said, clearly endeavoring to remain calm. "Why don't you take Ayotunde upstairs and find her something to wear that's a little more stylish and a little less smells like it hasn't been laundered in three hundred years." She forced a smile and encouraged them away with a gentle flapping of her hand.

Once they were upstairs, a door flew shut, and Morgan turned to Hazel and Raven. "I've confined them to the room till I have the time and patience to deal with this latest snafu."

Still dazed, Hazel motioned for the vodka bottle and poured herself a shot.

Morgan turned to Raven with a grave expression. "Sarah and Ayotunde need to go back, and they need to take whatever came through with them. The realms are shifting. Damage the likes of which we've never seen before is occurring, and it may soon be irreversible. I'm not powerful enough to stop it alone."

Raven leaned forward. "What do you need?"

Morgan opted out of the juice this time and filled her glass with vodka, finishing it again in one gulp. "There is only one night with enough mystic energy to send everything back where it belongs."

"All Hallows' Eve," Hazel said absently, then tried to ignore the way Raven's eyes studied her face.

"Smart girl." Morgan lifted her glass in salute, and it filled with vodka again.

"That's only three weeks from now," Raven said and sipped her coffee. "Not a lot of time for this type of mission. It has to happen on that exact date?"

"Yes," Hazel said. "Samhain, or Halloween, is the most powerful night of the year, the night when the barrier between the earthly world and the spirit world is at its most vulnerable, so if your goal is to drive all of the evil entities back at once, it has to be on Halloween."

Morgan and Raven stared at her, seemingly impressed into silence.

Hazel shrugged. "My degree is in occult studies."

"Indeed. Past, present, and future become one for a single wisp of time," Morgan added. "And it's our only opportunity to achieve our goal."

Raven nodded. "Just tell me what you need."

"You need to entice the entities back to the portal through which they entered: the hallowed ground of Salem." She leaned toward Raven, the gravity of the situation flaring in her eyes. "First, you must track down all three demons that followed Sarah though. We need to know what they're planning in order to draw them back to Salem."

"We already know where Lucien McCoulter is," Raven said as she rose from the table. "The others can't be too far off."

The thought of Raven going against the creatures they'd met a few days before without assistance nearly paralyzed Hazel with fear. "I'll go with you."

"No, you won't." Morgan slid another glass of vodka in front of Hazel. "You'll stay right here with me. You need to learn how to master your abilities. I can't have a rogue witch running around amidst all the other chaos. Most importantly, I need you to form a coven, master this spell, and rid the realm of these things."

Hazel pushed the drink away. "She can't go alone. It's too dangerous."

Morgan put her hand on Raven's arm. "Do you need protection, darling?"

Raven swept up the glass in front of Hazel and knocked it back in one motion. "No." She looked at Hazel. "Stay here and learn what you need to. I'll be fine."

The housekeeper came into the dining area with a frown of contrition. "Ma'am, I'm sorry to interrupt, but Madame Laveau is here to see you."

Morgan rose from her seat in a fluid motion. "Take her to the parlor." She looked at Raven. "You need to leave within the hour. We only have three weeks to make this happen, and we can't afford any more surprises."

Raven nodded, and she and Morgan strode out of the room as if on a mission.

Raven was almost to the stairs when Hazel stopped her. "I have a bad feeling about this."

"I'd be surprised if you had a good one." Raven's face softened as she put her hand on Hazel's shoulder. "I'm a shadowhunter. This is literally what I do. I'll be fine."

Hazel looked down at her hands. Her fingertips were glowing again. "About last night." She wanted to say so many things, but she wasn't sure how to put them into words.

Raven shoved her hands into her pockets. "Don't worry about it. It was a weird night." Raven stared with apprehension. She was guarding herself in a way she hadn't the night before when she'd allowed Hazel to sneak a glimpse of the woman beneath the armor. Hazel wanted to banish the trepidation staring back at her, to let Raven know she could be trusted in any situation. She pulled Raven's hands from her pockets and put them against her face, kissing the palms.

"Hazel, I—"

"Don't." She gently pressed her fingers against Raven's lips. "Don't write us off before we have a chance. Don't take a curse from several hundred years ago and allow it to dictate what's happening between us. Don't let black magic determine your fate. Give me a chance. Give yourself a chance."

Hazel felt the shift in Raven's emotions before she felt the lips pressing into her own. Last night, Raven was cautious, as if something in her was holding back. That wasn't what Hazel felt now. Raven's lips were hungry and determined. Wanting to express her approval and appreciation, Hazel put her fingers through Raven's belt loops and nudged her closer. Raven's hips pressing into her sent her mind careening in all directions. Hazel wanted more. She wanted to take Raven upstairs, lock the door, and take the time the two of them needed and deserved. She wanted to explore every part of Raven's body and mind. Hazel maneuvered her hands under Raven's shirt and felt her body hum when Raven's muscles tightened beneath her touch. It was agonizingly short-lived.

Raven pulled away, breathless. "I'll be back soon."

Hazel wanted to protest, to beg her to stay. "Okay," she said instead. "Please be safe."

Raven winked, then disappeared up the stairs.

❖

Sarah paced, periodically checking to see if the door to her guestroom had unlocked and she could return downstairs to offer Morgan more heartfelt apologies. She prayed that what she had done out of desperation hadn't heaped irreparable harm upon Hazel and Raven nor would further endanger them in their quest to rid the land of evil.

She stopped at the door of the bathroom adjacent to her room as the sweet sound of Ayotunde's humming emanated from inside. She closed her eyes and smiled at the purr of her voice, a soothing balm to her anxiety.

She tapped on the door. "Ayotunde, you sound utterly enraptured."

"Come in, Miss Sarah."

Sarah opened the door to Ayotunde smiling at her from the tub, her body covered to her neck in bubbles.

"Oh, this be a marvelous magic," Ayotunde said and blew a handful of bubbles toward her.

Sarah knelt beside the tub and smiled as she lightly flicked the bubbles. "'Tis just one of many enchantments."

Ayotunde's eyes were animated. "The water…it pour right out of the spout. And it be hot. Surely, something this pleasing be the work of the devil himself."

Sarah giggled. "I think it not. But if it be, people seem not concerned." She picked up a cloth and began gently washing Ayotunde's back, letting warm water droplets cascade down her russet skin.

Ayotunde let out a soft moan that sent a shiver through Sarah. She guided the soapy cloth farther down her back as her own body tingled with sensation.

"Your Thomas came for you," Ayotunde said after a while.

Sarah stopped, startled by the mention of her husband's name. "Did he?" She felt a sudden wave of shame because she had not thought of him much since her escape. "What say he to the jailors?"

"He ask what price for your release." Ayotunde went very still. "He yell and beseech the guards but they turn him away. He think you still be jailed."

Sarah sank to the floor in dejection, talking almost to herself. "My Thomas be a good man. Methinks he deserve a wife whose heart beat with proper warmth for him."

"And yours does not feel warmth?"

"Aye, it does. But not for Thomas."

At that, Ayotunde turned around and gazed at her with a soulfulness Sarah felt deep within her. Sarah leaned over the side of the tub and kissed Ayotunde's wet lips softly as a tide of passion rushed forward, a passion she knew was not hers alone.

Ayotunde's gleaming, soapy arm reached around Sarah's head and held it firmly as they devoured each other's lips with a craving Sarah had never dreamed existed. Her body screamed in a tempest of new, unusual sensations that startled her, yet she refused to pull away. She loved the taste of Ayotunde's mouth, hungered for more of what she hadn't known. All she felt was the desire to crawl into the tub so that they absorbed each other until they were one being.

"Miss Sarah," Ayotunde whispered. "I knew it be you my heart beat for. I be bound to you for all ages."

"Oh, Ayotunde, so much that I had not understood doth seem clear now, the melancholy I felt for so long since I marry Thomas. Then when father passed to his eternal rest and I discovered he will you to my brother against my entreaties to him…I thought my heart never to recover."

"But we here now, Miss Sarah."

"Aye. And I mean not to lose you again."

With a click of the lock, the guestroom door swung open, and Morgan appeared at the open bathroom door. "Well, here's a turn even I didn't see coming."

Sarah sprang to her feet, standing in front of the tub as if to shield Ayotunde. "Madame le Fay, 'tis not what it appears."

Morgan rolled her eyes. "Whatever it is, you do realize that in these times, and especially in this city, it's fine. Do your thing, ladies."

"I know not what you mean of these times." Sarah stepped aside, sensing she didn't have to hide Ayotunde.

"I mean, if you two love each other, go for it."

"I don't understand," Sarah said. "Our love be not an abhorrence?"

"Oh, I didn't say that," Morgan replied. "Some still say it is. That's why our three rogue demons have enjoyed such a quick ascent to power in this society, by manipulating ignorance and thus bending the gullible to their will. Which brings me to my purpose in crashing your little bubble party. Sarah, you need to join Hazel in a little seminar I like to call…" She spread her hand across the air as though seeing it on a marquee. "'Harnessing your witchly powers.' Pronto."

"And as for you…" She compelled Ayotunde to stand, bubble-covered, in the tub and tossed her a thick bath towel. "We have to meet with Madame Laveau to decide what we're going to do with you."

"I beg of you, Madame le Fay, please do not send her back."

Morgan glared at Sarah. "I think you've made enough of the decisions in this matter for now. Why don't you leave it up to the experienced ones to decide what's next?"

Sarah bowed her head and curtsied. "Aye, Madame."

Morgan exited the room in a flourish. Sarah and Ayotunde exchanged nervous smiles.

"I fear Madame Laveau be sending me back," Ayotunde said softly.

"No, no. I shall not allow it, Ayotunde," Sarah said, her throat thick with sadness. "I can't lose you again."

"Like so much, the choice be not ours. But may it be that the power of my love for you forever keep me by your side."

"May God hear our prayers." Sarah took the towel from Ayotunde and gently patted her chest and shoulders dry.

"Next time, it be your turn for a back scrub," Ayotunde said with a knowing grin.

"Aye," Sarah said, giggling through her tears.

CHAPTER THIRTEEN

Raven watched out her window as the small plane descended into the Roanoke airport. One of the many benefits of being able to utilize Morgan's personal plane was that she could make this trip in just two hours instead of the twelve-hour drive she otherwise would've had to endure. The other major benefit was that she could bring all her necessary weapons without having to deal with TSA. It was never an easy task having to explain to a perplexed agent why she needed a dozen different types of blades, wooden stakes, and an assortment of silver- and gold-infused weaponry. If she were being honest, flying on a private plane made her feel rather important. If it weren't for Morgan, she'd be stashed away on a middle seat somewhere over Nebraska waiting to change planes and undoubtedly sitting next to someone who didn't take a great deal of concern regarding their personal hygiene.

She thanked the flight crew and waited while one of Morgan's guys dropped her bags into a small rental car.

"Didn't want to spring for an SUV, huh?" she asked as she walked around to the driver's side.

"Take it up with the boss, Dare," the bulky man said as he walked back toward the plane.

She'd been kidding, but clearly her brand of sarcasm was lost on the new guy. She'd tried to talk to him while they'd been on the plane, but he'd either nodded or shaken his head in response to her questions. She couldn't even get him to reveal his name. Rude, she'd thought as she sipped her champagne, another perk of Morgan's private transport.

Raven drove the car off the tarmac and toward the outskirts of town. The first thing she needed to do was locate the demons, and to do that, she needed to retrace their steps. The only way to accomplish that was to double back to where she'd last seen Lucien. The thought of Lucien alone sent a shiver up her spine. He was unlike any demon she'd ever encountered. Demons tended to be simpleminded, unambitious followers. That was not what Lucien was at all. Was there a new, modernized breed of demon? Was that what the shift was? Had Sarah inadvertently started a chain reaction that none of them could have foreseen? She rolled her shoulders, trying to release some of the foreboding tension from her body. She reached into her backpack when she came to a stoplight and checked to make sure her weapons were in easy reach. They always were, but the reassurance was nice.

She rolled down the window of the car, allowing the brisk, early fall air to hit her face. It smelled of recent rain and woodsmoke. It was the same smell that had filled her senses the night she'd met Hazel. She'd been trying to push thoughts of Hazel out of her mind since she'd left her a few hours ago, but they were here now. Before she left, Hazel had told her to give her a chance, and in that moment, it had seemed like a lovely premise. Raven took lots of chances with her life, with her safety, with the realms. But never when it came to matters of the heart. Entertaining the idea, even for a passing second, made her a bit queasy. Even if she allowed herself to fall for Hazel, it would never come to anything. She was bound to Morgan in perpetuity. If she dissolved their relationship, walked away from being a shadowhunter, her uncle would die. She couldn't and wouldn't do that to him. Plus, Morgan would never allow it. No, it had to be just those few stolen moments, those few fleeting seconds of promise. Raven had allowed herself brief encounters with women over the years, but they never lasted more than a night or two. That was all Morgan would allow. She'd never have more, and it was pointless to wish for it. Hazel was new to this world, to understanding that curses, no matter how old, still carried their original significance. *But those eyes.* They held so much hope, acceptance, concern. No one had ever looked at her the way Hazel had before she left; no one had ever looked so directly into her soul.

Raven turned into the parking lot behind the convention center. She leaned forward on her steering wheel and looked up at the building. *This is as good a place to start as any.* She grabbed her bag and opened the door.

Her senses took over as she stepped from the vehicle. A high-pitched howl emanated from somewhere behind her, and the smell of fire and death filled her nose. She withdrew one blade from her backpack, another from her waist, turning to face the beast gaining on her with each passing second.

Only one creature made that sound, only one with a stench so foul she could identify it from miles away. Only one that had the capability of tracking down a shadowhunter: *hellhound*, about as nasty a creature as one could encounter. Raven had only ever seen one hellhound before this, and it had belonged to Morgan. They were used by the witches to drag misplaced demons back to Hell. This fact alone sent a million questions through Raven's mind, none of which she had the time to process now. It didn't matter if the hellhound was from some rogue witch or Morgan herself.

It moved into her peripheral vision and looked to be about five feet, even on all fours. Its teeth would put an alligator to shame. They were like small spikes erupting from frothing jaws. With paws the size of shovels, its nails looked like they could rip through prey as if they were nothing more than tissue paper. Whatever it wanted, she wasn't going to let it tear her apart like a cheap carnival prize.

As the thing charged her, extraordinary muscles rippled through its shoulders and legs, while its eyes burned red hot with hellfire. If it wasn't planning to obliterate her, she'd be awed by such raw, mesmerizing beauty. Raven tightened her grip around each of the blades, one infused with silver, the other gold. The hellhound lowered its head as it got closer, showing the teeth that could rip a car door off its hinges. Raven ran straight at it, hoping the change in the sport of predator versus prey would throw the hound off its game.

As they collided, she felt the scorching breath on her neck as the beast struggled against the gold blade at its throat. The more it struggled and pushed, the more intense the aroma of burning hair and flesh became. The hound seemed unfazed as its teeth snapped for her face and throat. Raven's feet were slipping as she struggled to find a weak point of some kind, anything to create an advantage. She didn't want to kill it. She needed to see who had sent it, to know who wielded this level of power.

The creature lifted a massive paw and batted Raven to the side. Claws ripped her from her ribs to her brain, and she let out a bloodcurdling scream at the blinding flash of pain.

She had less than ten minutes to treat the wound before the poison devoured whatever soul she had. A gash of this magnitude from a hellhound was enough to kill a shadowhunter. Holding her side, she tried to bring her vision back into focus, the pain blurring everything around her. She knew it was coming back. Even through the pain, her skin prickled its warning. She gritted her teeth through the agony, turning both blades upward. It leapt at her again. She watched through one eye, the other stuck fast by blood as the hellhound's teeth rushed for her throat. The only way to defeat a hellhound was to plunge a silver and gold knife into both of the creature's hearts at the same time. She'd only have one opportunity. Rallying the last of her energy, she thrust the blades under both of its shoulders. It yelped, staggered for a few feet, then collapsed on the ground, a writhing mass.

Raven crawled to the body to inspect the brand that was always burned into a hellhound's hindquarters. She wasn't sure if the injuries she'd inflicted would be lethal, but if they were, the creature would dissolve into ash before she had the chance to identify who was responsible.

Every movement sent another shock of excruciating pain through her body. The poison was working faster than anticipated. She needed to get to her bag and retrieve the vial that contained the antidote, but the creature was twitching as it gave in to its final breaths. Ignoring the flash of white-hot pain, she reached out and dug through its fur.

"Holy shit," she said as a myriad of thoughts rushed through her mind.

She made it the few feet back to her bag and prayed her hands wouldn't stop working before she could obtain the vial and save herself. Every part of her body began stiffening, seeming to atrophy before the other realm had officially claimed her. She bit off the cap from the vial and dumped the contents into her mouth. She lay back on the pavement and waited for the medicine to combat the poison.

Staring up at the sky, she smelled the infected pus as it ejected from her body and dripped onto the pavement. The medicine was doing its job. As she struggled to remain conscious, images of Hazel sputtered behind her eyelids. Hazel watching her, reaching for her, touching her. Then, the brand on the back of the hellhound, a single flame, curved into the letter B. This only meant one thing, and she wasn't even sure it was possible.

❖

Lucien paced in the small room, running his fingers along a compact knife. He felt his knees give out, and his body fell to the floor. Blaise entered the room as a wave of heat and anger engulfed the space. Blaise snapped his fingers, and Tammi Lee and Dirk appeared alongside Lucien, their bodies posed in the same position.

"Master, to what do I owe this honor?" Lucien choked out through labored breath. The heat in the room was suffocating.

"It has been several days, and you've given me nothing," the voice roared. "Where is my witch, my shadowhunter? You disappoint me."

Lucien tried to lift his head to look at the all-powerful entity he had pledged his soul to, but he couldn't move against the force. "I sent your hellhound to find them. It shouldn't be long now."

Tammi Lee seemed to be struggling against the same weight Lucien was feeling. He saw her trembling as she tried to speak. "It would be much faster if you could tell us where to look."

Blaise banged his massive staff into the floor. "The shadowhunter belongs to Morgan. I am unable to see or feel her. White witches are cloaked from my vision. Do you honestly think I'd be wasting my time with you three if I could handle this myself? Your incompetence is mind-boggling."

"We'll take care of it, Master. You have my word." Lucien tasted the salt of his sweat coating his lips. Blaise's power knew no bounds, and it was intoxicating. "We will not fail you."

Blaise took a step toward him and apprehended him by the neck, lifting him off the ground. "If you fail me, your soul will be forsaken to a corner of Hell that even the most prolific poet could not dream into existence. The only thing you will be able to feel is the skin melting from your bones and demons devouring your scorched flesh." Blaise released him and disappeared.

Lucien fell, pawing at his throat. He rolled over on his side, watching Tammi Lee and Dirk try to catch their breath. He crawled to the table and retrieved three bottles of water. He guzzled his, desperate to rid himself of the burning sensation deep in his lungs as the other two did the same.

Dirk forced himself up and leaned against one of the cabinets, wiping sweat from his forehead. "What's the plan? I have a feeling Blaise won't be so generous with us the next time he summons us."

Lucien was pensively silent. He had an idea, but it meant placing Dirk in harm's way. The father in him bristled at the thought, but the part of him who wanted to please Blaise overrode the instinct. "You're going to reveal yourself as a dark witch." He glanced between Dirk and Tammi Lee but saw no protest, so he continued. "This should turn their attention on trying to capture you in order to get information. If we can lure them out, we'll be able to strike first."

Tammi Lee squinted in his direction, seeming unconvinced. "And if we can't?"

Dirk smashed the water bottle between his hands and tossed it over into the corner. "Then I'll die."

Lucien knew he should reassure Dirk but couldn't find it in himself to do so. "Yes, then you'll die."

Lucien thought he might object, but when he didn't, Lucien smiled with fatherly pride.

"My rally is at the end of the week," Dirk said. "There will be a ton of television cameras, and I'll make sure they get a glimpse of my tattoo. That should be enough to get them to come after me. Tammi, I need you to promote it on your podcast, say you'll be there. They already think you and Lucien are linked; that should pique their interest enough."

Tammi Lee tossed her empty water bottle into the same corner. "I think we should wait on the hellhound. I don't want you to put yourself in danger."

Lucien stood and hurried to a cloth bag sitting on a table in the corner. "There's no time. We can't afford any mistakes. We'll go with Dirk's idea." He pulled a small necklace out of the front pouch and tossed it to Dirk. "Wear this, so I'll be able to locate you."

Tammi Lee put her hand on Lucien's shoulder. "There has to be another way. Can't I drop some sort of code on my podcast that will signify us?"

Lucien shrugged her off. "That will only work if they happen to be listening. We can't chance it. We haven't the luxury of time. This plan will yield the fastest results."

"But Dirk—"

Lucien stopped her mid-sentence. "Dirk is a grown man, and he will do as he pleases. Need I remind you we are here to serve Blaise?" Tammi Lee crossed her arms and shook her head.

"Then I don't want to hear anything else about it."

"I hope you know what you're doing." She shoved Dirk ahead of her and marched him out of the room.

CHAPTER FOURTEEN

Sarah stood in the courtyard behind Morgan's house, studying the gray, cottony substance dangling from the tree canopying the yard. Spanish moss, they called it, but to her, it resembled untidy clumps of dust and seemed a more fitting adornment for the lair of a fiend. She couldn't keep her limbs still, anticipating the lesson in harnessing their white witch powers set to begin momentarily.

As dusk spread its amber glow over New Orleans, Hazel practiced something called yoga, stretching off to the side along the fence, but Sarah's eyes kept drifting back to Ayotunde, who was lovingly studying a monarch butterfly perched on her fingers. Her outfit, consisting of tight violet workout pants and an equally clingy T-shirt, emphasized the beautifully curvaceous body Sarah never knew she'd possessed, as it had always been ensconced under a dowdy frock. After a while, Sarah forced her eyes away, feeling the sting of shame at the way her body was responding to such a breathtaking sight.

Their instructor, a statuesque brunette with luminous green eyes, and curiously dressed in a breastplate of armor, was arranging crystals around a sculpted wooden owl on a table, her attention clearly engrossed in her task. Her graceful movements told of boundless assurance and physical strength, and she had an air of magnetism that seemed to draw in all of the energy around her.

Sipping a mint julep, Morgan sashayed through the curtains blowing around the open French doors and joined them outside. "Gather 'round, my sister necromancers. My dear friend Athena is now ready to commence your education."

Hazel's face lit up. "Athena, as in the Greek goddess of war strategy?"

Morgan and Athena exchanged condescending grins.

"I prefer the moniker Goddess of Wisdom, but what's in a name, huh?" As Athena smiled, her triceps seemingly flexed of their own accord. "My talents are most often called upon to counsel in the avoidance of war. However, when war becomes inevitable, as it is in this case, I always assist the forces of good, like when I aided the Greeks in their thrashing of the Trojans." She smiled reminiscently. "Good times."

"It pays to have friends in high places," Morgan said, chewing her straw. "Get it? High places?" She waited. "Mount Olympus? C'mon, nothing?"

Sarah shrugged, completely unaware of the reference.

Hazel smiled respectfully at Morgan. "Forgive me, but I'm a little slow on the uptake when standing before a mythological immortal hero I learned about in high school." She turned to Athena. "But you're not a witch. How would you know about our powers?"

"I'm freakin' Zeus's daughter," Athena replied with a cocked eyebrow.

"Trust us, Hazel," Morgan said. "We know what we're doing. We each have centuries of combined experience in battle, not to mention a brief personal history." She shot Athena a lusty grin that Athena happily returned.

"Oh, right. Okay. Sorry." Hazel stood in place, shaking out her hands and feet. "I'm just a little nervous."

"You should be more than a little nervous given what you're all up against," Morgan said. "Athena, I now leave my ingénues in your capable hands. Do with them as you wish." She walked over to a swinging love seat and sprawled.

"All right," Athena said as she marched in front of them making eye contact like a stern task master. "Hazel, Sarah, and Ayotunde, you each possess untapped capabilities that will enable you to become more powerful than you've ever imagined, agents of change in a world that, at present, is changing but not for the better. So tonight, we're gonna tap them." At that point, an owl flew onto her outstretched arm. "From what Morgan tells me, the entire realm of the white witch is in jeopardy right now, and if you fail at your mission, evil will win, and Earth will be locked in its stronghold for eternity. Hazel, I'm sure you've already noticed the shift over the last couple of years."

Hazel nodded with a frown.

"Sarah and Ayotunde, not to call you out or anything, but it was your scheme to save Sarah from the hangman's noose that set all this in motion. Those insolent demons had been salivating for the chance to slip through a portal, and Sarah, you gave it to them."

Hazel stepped forward. "Uh, my aunt is painfully aware of her role in this. There's no need to time travel shame anyone here."

Athena turned toward her with a mildly irritated look, and in sync with the slow rise of Athena's hand, Hazel's body levitated off the ground and floated back to her place in line.

Sarah placed a protective hand around Hazel's shoulder and looked at Athena. "Aye, your grace. The fault indeed be mine, but I meant not to wreak such havoc upon my fellow man. And pray, please blame not Ayotunde. She, too, knew not of the consequences our scheme hath wrought."

"I didn't even know I could do it," Ayotunde added. "I recited the incantations me mother taught me and then, na wa o! Poof! She be gone."

"'Tis true," Sarah said. "One moment I be withering in a cell, and the next, I wake on a bench in modern day Salem." She finished with a shrug.

Athena stood with her mouth agape. "Some days I can totally empathize with my father for wanting to smite the whole lot of you," she mumbled. "As I was saying, it is up to you and Morgan's shadowhunter to banish these scourges, and the only way that's happening is by you three understanding and mastering your powers. Ayotunde, please come hither."

"Aye, ma'am." She stepped forward, her head bowed, her toned arms glistening in the twilight.

"Look at me, Ayotunde," Athena demanded. "The first thing you must learn is that you are a superior being. You are marked to become a voodoo high priestess, and you will bow down before no one ever again, mortal or otherwise."

"Aye," Ayotunde answered with a confidence Sarah had never before witnessed in her.

Sarah's heart melted with pride to see Ayotunde's posture grow erect and her head held high.

"You held a butterfly's rapt attention earlier," Athena said. "That creature hadn't left your hand until your will freed it when Morgan called you all over. You have the power to charm, to compel things to your will."

"Aye," Sarah whispered to Ayotunde. "Your dancing poppets."

"I never thought it be sorcery," Ayotunde said. "I thought it be a trick my mother learned me."

"Sorcery, trick, or voodoo, as they like to call it down here in the bayou," Athena said. "Call it what you will, but it is an awesome power that you possess. You see my owl sitting upon the edge of the bird feeder?" Everyone's head turned.

"I want you to compel Hazel to throw a rock at it."

"What?" Hazel said. "I will not. That's cruel."

"Sarah, put a rock in Hazel's hand," Athena said.

"But I…" Sarah hesitated, disturbed by the direction this was taking.

"Do as I say, Sarah," Athena said. She held Sarah back when she motioned toward the garden. "Not with your hand. Use your mind."

Sarah stared at the rock, immobilized by fear and confusion. How was she to honor Athena's command when she hadn't the foggiest idea as to how to begin? "Your Excellency, I know not how to rein these powers you speak of. I am but a humble Christian."

"Sarah, how did you invoke your powers at the arena?" Hazel said.

Sarah shook her head, agitated. "'Twas an impulse. There be no time for forethought when danger arose."

"It's within you, Sarah," Athena said. "You must envision your will and then concentrate. You have to believe your will alone is as powerful as your physical body and is capable of moving that rock."

Overwhelmed nearly to tears, Sarah focused on a rock the size of her fist in the garden. She stared at it until it was almost a blur and then imagined it lifting from the soil into the air and floating over to Hazel's open hand.

"Oh my God," Hazel whispered as it landed in her palm.

"Ayotunde," Athena said. "Now compel Hazel to throw it at the owl; aim it right at the bird."

Clearly upset by the command, Ayotunde looked between Athena and Hazel.

"Do it!" Athena shouted.

Ayotunde closed her eyes and acted out the motion of her arm winding up.

Hazel was visibly shaken. "Look. I know what you're trying to illustrate here, but I categorically refuse to hurt..." Before she could complete her thought, she sent the stone rocketing toward the bird. It narrowly missed and pelted the feeder's pedestal instead. "This is insane," Hazel said, clearly astonished.

A smile crept across Athena's face. "Excellent."

Sarah stared at her own hands as if the answers she sought would somehow spring from her palms.

"As you all can see, Sarah's power is telekinesis."

Sarah shook her head in amazement. "I envisioned the rock floating toward Hazel, and thus, it floated."

Morgan called out from the swing. "A rock is nothing, girl. You've already sent demons hurtling through the air."

"I can't believe what I'm seeing," Hazel said. "If I didn't already have a vague knowledge of my female ancestors, I'd swear I'd completely lost my mind."

Athena flicked her hair off her shoulder. "That brings us to you, Hazel. Based on what Morgan's told me, every time you've complained about it being too hot for October, a cool breeze kicked up; I'd say you possess the power to harness the weather."

Sarah turned to Hazel excitedly. "The arena."

Hazel said to Athena, "We both used these powers to fend off the demons that were attacking Raven, only we had no idea what we were doing."

Athena opened her arms wide. "Hence, this training session. Now, Hazel, let's see what happens when you deliberately manipulate the weather."

Hazel looked around the courtyard with a puzzled expression. "Uh, hmm, okay. How about a little thunder and lightning?"

"Have at it," Athena replied and took a step back.

Hazel closed her eyes, and her hands started to shake at her sides. A low rumble of thunder hummed in the distance.

"Make it stronger," Athena said. "Louder."

Hazel's hands shook harder and began to slowly rise above her head. The sky above them sounded as though it had cracked wide open. Sarah and the others looked heavenward in amazement. Hazel then swung her arm down, and a bolt of lightning zapped a tree in the far end of Morgan's courtyard, and it burst into flames.

Hazel's jaw fell open, and she turned to Athena. "I can make lightning bolts just like your father."

"You sure can," she replied. "Except he can do it without setting a whole city on fire. You better drop some rain on that."

"Oh crap. Okay." Hazel waved her arms in a crisscross and the sky opened in a downpour over all of them.

"Just the tree, you boob," Morgan called out from the swing.

"Ugh. I'm never gonna get this right," Hazel said.

Sarah approached her with a comforting hand on her shoulder. "Your abilities do leave me in awe, Hazel. Destiny hath forged in you a most formidable witch. You need only hone your skill."

Hazel smiled warmly at her. "Thank you, Aunt Sarah. Coming from you, that means a lot."

"Good work, ladies," Athena said. "Now that you understand your abilities, you must cultivate them, gain complete command of them to avoid any accidents that can occur when novices get overconfident. You think I was ready to roll that wooden horse full of Greeks into Troy the instant I popped out of Daddy's head? Even I wasn't that arrogant."

"Amen to that," Morgan said as she approached the group. "Hazel, I don't think I have to remind you about that hurricane we had down here in aught-five. A young upstart I was training named Katrina got a little too cocky for her corset, and before I knew it, voilà, the entire Ninth Ward was under water."

"These powers are to be taken seriously," Athena said. "They're weapons intended to be used only to redress wrongs and defend the good. You must exercise the utmost wisdom and caution when you summon them, and for the goddesses' sakes, do not unleash their full potential until you've sufficiently practiced and mastered wielding them." She flashed Hazel a warning glare.

"How long will that take?" Hazel said. "It's not like we have time on our side."

"After we're done here, take a walk over to Bourbon Street and engage in some field exercises with the drunks," Athena said. "You can mess with them, and they won't remember a thing. It worked like a talisman for Dionysus."

"And, Sarah," Morgan said gravely, "if anyone takes out a cell phone and tries to record any of you, you must divest them of it at once. We can't get sloppy and end up all over the internet. This is a covert operation."

Hazel exhaled deeply as she glanced at Sarah and Ayotunde. "Ready to do this?"

"Aye," Sarah said and tried not to make too much of the look of apprehension on Hazel's face. "May God be with us."

As they exited the gate to the street, Sarah took Ayotunde's hand, and they both seemed to relax as their fingers folded around each other's.

With the rising full moon behind them, Hazel, Sarah, and Ayotunde walked down Canal Street headed toward Bourbon with Hazel taking the lead through the city. It was a noble attempt to shield poor Sarah and Ayotunde from the debauchery they would likely witness once they'd reached their destination, having barely recovered from learning the depth and implications of their powers and that Athena was a goddess in existence longer than *the* God. That way, she'd have a chance to warn them if a topless, intoxicated reveler came screeching toward them with strings of multicolored beads bouncing off her breasts.

As they walked, Hazel couldn't help turning around and stealing glances at them since she'd noticed their connection during the training. It was obvious they were into each other and so adorable the way they looked at each other: the awe, the pride, and the yearning. Now they were walking so close together, they could've been inside the same pair of pants. Hazel had so many questions. She knew Sarah had a husband, but all that meant was their attraction to each other was more dangerously complex. Had their love affair dated back to the colonial days, or was it only blossoming now? If it was the former, it certainly explained their desire to escape to an era in which they would be free to love each other. Whatever the case, their bond filled Hazel's heart with warmth and feeling for Raven, whom she was currently missing to an alarming degree.

She stopped when they reached the corner of Canal and Bourbon and turned around. "You know, you guys didn't have to stop holding hands. People do that in public sometimes. It's not a big deal in the twenty-first century."

Sarah and Ayotunde exchanged embarrassed grins.

"Not that I'm suggesting anything about you two," Hazel said, sensing the embarrassment she'd stirred up between them. "Just saying."

Sarah continued as though ignoring the suggestion that Hazel hadn't made. "It appears we have arrived at our destination." She pointed at the street sign.

Hazel nodded. "Let's review the plan." She looked down when she hit her elbow on the newspaper bin next to her. The headline immediately caught her attention: "More Rally Violence, One Dead." She read the location through the glass and gasped when she saw it had occurred in Roanoke, Virginia.

"Raven," she whispered. Raven had been on her mind constantly. Her only reprieve had been the intensity of the training session. She wanted so badly to hear her voice or at least to text her and read that she was fine. The deeper they got into this mission, the deeper her feelings for her seemed to go, taking root at a subterranean level. She ached to see her.

"Hazel. The plan?" Sarah said.

She snapped back to reality and waved them closer. "Okay. So, we're going to stroll casually down Bourbon Street and take in all the sights and sounds just like any old tourists. As soon as we see an available outdoor table at a café, we're gonna park ourselves, order some drinks, and see what kind of mischief we can conjure."

"Conjure," Sarah repeated solemnly. "This feel like the devil's work we be doing. I fear the prodigious sins I commit in this new world. Have I become too lost in the wood for redemption?"

Ayotunde nodded. "Aye. If we be sent back to the Salem Village and be hanged, they be righteous hangin's for sure."

"No, no, no," Hazel said, worrying she was starting to lose them. "Those hangings were bogus, complete ideological horseshit. History proves that. Look. I know in your Puritan belief system that sorcery and mystical powers were interpreted solely as the work of Lucifer, but you have to understand something. Just like evil can manifest these powers, so can good. It's the only defense we have. Conjuring them so good can prevail isn't a sinful act, not if it will save humanity from its final descent into destruction." She pointed to the headline inside the newspaper bin. "And recently, it seems the descent has kicked into warp speed."

Sarah studied Hazel for a moment, then nodded. "My faith be in you, Hazel. Instruct us."

After one more glance at the troubling headline, Hazel led them down Bourbon Street in search of a base of operations. Although it was early by normal bar standards, the open-air clubs and cafés lining the street teemed with tourists and spilled bluegrass music and people out onto the sidewalk and off the curb in equal proportion.

"This is ridiculous," Hazel said. "We're never going to find a place to sit." She stopped and looked at her shoes resting in a puddle of something offensive. Noticing a drunken couple sitting at a round table sipping blue slushy drinks in tall plastic tubes, she tapped Ayotunde on the shoulder. "What do you say you start practicing your power to compel right now?"

Ayotunde smiled knowingly and turned toward the oblivious couple, her eyes boring into them. Hazel leaned eagerly into Sarah as they awaited the results. Ayotunde's index fingers made one swift flicking motion, and seconds later, the couple got up and staggered off.

"Yes," Hazel hissed and offered them both high fives, which she had to teach them how to do.

Ayotunde stared at her hands as they sat around the table. She looked at Hazel with sudden sadness. "Had I known of this power, I would save my blessed mother from the slave traders."

Hazel placed her hand over Ayotunde's. "I know you would've."

Sarah held her other hand. "Ayotunde, you were but a child of six when you and your mother were captured and sold to those vicious heathens masquerading as Christians. You mustn't wallow in regret."

"They separate us not long after."

Hazel and Sarah exchanged glances of unspoken shame and indignation. Hazel opened her mouth to speak but knew her words would ring hollow.

"'Twas my father who purchased you, stripping you from your mother's arms," Sarah finally said.

Hazel grew queasy at the confirmation that one of her ancestors had indeed owned another human being. She shifted in her chair, wondering where their drink server was.

"Aye, but your father treat me kindly, Sarah. He be strict, but I never felt no crack of the whip in his house. I think it be a blessing he take me in."

Hazel shook her head in disgust. "Only in the good old American system of institutionalized slavery can a person feel gratitude toward a *kind* master."

"A devout Puritan my father was and a good man as well," Sarah said. "He taught me reading. He believed girls had minds for contemplation despite the instruction of the Scripture."

"That explains so much about you, Sarah," Hazel said. How awesome that the seeds of feminism were apparently sprinkled far back through her lineage. What would Sarah be able to accomplish today if she were born in Hazel's generation?

Sarah smiled. "'Tis is a relief to sit, but my thirst doth rankle me."

Hazel pretended to think. "Hmm…if only there was a way to get a server over here."

Ayotunde smiled and glanced at a woman carrying a tray laden with cocktails, who instantly changed direction toward them.

"*Bonjour.* What can I get ya gals?" the server said in a slightly strained voice.

"Let's make it easy," Hazel said. "Hurricanes all around." She felt sorry for the woman as she started to struggle balancing the heavy tray.

She turned back to Sarah and Ayotunde in time to catch their eyes locked on each other. She wasn't sure if the thick heat blanketing her was from the sweaty mob of tourists or the sexual tension simmering between them. She cleared her throat to remind them of her presence.

Sarah broke the gaze and noted her surroundings. "This city doth have its charms."

"And its foulness," Ayotunde said, waving a hand in front of her nose.

"Hashtag life below sea level," Hazel replied and flared her nostrils at the aroma wafting from the street. "I know what we need. How does a gentle breeze to cleanse the rancid air sound?"

Sarah and Ayotunde nodded with enthusiasm.

Instead of concentrating and willing the breeze to kick up slowly and steadily, Hazel wound her arm up like a Division I college softball pitcher. A gust of wind roared down the street, knocking over loaded garbage cans, clearing tables of their napkins and drinks, and sending the sundress of a woman who'd made the unfortunate decision to go commando sailing above her waist. When everyone around them stopped screaming and regained their footing, Hazel sucked at her cheeks in embarrassment.

Sarah smiled politely at her, then straightened her posture. "Hark. I believe our wench doth approach with a strange blue potion."

Ayotunde covered her mouth over a smile. "Miss Hazel, the next time you conjure the wind, we batten down the hatches first."

They all giggled. Hazel raised her hurricane drink in agreement and took a long sip until she felt the glorious stab of brain freeze. "I'm gonna take a break and work on my technique. In the meantime, Sarah, you can razzle-dazzle us."

As soon as Sarah sipped her drink, her entire face puckered in horror. "What infernal potion hath the wench proffered?"

Hazel laughed heartily as she brought the drink to her mouth. Before her lips could make contact with the straw, all three of their drinks floated away toward the gutter and upended into the sewer.

Hazel was shocked. "What are you doing, Sarah? Do you know how much those cost?"

"Aye. The price of our souls be a steep one." Sarah guzzled a glass of water.

"Okay. You guys are sticking with wine from now on," Hazel said and tried to signal for their waitress.

Ayotunde tapped Sarah on the arm and pointed to an argument brewing in the street in front of them. "That angry man be hollering at the women."

Hazel stood as she saw an apparently intoxicated guy yelling at two young women. "Where are those cops we saw on horseback before?"

Sarah shrugged as she continued staring at the altercation.

"We should do something," Hazel said.

"Pray, be still," Sarah said, holding out an arm to keep Hazel back.

The man shoved one of the women, and Hazel and Ayotunde gasped. Sarah extended her arm, molded her fingers into a claw, and drew her arm back. As if he was attached to an invisible cord, he stumbled away from the women as the gathering onlookers cheered.

Ayotunde then flicked her index finger at him as though he was a mosquito. He finally lost his footing and fell backward, landing in the remains of a horse manure pile.

"Oh no, you didn't," Hazel said, covering her mouth in amusement. "We better go do our homework somewhere else before someone figures us out."

As they all turned to leave, Hazel twisted her arm in the air as though pulling something down from the sky. "We can't leave him all soiled like that. It's gross." Rain began to pour only over him as he struggled, slipping and sliding, to his feet.

Sarah grabbed Ayotunde by the hand, and they rushed through the throngs of people, riotous with laughter.

When they arrived in front of Morgan's house, they stopped when Hazel's text went off. She smiled when she saw the words *I'm okay*. She was so happy to hear from Raven that she wasn't even annoyed that that was all it said. She typed back *I miss you so much*, with a heart emoji before she had time to think better of it. She knew she shouldn't have. Raven had made it abundantly clear that she wanted to remain friends only, but Hazel decided she'd deal with any and all consequences later.

She shoved her phone in her pocket and looked up to see Sarah and Ayotunde linked in silhouette from head to toe. A sliver of moonlight filtered between them as they stroked each other's faces and kissed.

Hazel smiled and quietly disappeared through Morgan's front gate.

After she and Ayotunde went up to their room, Sarah lit several candles. She knew she could press the light switch and illuminate the room much brighter, but after holding Ayotunde in her arms and kissing her for the first time under a starlit sky, the candlelight seemed more fitting. Ayotunde stood by the bed holding on to one of the posts. She licked her inviting lips, but her eyes reflected hesitation. Perhaps she was feeling the same as Sarah, warm and alive inside but marred with guilt and fear, as if they'd become lost within a maze of forbidden longing. Despite Hazel's assurances that in these modern times, passionate love between a woman and her friend was accepted, her mind whirled at the opposition between what her heart wanted and the teachings that her faith had instilled in her.

"I much enjoyed our kiss," Sarah said from safely across the room.

"Aye." Ayotunde smiled. "It sent my heart soaring."

"Do you practice your power to compel now? On me?"

Ayotunde bowed her head shyly. "My brain be too mixed up for conjurin'."

"Well then," Sarah said as she started across the room. "I must confess that some other force doth strongly compel me to you."

"I feel it, too."

Ayotunde rushed to meet her halfway. They collided, and Sarah swept her into her arms and into a soul-searing kiss. The taste of Ayotunde's lips whetted appetites brand-new to Sarah. She hadn't ever known how badly she'd been starved until Ayotunde's touch awakened such pangs of hunger in her.

Abandoning everything, they dove into the delights of the flesh she'd been warned about all her life. Sarah traced the contour of Ayotunde's strong jaw, her thumb lingering over her full bottom lip. She stared deeply into her eyes, ready to forsake the possibility of eternal salvation for this taste of euphoria they'd tumbled into together. How good it felt to succumb to the thing her heart had yearned for.

"Nobody never kiss me like that before," Ayotunde said. She licked her lips and stared at Sarah from under eyelids heavy with passion.

"Though I be married some time, never have I felt the strength of a kiss such as with yours, Ayotunde. I do fear I've learned of the lust that our minister speak of, yet I want not to resist."

"Aye, Sarah. My body hunger so for you that nothing can frighten me away." Ayotunde cradled Sarah's face and lunged at her mouth as she guided her toward the bed.

Sarah gasped at the excruciating pleasure of Ayotunde's body pressing down on hers. Her tongue snaked into Ayotunde's mouth like the serpent tempting Eve in paradise. An infernal flame of desire licked at the place between her legs that had been forbidden to anyone but her husband, but Ayotunde's deep kisses weakened her into complete submission.

Ayotunde sat up astride Sarah and pulled off her T-shirt, but it took both of them to claw at the vexing garment around her bosom Hazel called a sports bra. Once her breasts were freed from their confinement, Sarah reached up and received them like manna from heaven. Ayotunde's nipples hardened under her fingertips, sending an ache rippling through Sarah's nether region. When Sarah tightened her grip on her breasts and squeezed, Ayotunde moaned as though possessed.

She rolled off her, and they proceeded to divest each other of every last stitch of their workout gear. Sarah's fingers were wet as she stroked the silky gem she discovered between Ayotunde's legs.

Sarah groaned as Ayotunde's hand mimicked her movements over and all around her secret place. She started breathing heavily as a swell of the most intense physical pleasure she'd ever experienced began building with such force, she could do nothing to stop it. She began crying out as her back arched, and their hands moved faster and harder in each other's wetness. Screeches and moans shattered the silence of the room as the explosion of their dual pleasure shook them into convulsions.

After their physical act, they lay in each other's arms, spent, catching their breath. Sarah held Ayotunde tighter when she felt her fingers dancing across her stomach. She wanted to speak but couldn't induce her mouth to form words. What words could possibly capture what she was feeling anyway? She lay still as part of her wanted this moment to last forever while the other part trembled in anticipation of what might happen next. She wanted Ayotunde again. Once had not been enough to satiate the need in her, but as Ayotunde caressed the inside of her thighs, she willed herself to be patient, biting her lip at the sweet torment.

She wouldn't have been surprised in the least if the floor opened up, and they plummeted, bed and all, into a fiery abyss, never to be heard from again. She waited, her eyes clenched shut in fear of what unspeakable horrors were about to consume them in the wake of God's wrath.

But nothing unspeakable occurred. Her eyes sprang open when Ayotunde let out a soft sigh, but that only signified the coming of sleep as she lay in Sarah's arms. She began entertaining a notion that a trick might have been played on her in the past, one that had promised an eternity of prodigious suffering if one allowed herself to partake in earthly happiness rather than live a somber life of piety and self-sacrifice. What if that had not been what God intended for His children? What if ministers only spake with such fervency to keep the meetinghouse full and their pulpits secure?

She shuddered at her abominable thoughts. Was lust so powerful that it had prompted her to question her religion? What could she know of God? Learned men who'd spent many a year studying the Word with eager devotion scantly understood His will. She enveloped Ayotunde tighter. All she knew was that the feeling Ayotunde filled her heart with was worth any consequence God saw fit to deliver.

"Sarah, you tremble so," Ayotunde whispered.

"'Tis you who make me tremble," she said with a smile.

Ayotunde ran her fingertips down Sarah's cheek. "My love, I hold no talisman over you."

"Aye but you do." Sarah shifted to look at her. "In my dreams, we have been this close, but always would I wake in terror, fearing the devil hath sent your spirit to tempt me into his wickedness."

Ayotunde raised up on her elbow in fright. "No, Sarah. My spirit no leave my body. I never torment you."

"Peace," Sarah said, rubbing her back. "I know it be not so now. But my dreams of you would unsettle me so as Thomas lay next to me. I thought of no other way to explain such sinfulness in my heart."

"That be how they think in Salem Village. They don' feel what we feel, Sarah. They too busy fearin' what God gonna do to them each day. They blind to the joys in the world when they always lookin' out for the devil."

Sarah lay in the peaceful darkness, stroking Ayotunde's back before breaking the precious silence. "Madame le Fay says we must go back to Salem Village. That is the mission we are preparing for with Raven and Hazel."

"No, no." Ayotunde frowned. "We help them send the demons back. We stay here and be free."

"Aye. We must beseech Madame le Fay to allow us to stay with Raven and Hazel. Now that I have you, I shall not let you go."

"Hold me, Sarah. Hold me with all your might."

She kissed Ayotunde until her frown dissolved into the warm look of desire she'd observed smoldering in Ayotunde's eyes when they closed the bedroom door behind them.

CHAPTER FIFTEEN

Raven stared at her naked reflection in the steam-streaked mirror. She traced her fingers over the gashes in her skin, wincing at the contact. The claw marks were healing, but they remained puffy, red, and swollen at the site of impact. She leaned forward, holding her weight on the counter after becoming lightheaded from the wave of pain and nausea that swept through her when she examined her wound.

After her vision cleared, she shuffled to her suitcase and gathered a few medical supplies. She pulled a gauze pad out and ripped the wrapper open, gently covering the gashes with the sterile material. She placed a few pieces of tape along the edges to secure it in place. She grabbed her almost threadbare Def Leppard shirt from her bag and carefully slipped it over her head, vigilant not to pull the gauze off with her movements. She sat on the bed and ran her fingers through her hair. The water droplets that fell from the tips of her locks and onto her neck helped cool the heat beginning to creep up her body from her efforts.

She picked up her phone off the nightstand and opened the notifications. *I miss you so much*, with a heart emoji. She had texted Hazel before she forced herself into the shower, not wanting her to worry, or worse, try to use her witchy powers to see what she was doing. She wasn't sure if Hazel had those capabilities or not, but she didn't want to take the chance. She read the message over and over again. The simplicity in the statement warmed Raven's chest. Hazel missed her. Her thumbs hovered over the keyboard, trying to decide how to respond. She wanted to tell her that she missed her, too, that she'd thought about her every moment since they'd been apart. She wanted to tell her that when she was slipping into what she thought might be her final moments, Hazel was all she could think about. She stared down at the winking emoji that was coyly blowing a kiss and pushed the button, sending it into the text box. She only allowed herself a fleeting second to think about her soul not belonging to her. She pushed send before she could talk herself out of it. She shrugged and put the phone back onto the nightstand. *It's just an emoji; don't overthink it.*

She got the map of Roanoke from her bag, opened it, and smoothed it out on her bed. She needed to tell Morgan about the brand she saw on the hellhound, but she needed a little more information first. Raven took the necklace from around her neck and hung it over the map. She took several deep breaths and focused on the demons she needed to locate. The small stone spun in a large circle but didn't slow. She shook her head and tried to refocus her thoughts. Again, after several deep breaths, she tried to clear her mind. Nothing.

Raven didn't understand what she was doing wrong. Sitting for a few minutes, she racked her brain as to whether or not she was missing a step in the location process. Then a thought occurred to her. *No, that's not possible.* She picked up the necklace again and focused on dark magic. Even as the thought passed through her psyche, she felt goose bumps crawl up her arms. The stone at the end of her necklace began to spin a little faster until halting altogether. She looked down at the map. The address was only a few miles from her motel. She heard ringing in her ears and closed her eyes, trying to force the foreboding thoughts from her mind. She wasn't dealing with demons at all; she was dealing with dark witchcraft. *Fuck.*

She needed to get eyes on them, find out what they were plotting. At the very least, she had to get to the bottom of the Blaise issue. Raven didn't think it would be possible that he was still alive. It was probably some hoax these three morons were trying to pull to make themselves seem more powerful than they really were.

She stood to leave when the pain in her side forced her back onto the bed. She gritted her teeth, the desire to find the dark witches nagging at her, egging her to move forward and ignore the pain. She withdrew one of the blades from her bag and inspected it, giving herself a minute to think. If these three were who she thought they were and they discovered her there, spying on them, she wouldn't be able to protect herself in her current condition. She lifted her shirt and pulled open the gauze. The wound would be healed by morning. She cursed under her breath and tossed the knife back into her bag. Ten hours. In ten hours, she could go find them and hopefully get some answers to her questions.

She shot Morgan off a quick text. *Found them. Let you know more tomorrow.* Sure, she left out major pieces of information, but there was no reason to alarm Morgan. The mention of dark witchcraft would send Morgan into a fit of rage, and if she added in the other part about someone pretending to be Blaise, Morgan would be downright apocalyptic. Raven figured she was doing everyone a favor at this point.

The response from Morgan was almost immediate. *Looking forward to hearing all about it.* Raven grunted a laugh and shook her head. She could hear Morgan's seductive purr even through text message.

She leaned back against the bed and opened her contacts. She scrolled until she found Hazel and stared at the name. She wanted to hear her voice, to know how her training was going. She just wanted to feel connected to something, even if it was only temporary. She pushed the name and held the phone up to her ear.

Hazel answered on the second ring. "Hey, there."

Raven smiled. "Hey. How was your day?"

She heard Hazel moving around. "Did you know Athena is real?"

Raven traced circles on her leg with her thumb. "Ah, Morgan brought in the big guns for your training."

"She's, like, a real-life person," Hazel whispered.

"I think she prefers the term goddess, but yeah, it's a lot to take in. How are you holding up?" Raven smiled when she heard Hazel blow out a long breath.

"Let's see, Ayotunde can compel people or things into movement, Sarah has telekinetic abilities, and I can control the weather. So, you know, just another day." Hazel let out a nervous laugh.

"You're also psychic. All the most powerful witches are. You can sense, and if need be, control people's emotions. I've only ever known Morgan to be capable, but you have it, too."

Hazel was quiet for a minute before she continued. "How do you know that?"

Raven lazily rubbed her arm. "Because you've done it to me.

You've calmed me when I needed it. Granted, I'm more sensitive to your power because I'm a shadowhunter, but believe me, it's there. Give yourself some time. You'll figure it out."

Hazel took a deep breath. "I could go on and on about how overwhelming all this is, how I feel completely out of my depth, and how scared I am of how much this will change my life. But I really want to know how your trip has been so far. Find anything interesting? I miss you."

Raven leaned her head back against the headboard. She felt compelled to tell Hazel everything and desperately fought against that instinct. "I'll know more tomorrow." She closed her eyes after she said it, willing herself not to tell more.

"You're in pain." It was a statement, not a question.

"I'll be okay," Raven answered.

"My abilities, can I take your pain away from this far? Is that how they work?"

"I'm not sure," Raven said. "It's hard to say how powerful you are. You're still learning."

"Can I try?" Hazel's voice was soft and careful.

The thought of allowing Hazel to sense her physical pain, much less her emotions, was a rather terrifying premise, but the more control Hazel had over her powers, the better off they'd all be. "Sure." She let out a long breath. The other line of the phone went quiet except for Hazel's deep breathing, and Raven found herself mimicking her breathing patterns.

"The pain is near your rib cage." Hazel's voice was husky as if she'd just woken up from a long nap. "It's deep, but it's healing."

"Yes."

Raven's body became warm, the feeling of a summer day creeping up from her legs through her neck. She could smell the lingering aroma of the beach: warm saltwater with a mix of sunscreen and fresh waffle cones. She felt the smile start on her face when she heard the waves lapping against the sand and children laughing in the background. She wiggled her toes as she felt wet sand begin to swallow her feet.

"Raven?" Hazel sounded far away.

Raven turned her hands over as she felt the sun warm her skin and the breeze from the ocean kiss her face. "Hmm."

"Raven, are you okay? Did it work?" Hazel's voice was louder now, as if she was getting closer.

Raven was dropped back into reality. She was alone in her motel room, and the alarm clock that sat next to the bed was making the same low and annoying hum it had been since she'd arrived. There was no sunshine, no ocean, no smells of summer. She took a second to swallow the disappointment that filled her throat.

"Yeah, I'm here." Raven gingerly touched her side and was surprised to discover it no longer throbbed with pain.

"It worked?" Hazel asked, but her voice indicated she already knew the answer.

"I've never felt so completely engulfed in a projection like that before. How did you do it?" Raven didn't say what she really wanted, to be sent back.

"I focused on finding your happiest place, wherever it's buried in your mind, and sending you there." Hazel seemed almost embarrassed by the revelation. "I'm not really sure of what I'm doing. Sorry if I crossed a line."

"Could you see it, too? Could you feel it?" Raven wasn't upset that Hazel had been able to tap into her. She wanted to know they'd shared it together.

"Yes. I just wasn't sure if I was the only one who could see it. Where were we?"

Raven let her body cascade down the headboard a bit farther. "A beach I used to go to as a kid. I spent the best summers of my life there before everything changed."

"Before what changed?" Hazel's voice was filled with compassion and concern.

Raven picked at the loose threads coming off the comforter. "My parents used to take me to the beach for three weeks every summer. I'd play in the sand or walk along the boardwalk from the very first glimmers of daylight until my parents would force me back home for dinner and bed. Those days were filled with laughter, sunscreen, and the ocean. I could smell and taste it all again, just now."

"Why did you stop going?" Hazel's question was tentative.

Raven pinched the bridge of her nose, an attempt to keep the memories from escaping her eyes in the form of tears. "They went out for a date when I was eight years old and never came back. They were killed in a car accident. I went to live with my uncle after that." She tried to laugh to keep from crying. "He wasn't what you'd call conventional, but he loves me, and he's all I have."

"He's a shadowhunter, too?"

Raven crossed her arms, a pointless attempt to shield herself from the memories of her parents and her lost childhood. "Yes. I'd have to go with him when Morgan sent him out on little missions. At first, I'd stay in the motel room, but when I was about twelve, he let me go with him. I've been chasing demons around ever since." She cleared her throat, realizing that her words made her uncle seem neglectful and reckless. "I did graduate high school. My uncle homeschooled me, and I actually graduated early. I know this seems odd to people, but my uncle loves me and would do anything for me."

"And where is he now?" Hazel asked.

Raven traced the tattoo on her arm. She followed the lines of the pentagram down to the tips of the knives. "He was attacked by a very powerful demon. Morgan saved him. I took over his mantle to keep him alive. He's in suspended animation, healing."

Hazel was quiet for a long moment before she spoke. "I want to ask you something, but I don't want to upset you. Please understand that this just comes from a place of concern and care for you."

"Okay," Raven said.

"What happens when he's healed? Will Morgan let you go? Is that what you want?"

Raven knew this question was coming, but it didn't make it any easier to say out loud. "There can only be one shadowhunter. Those are the rules. My uncle is almost fifty. He can't sustain this lifestyle anymore. When Morgan deems him fit, she'll bring him back, and he can retire. Granted, he won't remember any of this life. Morgan will fill his head with false memories. He'll think he worked for the phone company or something like that. But he'll be alive. He'll be released from the curse and hopefully, find a nice woman, settle down, travel some."

Hazel gasped. "And what about you?"

Raven shook her head. "What about me? I'm saddled with the Dare curse. It has to be one of us until there are none left."

"Aren't you lonely? Don't you want a life of your own?" Hazel sounded as if she was going to cry.

Raven closed her eyes and took a deep breath. "I'm the last in my family line. It brings me comfort to know the family curse will end with me."

Hazel's voice was soft and comforting. "Just because something has always been done a certain way doesn't make it the right way. You can choose how your life ends up. Don't resign yourself to these circumstances because you never imagined anything more was possible."

Raven sat up in bed, feeling defensive. "You've been aware of the realms for like ten seconds. You have no idea the power these curses wield and the finality of all of it." She knew her anger was misplaced, but she couldn't stop herself. "You have the blood of the most powerful witch who has ever lived coursing through your veins. You have no idea what it's like to be me, to be trapped. So please, Hazel, save your hopes and dreams speeches for someone who hasn't spent their lifetime on the receiving end of this bullshit."

"Raven, I—"

Raven cut her off. "I have to go. Big day tomorrow. I'll talk to you later." She hung up before Hazel had the chance to say anything else.

Raven got out of bed and started pacing. Who did Hazel think she was? Lobbing out unobtainable possibilities tied to determining your own fate and bucking the system. She didn't understand the ancient forces she was dealing with, and she never would. Even if Hazel mastered her craft, she still wouldn't get it because her place in the realms would always be superior to Raven's.

She stalked into the bathroom and flipped on the light. She steadied herself against the countertop and pressed her fingertips in to the cold hard surface. Glaring at her reflection, she grew angrier when she recognized her mother's eyes, her father's nose, and scars from a life her uncle had brought her into. The suffering and rage singed her skin while the loneliness bored a hole deeper into the pit of her stomach. She stared harder into her own eyes as the tears started to form, pooling at her lids. Finally, she let out a scream as she sank onto the floor.

It didn't matter how many demons she succeeded in banishing to

Hell. She'd never chase down the ones that lived in her memories and clawed at her mind.

❖

Hazel tossed the phone down on the bed and covered her face. *Shit.* She'd pushed Raven too far, and she wasn't sure she'd ever be able to fully get her back. Her intention hadn't been to harm but to shine light on a path she might not have considered before. She thought briefly about calling her back but changed her mind. Hazel wasn't sure if she'd do more harm by trying to push.

She walked to the closet and pulled out her family grimoire. She was still amazed by the way the pages came to life as her fingers traced the old paper. She wasn't sure what she was looking for but knew she was searching for a way to help Raven. Surely, there had to be something in this old book that could release Raven from this ridiculous curse.

As if Morgan knew what she was doing, she appeared in her room. "Anything I can help with?"

Hazel almost fell off the bed. "Jesus, do you ever use the door?"

Morgan waved her hand. "No." Her slight smile showed her amusement.

Hazel didn't want to tell Morgan what she was looking for but thought better than to lie. She didn't understand Morgan's full range of capabilities and figured she might as well answer a question that Morgan probably already knew the answer to. "I'm trying to find a spell to release Raven from this ridiculous curse."

"Is that what Raven wants, to be released?" Morgan cocked an eyebrow.

"How could she not?"

Morgan pushed a strand of hair out of Hazel's eyes and smiled at her. "I'm all Raven knows. This life, it gives her purpose. What would you have her do if she wasn't chasing down demons?"

Hazel felt Morgan trying to sneak into her subconscious and pushed back against the effort. "Whatever she wants. It wouldn't be up to me."

Morgan leaned back on the bed and crossed her legs. "Rather bold to make decisions for someone, don't you think?"

Hazel kept flipping through the pages of the grimoire. "Says the woman who cursed an entire family line to servitude."

Morgan laughed. "Your audacity is impressive. Do you really believe that you know Raven better than I do?"

Hazel tried to suppress her eye roll. "It's not about knowing her. It's about what's right."

"What's right for her or for you?" Morgan dragged her finger down the side of Hazel's face. "I see the way you look at her, the way your eyes fill with lust. I can see how your body reacts when she's around. It's so blatant I can smell it on you now."

Hazel didn't want to shiver at Morgan's touch, but her body betrayed her. "What bothers you exactly? How I look at Raven or the way she looks at me?" Hazel was surprised by her words. She hadn't known everything Morgan could do, but she was pretty sure turning Hazel into a pile of ash or even a frog was well within her capabilities.

Morgan cocked her head and studied her. "I'm not sure if you're terribly brave or insanely foolish." She stood and walked toward the door. "Raven may think she wants you, she may even act on a few primitive impulses, but make no mistake, she belongs to me. I've known Raven in ways that you sit in your room and fantasize about. I've felt her touch on my bare skin and her lips on my neck. I've felt her body tremble from an orgasm so intense, no mortal has ever even imagined, never mind experienced it. You, my dear, may very well turn out to be a tremendously powerful witch, but you will never be me." She gave a small wave and shut the door behind her.

Hazel picked up a pillow from the bed and screamed into it. Morgan was infuriating. She looked down at her hands and was no longer surprised to see her fingertips glowing and crackling. She took several deep breaths and focused on isolating the sensation she was feeling.

She moved her hands and watched the exchange of electricity between them. It was as if she was creating miniature bolts of lightning. She smiled to herself, pleased she was able to control the power with more ease now. Instinctively, she picked up her phone to call Raven, to tell her of the small amount of progress she'd made. But she changed her mind, remembering their last exchange.

Hazel shook her head, an attempt to clear the last hour from it, and went back to studying the book in front of her. Morgan was right about one thing: Even if Hazel could help Raven, the decision would still need to be hers. She just wanted to be able to offer options, which was already more than Morgan had ever done for her.

She continued to skim the pages until she came upon something that made her ears ring and the hair on the back of her neck stand up. *This is exactly what I've been looking for.*

CHAPTER SIXTEEN

R aven sat up, her breathing labored. The sweat from her fitful night of sleep forced her shirt to cling to her skin. "Fuck."

She rubbed her face as she got out of bed and made her way into the bathroom, trying to shake the images of demons disintegrating into a pile of ash from her mind. She pulled off her shirt as she watched herself in the mirror. The minor bruises and scrapes had disappeared overnight, and she held her breath as she removed the gauze pad from her ribs. Only minor scratch marks remained, looking more as if she'd had an unfortunate run-in with a housecat. She tossed the pad into the small wastebasket, wondering not for the first time why the scars in her mind couldn't heal as easily.

She brushed her teeth and walked to the nightstand, picking up her phone. She opened the text from Hazel in her notifications. *I'm sorry for upsetting you last night. I just want you to be happy, whatever that means. Please be careful today.* Raven felt her face warm as it always did when she thought of Hazel. She'd overreacted last night, a combination of her injuries and a lifetime of feeling tethered to a fate she never chose. Hazel had a way of highlighting her resentment toward her predetermined path. Maybe it was because no one had ever cared about what she wanted before, or maybe it was because Hazel made her want other things. Either way, it was her burden to bear, not Hazel's.

I'm sorry for getting upset. It was a long day. I'll be back soon. Her thumbs hovered over the keyboard. She wanted to tell Hazel that she missed her, to let her know that if they'd met in a different place or in a different time, things would've been different. But she opted to say nothing, tossing the phone next to her bag.

After examining the map again, she packed up her few belongings and headed for the door. She was going to need a clear and focused mind today. She could dwell on the what-ifs later.

It didn't take long to get to the apartment building her necklace had pointed her toward. She sat in the parking lot for several minutes, watching as people walked in and out of the building. Everyone seemed to be going about their day, unaware of the dangers unfolding right beneath their noses. Raven never stopped being amazed by this fact. Sometimes she wished she could trade places with any of these people, anyone who had the privilege of living their lives, complacent of the realms and their significance. She shook her head at their blissful ignorance.

She checked her weapons, attached two to her hips, one to her leg, and walked into the building. She stood in the lobby and closed her eyes, taking a deep breath to let her senses take over. The abilities that came along with the shadowhunter gig were limited, but she could sense, locate, and determine where demons and dark magic hid. It only took a few moments for the hair on the back of her neck to stand up and for an apartment number to appear in her mind.

She walked over to the elevator and rode it up to the fifth floor. She had to keep herself from laughing as the sounds of Muzak filled the small space. Here she was, ascending five floors to torture information out of a dark witch, listening to a terrible rendition of "Every Breath You Take" played on something that only slightly resembled an instrument.

The doors opened while she was still laughing at the irony of it all, and there in front of her stood Lucien McCoulter. She froze, surprised by his presence. To his credit, he had the decency to look panicked before he turned and bolted.

"God dammit," she said under her breath as she sprinted after him.

He darted for an apartment and fumbled with his keys. She caught up as soon as he got the door open. She shoved him inside, turned, and locked the door behind her.

"Did you really think I wouldn't catch you?" she asked with her hands on her hips.

He walked backward until his knees hit the sofa and then tried to stand a little taller. "You should be dead."

She took the gold-plated knife from its sheath and used the butt to scratch her head. "And why is that? Was it you who sent the hellhound? I sure hope not. I just came here for information, but if that's the case, I'll have to kill you, and I really didn't want to kill anyone today." She pointed the knife at him.

"You have no idea who you're dealing with." Lucien stuck his chin out, a small act of defiance.

She drew the other knife from its holster and made a show of examining it. "Oh, I think I do. In fact, you're sorely underestimating how much I do know. For instance, I know you're Samuel Cranwell and that you followed Sarah Hutchinson here from Salem Village after dragging her into the witch hysteria." She tapped the blade to her chin, enjoying the ability to toy with him. "Which, by the way, what the fuck was wrong with you people?" She shook her head. "I also know since you've been here, you've been sowing the seeds of discord, riling people up with your religious extremism, inciting their fear into violence. And I know that you came here with two other whack-jobs, or as you call them, your kids, and that you think you're going to win." She closed the distance, putting the tip of her knife under his throat. She changed her voice to a whisper. "But I have really bad news for you, Sammy. This is my world. You don't belong here, and I can't wait to send you back."

He eyed her up and down with a look of disdain, as though she, a woman, could never be a worthy adversary. "We're not going anywhere. It's you who will be banished to Hell. Count on it."

Raven smiled and pushed the tip of the blade a little deeper into his skin. "They must not teach you much about shadowhunters at dark magic school. You're not banishing me anywhere. You couldn't summon the power to kill me even if you had the brains for it."

He licked his lips, his tongue white and pasty from fear. "That may be true, but Blaise does."

"What are you talking about? Morgan killed Blaise hundreds of years ago." She searched his eyes for an indication that he was lying but didn't find one.

"You sure about that, shadowhunter?" He put his finger on the tip of her knife and pushed it down. "I assume you defeated the hellhound since you're standing in front of me and that you're smart enough to have checked its brand. Where would I have gotten it?"

Raven took a step back and looked him up and down. "Another witch is fucking with you. Blaise would have shown himself by now if he was still alive."

"You sure about that? Sure enough to bet your life on it, or Morgan's? Or Hazel's?"

She stepped to him again, bringing both blades to his neck, crossing them over one another. "I really need you to give me a reason not to kill you right now."

The room became unbearably hot. The air was forced out of her lungs by a presence so powerful it could only be forged in the darkest recesses of Hell. She fell over, grabbing at her throat, willing her body to do what it was designed to do and breathe. She heard a crackling noise and strained to look up.

A figure stood in front of her, draped in a black cloak. An aura of red emanated from somewhere behind it. The room smelled of sulfur and wet dirt, and she gasped as her chest constricted.

"You dare to be so arrogant and doubt my existence?" The voice was intoxicating. If melting butter had a sound, this would be it.

Raven tried desperately to stand but was held in place by a force she couldn't see. "It's impossible."

"Yet here I am." He moved closer.

Raven looked up. Her vision was blurring, but she could make out a stream of electricity transferring between the entity and Lucien. Lucien seemed to be in a trance of some kind, but Raven couldn't determine what was happening between the two of them. She'd never seen anything like it.

He moved his left hand out of the cloak and toward her face. His fingers were gnarled and cracking at the knuckles. "Who am I?"

Raven coughed, fighting against her involuntary need to respond. She bit her tongue, not wanting to give this thing the satisfaction of an answer.

He gripped her chin and squeezed. His fingers were soft despite their appearance. "Who am I?"

Raven's hand shook against the force holding her as she groped for her blade. He'd released his hold on her voice, wanting an answer. "A guy who really needs to work on his pickup game?"

Red balls of fire ignited under the cloak where his eyes should be.

He tightened his grip and jerked her into a standing position. "Say my name."

The smell of her searing flesh filled her nostrils as she railed against the pain. "No."

He tossed her backward, and she landed on her back, knocking the wind out of her. He was suddenly on top of her, his mouth next to her ear, his finger dragging down her stomach. "I'll make sure you never forget who I am and what I'm capable of."

Smoke billowed from her stomach as the sound of her skin sizzling from the brand filled the air around them. The onslaught of blinding pain pulsed though her body. She stifled a scream and clenched her jaw. "You will lose."

He placed his hand on her forehead, his index and pinky finger latching on to her temples. "Make sure you tell Morgan that I'm back."

It couldn't have been more than half a second until she felt wet grass under her head. Raven rolled over onto her side, unable to stop the coughing fit raging through her body. She looked down. Parts of her shirt had been burned away. She tugged at the material to see what he'd done. Her flesh was raw, open, and blistered. The edges of the wound were singed black, and blood dripped from the sections he had taken a bit longer at.

"Raven?"

As it came closer, she recognized the panicked voice as Hazel's.

"What the hell happened?" Hands were on her a moment later, rubbing her body up and down.

"Take me to Morgan." Raven tried to stand, but the pain was crippling.

"You need medical attention. I'm calling EMS." Hazel was trying to hold her in place as she fumbled for the phone in her pocket.

Raven reached for her hand. "Hang up the phone and take me to Morgan. A hospital isn't going to do me any good."

Hazel seemed to remember who she was and where they were. She nodded. "Instead of trying to move you and risk hurting you more, I'm going to get Morgan."

Raven nodded and grazed Hazel's arm again before she left. "Thank you."

Hazel gave her a smile that seemed forced, then disappeared. No more than a minute later, Raven found herself lying on the floor in Morgan's parlor.

Morgan carefully opened her shirt. "What happened?"

Raven forced the words out through the pain. "Blaise."

Morgan's eyes grew larger than Raven ever remembered seeing, and after swallowing hard, she said, "That's not possible."

Raven clutched her hand. "Please fix this so I can tell you everything I know."

Morgan blinked a few times and then focused. Her hand glided over the burnt flesh. "Try to relax and open yourself to me."

Raven felt her skin cool, and she almost wept at the relief. After a beat, she looked up at Morgan and searched her eyes, unnerved by what she was seeing. "What is it?"

Morgan shook her head. "I healed the wound, but I can't seem to do anything about the brand."

Raven wrenched her neck to get a better look. Her flesh was no longer burned, but an eight-inch scar in the shape of a B stared back at her.

"What does that mean?" Hazel asked as she leaned over, her eyes full of panic and anger.

Morgan looked disturbingly out of sorts. "Blaise is alive." She hugged herself. "He wants to seize control of the realms."

"Which realm?" Hazel asked.

Morgan looked up, her pupils large with foreboding. "All of them."

Hazel sat on the couch, allowing her body to rest against Raven. She hadn't meant to do it, but the information was all so much, it was completely overwhelming. She'd been listening to Morgan talk for almost thirty minutes straight, and she still couldn't believe what she was hearing.

Hazel finally raised her hand. "I just want to make sure I'm understanding everything correctly. Blaise was the wizard you trained back during your time with King Arthur. I didn't think that was a real thing, but we can get back to that later." She took a deep breath before she continued. "You overthrew Blaise when he became too powerful and banished him to Hell. Now, thousands of years later, he's back."

Morgan continued pacing. "I cannot fathom how this is possible, but yes, that's the abridged version of events."

Raven put her hand on Hazel's knee, an apparent attempt to stop it from bouncing up and down. "I'm not so sure he actually is." She held her hand up before Morgan could interrupt. "I couldn't figure it out exactly, but I think he's drawing his power from Lucien. I saw a current of energy between the two of them. The brighter it got, the more powerful Blaise seemed to become and the more catatonic Lucien was."

Morgan stopped at the bookshelf and selected several volumes with a single swipe of her hand. "That actually makes sense. I couldn't completely kill Blaise because his power is the very essence of evil. There has to be balance, blah, blah, blah. He's siphoning from dark witches and projecting himself into this realm."

Hazel took a deep breath. "How does that make any sense at all?"

Morgan continued to scour the books. "He needs the dark witches because he can't exist without their power. He's counting on us not being able to banish all of them. He thinks we'll never be able to completely rid the realm of his presence. He's like a cancer. He must have infected hundreds of them by now."

Feeling nauseous, Hazel leaned a little harder into Raven. "What are we supposed to do with that information?"

Morgan didn't bother looking up from her books. "They're going to have to send a signal of some kind, alert the others. If Blaise is going to make a real comeback, he's going to need all of their power."

CHAPTER SEVENTEEN

When Sarah and Ayotunde entered the Roanoke hotel suite they'd all be sharing while undertaking the newly revamped mission, Sarah froze at the dire expressions on the faces of Morgan, Hazel, and Raven. She shivered at the palpable tension in the room and reached behind her for Ayotunde's hand.

"How was your flight?" Morgan asked.

Morgan's half-cocked smile seemed a contrivance at best, but Sarah tried to relax in light of it. "'Twas a bit more frightening for Ayotunde, I suspect. Lingering purple finger marks on my thighs do betray her."

Ayotunde shook her head. "That ride in Satan's flying carriage be more ghastly than my travel through the portal of time."

Morgan handed them both glasses of bourbon straight up. "Sorry, but we're not allowing Sarah anywhere near portals of any kind until further notice. She comes in too hot and drags the worst of the preternatural flotsam and jetsam with her."

"I shall be quite pleased never to enter another portal again as long as I walk the earth," Sarah said.

"Yeah, that's a conversation for another time," Morgan said.

"Here's the part I don't understand," Hazel said as she ran her hand through her hair and stared out the window. "They didn't actually come with Sarah. It seems like they've been here much longer. They'd have to be to build such a following."

Morgan crossed her legs and leaned back in the chair. "Sarah was brought to this time because of her familiar link to you. The three buffoons had a familiar link as well, although they must not have stumbled on to them the way Sarah did to you. Time traveling isn't an exact science. I'm not entirely sure why they showed up here a few years ago, and Sarah a few weeks ago. But you can be sure, Blaise sensed them immediately and took advantage. Darkness calls to darkness, and it was alive and well in them." Morgan waved her hand around. "That's all I know. Traipsing through time is forbidden because of the damage it can do, so I don't have a lot of other information." She glared at Sarah.

Raven stood up from the sofa and was all manner of business as she addressed Sarah and Ayotunde. "Our mission now has an additional element of danger, one that's going to require a quadrangle of white witch power along with the shadowhunting skills of yours truly."

"That's why I'm now on the team instead of calling the shots from the comfort of my French provincial lair," Morgan said. "It's also going to require even swifter action than previously anticipated. If Blaise is trying to restore his original power by feeding off the evil energy of Lucien McCoulter and his offspring menace, we have to stop him before Blaise gathers enough strength to anchor a foothold here."

Sarah shuddered inside. The thought of Samuel Cranwell aiding the almighty evil being in his rise against good filled her with rage. Many a time she'd regretted her part in this mission until she'd reminded herself how her husband and she had done the charitable Christian thing and opened their home to Samuel only to have him steal from them and lay false claims of witchery against her. Whatever mark her involvement in this plan would lay upon her soul, she was resigned to settle it with God once they'd succeeded in their plan.

Hazel chimed in as she read from her phone. "Tomorrow night Tammi Lee Sanderson is recording a live podcast with McCoulter and Dirk Fowler. She's calling it 'The Politics of Religion.' It seems like it's going to be another pro-conservative platform where they incite evangelicals against all the presidential candidates who are allegedly undermining their religious rights."

"Don't they ever get tired of saying the same things over and over?" Raven said.

"You know what happens when you repeat the same message," Hazel said.

"An ideal situation. We need to get into that studio," Morgan said. "We can't waste any more time. We must lure those three sycophants back to Salem and promptly return them to 1692 before they wreak any more havoc."

"It's a ticketed event, and it says it's all sold out."

Morgan grinned and moved next to Ayotunde. "That's where our dear Ayotunde comes in." She draped her arm around her shoulder. "Your powers are going to get a good workout tomorrow night, my dear. Hazel and Sarah, after Ayotunde gets us past security, it'll be up to you two to make sure we can get access to the three of them. While you're handling that, Raven and I will keep Blaise and his bloodthirsty mutts at bay."

Hazel seemed not to like that part of the plan, but she turned toward Sarah. "Are you okay with all this, Sarah?"

Sarah jumped at her name. She wrung her hands together as she grappled with whether or not she should share her troublesome feelings. "This talk of encountering demons face-to-face doth cause me to quake inside. My heart be in the mission, but I fear letting you all down if I haven't the strength to fight such forces."

Hazel took one of her hands. "Morgan, Raven, and I would never put you in harm's way if we didn't believe in you and your powers."

"Hazel's right," Raven said. "Look at what you accomplished at the arena. You and Hazel rounded up those demons chasing us without missing a beat. I would've been killed if you weren't there."

"Aye, but I knew not what I were up against. I had not proper time to think. 'Twas instinct that impelled me to act."

She bowed her head but heard Morgan mutter to Raven, "You better do something about this."

"Miss Sarah," Ayotunde said. "You be de strongest woman I know. You help the frightened, pained young women deliver their babies and don't let them quit till the job be done. Those demons will pale against you."

Sarah beamed at Ayotunde, who was smiling back at her with complete adoration. After a minute, she tore her eyes off Ayotunde and noticed the three awkward expressions on the faces of their onlookers.

"We good?" Morgan glanced impatiently between Sarah and Ayotunde.

"Aye. We good," Ayotunde said, squeezing Sarah's hand.

"Fantabulous," Morgan said in an impatient drawl. "Why don't we all retreat to our rooms for a bit to settle down and gather our wits, and then we can head out to dinner."

"Good idea," Hazel said. "God knows I could use it."

Sarah nodded, resolving to choose bravery over fear. She might have unwittingly unleashed this evil into the world, but no matter how daunting the task before her was, she would dedicate whatever abilities or charms she'd possessed to help Morgan, Raven, and Hazel rid the world of it, no matter what it cost her.

In the meantime, she and Ayotunde rushed to their room, Sarah eager to spend any and every moment alone with Ayotunde that the Fates would allow. As soon as she closed the door, Ayotunde surprised her by lunging toward her and kissing her passionately.

"The more I have of you, the more I want," Ayotunde said. "Your lips be the sweetest nectar, the softest of petals."

"You mustn't, Ayotunde." Sarah half-heartedly tried to push her back. "Not now. You stir me so greatly that I cannot think when you be so close. I cannot control my desires against your touch."

"Aye," she whispered seductively. "My senses be lost when you be near."

"We must keep our wits about us," Sarah said. "The others count on us. Although, these strange urges you rouse in me do keep me in your grip."

Ayotunde wrapped her arms around Sarah's neck. "No witch in the world could conjure a spell more powerful than the love I feel for you, Sarah."

Sarah swept her up in her arms, and they tantalized each other with deep kisses before falling onto the bed.

❖

When Hazel and Raven went to their room, Raven collapsed on the bed, trying to conserve what energy she had in the face of her still-healing physical injuries. Her eyes were closed, but she sensed Hazel was agitated about something. Dared she ask? She exhaled deeply and opted to let it go.

"I don't like the idea of being separated from you," Hazel finally said.

Raven opened one eye. "Splitting up makes the most sense. The three of you are powerful together, and I can't leave Morgan without protection."

"I can't help but feel like it's just another way for Morgan to control you. I know I probably sound ridiculous, but I worry."

Raven struggled into an upright position. "Hazel, it has to be that way. In the likely event that Blaise tries to thwart us with another hellhound or demon attack, Morgan and I are the best team to fend them off. I have the actual weapons to kill them; you guys don't."

"Sarah and I did just fine against the demons at the arena; we can hold our own."

"I know," Raven said. "You guys were awesome at rendering and subduing them. But you can't kill them. Even if you could conjure up the skills, you don't have the weaponry to destroy them. Remember, they're not human."

Hazel's shoulders stooped in apparent disappointment. "I know I'm no expert, but to me it makes more sense to split the hellhound and demon killers with the ones who can subdue them. It just seems like a more effective method of attack."

Raven couldn't contain her amusement, and it escaped in a snort. "Would you like to tell Morgan your plan is better than hers?"

Hazel frowned. "No."

"I love your commitment, but your powers will serve best working in conjunction with Sarah and Ayotunde, doing whatever compelling and manipulating is necessary to get into the studio. You have to get close enough to Lucien and the other two. Once they realize Sarah and Ayotunde are on to them, they'll have no choice but to eliminate them if they want any chance of doing Blaise's bidding and winning a place in his immortal coven of evil. You and your aunt and Ayotunde are no match for Blaise. Only Morgan is."

"I don't like it, Raven. I don't like the way she flippantly uses you. It's like you're nothing but a toy to her, an action figure with moveable parts she can drop into any scenario she fancies, no matter how dangerous. She acts like she's in love with you, but forcing you into potentially lethal situations sure is a bizarre way of showing it."

Raven got up and met Hazel on her return from the other side of the room. "Hazel, I know it may look that way, but it really isn't. It's just like you said to Sarah—Morgan would never put me in a situation she knew I couldn't handle. I'm a shadowhunter. It's who I've always been."

"It's not who you've always been. It's what you've always done. You never had a chance to determine who you are. It was determined for you. Your uncle shouldn't have put you in this position. This lonely life of servitude to Morgan le Fay is no way to live."

Raven's empathy and patience faded. "My uncle is the most honest, honorable man you'll ever meet. He took his calling seriously, and so do I, even though it's totally fucked up my personal life. He's been my protector and my mentor ever since my parents died. I have nothing but gratitude toward him, and I won't have you blaming him."

"I'm sorry. I didn't mean to—"

"If you're jealous of Morgan, just own it. Don't drag a man who's—"

Hazel lurched toward Raven and kissed her with such force, Raven couldn't have escaped if she'd wanted to.

She gripped Hazel's ass and pulled her tightly against her, feeling her firm breasts mash against her own. She plunged her tongue into Hazel's mouth, savoring the sweetness and warmth as desire consumed her entire body.

Hazel groaned. "You don't know what you do to me." She bit at Raven's earlobe, sending shivers cascading down her back.

Raven didn't answer with words. She clutched handfuls of Hazel's hair as she flicked her tongue around in her mouth and shoved Hazel's thigh between her legs. "You should stay away from me," she whispered in Hazel's ear as she felt her body surrender.

"I can't," Hazel said, raking her teeth down the column of Raven's neck and sucking on her pulse point. "I know what you told me, but I can't pretend you don't drive me out of my mind."

"I can't give you what you want," Raven said.

"You don't know what I want," Hazel said breathlessly.

Raven began pushing her toward the bed. "Then tell me."

Hazel dug her nails into Raven's back. "I want you so fucking bad."

"This is a mistake," Raven said as she cupped Hazel's breasts.

"I hate Morgan. She has the worst timing," Hazel said as she pushed Raven down and crawled on top of her.

As Raven began unbuttoning Hazel's shirt, a knock on the door startled her.

"Come on, ladies," Morgan said from the other side. "Let's go get some dinner and cocktails and strategize."

She nudged Hazel off her and sprang up to the edge of the bed. "Fuck," she said, resting her head in her hands.

"I'm sorry," Hazel said and leapt up at the other side. "I don't know what came over me. I...I never do things like this. Honestly."

"Don't worry about it." Raven shook it off and gathered her usual arsenal of weapons. "Sometimes these types of missions can get really intense. It's easy to lose your grip and deal with the insanity in ways you'd never have guessed."

At first, Hazel looked wounded. "Yeah, yeah. I mean, that makes perfect sense. I'm sorry I got so *ah* about it." She made a gesture as if her head was exploding and then laughed awkwardly. She straightened her shirt before grabbing the doorknob. "Can we just forget this even..."

"Yeah, absolutely," Raven said, feeling awkward for her. She avoided eye contact until Hazel left the room.

Like there's any way either one of us will forget that. "Fuck," Raven spat as she looked toward the ceiling. "This is just what I need right now."

Hazel tried to calm her body and her mind. The rapid transitions of emotions and the intensity they'd just exchanged had her feeling out of sorts. The crackling in her fingertips was starting to become a good indicator of her being off-kilter. Raven had been bold and powerful. Hazel found that side of her invigorating, and she wanted more. She wanted as much as Raven was willing to give. She felt greedy for Raven and ravenous for her attention. But right now, she needed to push those feelings to the side. She knew they would remain close to the surface, bubbling with excitement, and longing for the next touch. But she could and would keep them at bay.

Raven had suggested they have their strategizing session over dinner at the restaurant inside the hotel, explaining that it wasn't prudent for the five of them to go roaming downtown Roanoke at night. Their collective energy would be so intense that Blaise and his minions could detect their presence and thwart their plans before they'd had a chance to set them in motion.

Hazel was especially amenable to the suggestion given that Raven still hadn't seemed herself. The gashes in her skin were nearly healed, but she moved slowly and deliberately as though still nursing some residual inner discomfort. The last thing she needed was to have to fend off a surprise attack from demons masquerading as radical right-wingers after sniffing her out as they trekked through the city in search of trendy wine bars.

They'd knocked back their first round of drinks in record time and in uncharacteristic silence. With everyone seeming a little more relaxed as they started on their second, Hazel shared the results of her search.

With her phone in one hand, she picked up her fresh cosmo and sipped as she read. "The doors open at five thirty p.m. tomorrow night and close promptly at six thirty. They begin the live podcast at seven. Should we get there when the doors open or right before they close?"

Raven plucked a garlic knot from the basket and tore it apart. "Right before it closes. Security's going to be tight, and we don't need a crowd of witnesses itching for a riot when Ayotunde puts the whammy on the guards."

"Good thinking." Hazel smiled, trying not to show Raven her emotions were still scattered from their earlier miscalculated encounter.

Ayotunde brought her glass of wine to her lips, then paused. "Pray, Miss Raven, what be a whammy you say I'm to put?"

"Your voodoo," Morgan said. "What a shame there isn't time to find out the identities of the security guards so you can slap together some dolls and get the operation underway ahead of time."

Raven looked puzzled. "I'm sitting here with two witches, their queen, and a voodoo priestess, and you guys can't pull that off before tomorrow night?"

Morgan scoffed. "You shadowhunters really gall me. You think we just snap our fingers, and bam, the whole universe bends to our will?"

Hazel gripped the table when it started shaking as Morgan grew more annoyed. Sarah stabilized her water glass while Ayotunde's quick hand saved the basket of garlic knots from falling off the table.

"If it's so easy," Morgan said, pointing at Raven's phone, "why don't you find out who they are on your little handheld box of man-made magic and then drop some laxatives in their iced lattes tomorrow afternoon?" She shook her head. "Do you want it done fast, or do you want it done right?"

Raven shrank like a wool sweater left in the dryer too long. "It was rhetorical, Morgan. I guess I should've been clearer about that."

"Okay, so once we're inside, what are the three of us supposed to do?" Hazel said.

Morgan seductively sucked an oyster out of its shell, leaving them in suspense as she chewed. Hazel wondered if they all found that as hot as she did. She looked away as she sipped her drink.

"You're going to introduce Samuel Cranwell to the new and improved twenty-first-century Sarah Hutchinson," Morgan said. "That ought to shut his cult-babbling piehole for a few minutes once he realizes she's not the obedient little wife of Thomas Cooper he remembers."

"So, what you're saying is the three of us will have to come face-to-face with the three of them." Hazel forced the bite of bread down her dry throat. "Where will you two be during this?"

"Morgan and I will be somewhere in the building fending off Blaise and whatever else he summons against me. Given that he failed at his last attempt to vaporize me, I'm sure he'll come at me with both barrels if given another chance."

"That's why she needs me by her side this time," Morgan said and winked at Raven.

Hazel bounced her knees again, agitated as much by Morgan's transparent effort to mark her territory as she was by the unfolding details of the plan. "What do we say when we meet them?"

"Tell Lucien that Sarah and Ayotunde are going to go back to 1692 Salem and kill him and his spawn before he has a chance to follow them through the portal," Raven said. "The objective is to get them to follow us back to the hallowed grounds of Salem, Mass." She turned to Sarah. "That's the portal you came through. You have to go back the same way."

Sarah and Ayotunde exchanged worried glances.

"You mean Sarah and Ayotunde actually have to go back?" The thought made Hazel feel queasy. She'd grown attached to her aunt in this short span of time. She wanted them both to stay.

"Of course," Raven said. "They'll reopen the portal, and you, Morgan, and I will shove all of them through it so they can face their original fates. Hopefully, order and balance in the white witch realm will be restored immediately."

"Sarah and Ayotunde can come back though, right?"

"Wrong," said Morgan. "Sarah's destiny never included coming into the twenty-first century in the first place. She had no more right to slip through that portal than those three miscreants. It was a mistake, an unfortunate result of two women playing around with powers they knew nothing about."

"I wanted only to save my Sarah's life, Madame le Fay," Ayotunde said. "I meant no harm with my conjurin'. Pray, I beg of you. Take my soul and let Miss Sarah stay here safe from de gallows."

Hazel's eyes blurred with tears. There would be no way to know the fate of her aunt and Ayotunde once they went through the portal. The realization felt like a vise around her heart and throat.

"I have no use for your soul, Ayotunde," Morgan said. "My one and only purpose is to correct the grievous anachronism that's thrown our realm into chaos and threatens the very existence of the white witch." She directed her fiery eyes at Hazel. "I don't think you have any inkling as to what this means for humanity if we don't win."

"Let's not get ahead of ourselves," Raven said. "Clear heads. We need clear heads if we're going to be successful accomplishing even the first part of this mission; getting access to Lucien McCoulter is priority number one."

"Right," Morgan said. "Once Cranwell realizes Sarah's going back to rid the world of them before they stumbled through to this time, it'll be a cinch to get them to follow her back to Salem."

"How will they follow if they know they are to return to the past?" Sarah said.

"They're not going to follow you to Salem to be sent back," Morgan said. "They're going to follow you to kill you." She raised her glass and smiled happily. "Now, let's enjoy the rest of our meal, perhaps a few more cocktails, and then go up to our suite and get a good night's sleep."

Hazel offered Raven a half-hearted smile of reassurance, but it was Sarah who had all of her attention at the moment. Although Sarah said nothing more, Hazel saw the distress in her eyes, uncertain if she'd been shaken more by the part about being killed or being sent back. Although she hadn't had time to adjust to life in this century, she clearly found it preferable to the life from which she and Ayotunde had both escaped. Hazel was beginning to know too well the profound ache of falling in love with someone she couldn't have. Sarah and Ayotunde were experiencing freedom unlike any Puritan had ever known. She couldn't imagine the agony they'd have to live with going back to such oppression and despair.

That was if they would even survive until the trials ended.

CHAPTER EIGHTEEN

In the green room outside the radio broadcast studio in downtown Roanoke, Lucien stared out the window at the distant glow emanating from the colossal Mill Mountain Star across town. This live podcast with Tammi Lee Sanderson was to be the culmination of all their painstaking planning to amass and install nationalist cells in major cities all across America. To his surprise, it hadn't been that difficult to accomplish. There was no shortage of angry, disillusioned, working-class people sick of liberal politicians insidiously infusing their socialist agenda into their government. The long-standing lax immigration policies, endless stream of welfare for the lazy, and regulations against American businesses had been a detriment to the economy and burdened hardworking Americans. Not to mention the flagrant ways these politicians catered to the gays.

He paced between Tammi, who was scribbling on a legal pad full of talking points for the podcast, and Dirk, seated next to Tammi, who was typing away on his phone.

"Twenty minutes," Lucien said, but mentally, he was still locked in his own head. Soon the social strife they'd been agitating for over the last decade would replenish Blaise's power, and Lucien would ascend to second in command of the dark realm.

Dirk finally rested his phone in his lap with a satisfied smile. "There. I've just blasted the Twitterverse with a dozen tweets and retweets about how the house speaker is about to give free Medicare to everyone and how the middle class will lose their private health benefits." He tilted his head back with a hearty laugh.

Still engrossed in her own matters, Tammi spoke without looking up. "We're leading with the correlation between corporate pollution regulation under Obama and the decline in job growth. Then we'll segue right into immigrant workers undermining the wages of skilled American workers. Dirk, you have the random callers lined up, right?"

"Yep. I got a redneck from Birmingham who's eager to gripe about his assembly-line job going to Mexico and the CEO of American Oil and Refinery Corp explaining how they've had to downsize their workforce because of the liberal panic about fossil fuel and the clean energy industry's pervasive bribes of senators."

Lucien basked in the pride of his son's impressive showing. "Well done. You both may have secured yourselves a spot in Blaise's ranks with tonight's event."

Tammi tossed her legal pad aside and got off the couch. "By this time tomorrow, the cells will have incited the multi-city riots and bombings, and then the fake socialist terror groups will claim responsibility."

Lucien dropped some ice cubes into a cup and poured from a silver flask. "Blaise will be so pleased with me," he said softly, already imagining the spoils he'd receive for his loyal efforts and demonstration of leadership.

"This is gonna really shake things up," Dirk said. "I'll be the most sought-after lobbyist in history. My firm will command the highest prices ever paid."

"Hmm," Lucien said. "This is the beginning of very big things to come for all of us."

"What is Blaise's actual plan once he's reached full potency?" Tammi asked.

Lucien wheeled around and regarded her as if she was simple. "To run for President of the United States, of course. What better way to destroy the fabric of global civilization than by installing the master of evil in the world's most influential position of power?"

"But it's only an eight-year term," she said.

Lucien laughed. "You really think the master of the entire realm of evil can't find a loophole if he wanted to? He's already laid the groundwork to get the Twenty-Second Amendment struck down through that nitwit he directed us to install in office in the interim. In only two years, we've managed to flip the Supreme Court over to a conservative majority." His face contorted with apparent resentment. "It still irks me that the Russians are getting the credit for helping destroy the democracy, but someday, history will portray the true story."

"And you're sure that shadowhunter isn't going to interfere with our plans again?" Dirk said.

Lucien shook his head. "Let her try. I have double the security staff ready to sniff her out if she comes anywhere near the building. If she is fool enough, they'll finish the job they started at the arena. Even Raven Dare isn't so mighty that she can fight off a legion of hellhounds. She and those two misfit witches got lucky that first time because I only had a few guards posted. This night, they are completely out of their league."

"Look at this." Tammi waved them over to the window. "There's already a riot outside, and we haven't even gone on yet." She smiled maniacally. "Our supporters are clashing with the protesters. That crowd out there is huge."

Lucien looked down and grinned at the sea of hand-decorated signs flowing into the street and stopping traffic as squad cars pulled up around them. "Can this night get any better? You need to open the show with this blatant attempt to suppress the free speech of our conservative following happening in real time right outside the studio."

Tammi smiled and flipped her blond hair back. "It's time."

The rioting crowd in the front of the building created a sweet, unexpected diversion. With so much commotion happening out front, nobody would be at all concerned with what might occur in the back. Raven watched the hulking security guard dressed in black slacks and blazer scan the sidewalk outside the employee entrance before going inside and closing the door. He wasn't dressed in the typical building security uniform with badge and walkie-talkie. He was clearly part of a private team, Lucien's team, and probably salivating at the opportunity to morph into his true form, a hellhound, at the first sign of trouble. She would have preferred the scent of a demon at this point. Demons were easier to control and to kill. Hellhounds were damn near impossible if they had the opportunity to shed their human form. It didn't matter now. They could only play the cards they were dealt.

Raven turned around to Ayotunde. "You ready?"

"Aye." Ayotunde's voice was rich with conviction, but her wide eyes and twitchy movements indicated otherwise.

"Hang on." Morgan whirled Ayotunde toward her by the shoulders and, after waving her hands in a flourish, Ayotunde's scoop-neck shirt was lower and tighter and her breasts much larger.

Raven glared at Morgan. "Really?"

Morgan rolled her eyes. "Yes, it's archaic, misogynistic, and offensive. But it's the way women have been bewitching men since the dawn of time."

"Yeah," Raven said. "Women who can't literally bewitch them."

"Tomato, tomahto," Morgan said. "Can we debate feminist philosophy later? We have to get in there."

Raven tried not to smile as Sarah's eyes fixated on Ayotunde's impressive new rack. "Sarah? You with us?"

"Aye," Sarah said with a start.

"How are we gonna get that guy to open the door for Ayotunde?" Hazel said.

"We're not," Morgan said. "You are, with a sudden gust of wind that'll blow the door wide open."

Hazel grinned. "I can do that."

As she was about to wind up her arm, Raven grabbed it and held it. "Cool your jets for a sec. Ayotunde, as soon as he comes to the door, run up to him like you need his help. And can you talk like a modern American to minimize suspicion?"

"Aye. Oh, I mean yes," she said.

"Here." Raven handed her a cell phone. "Tell him your car broke down, and your phone has no service. Then compel him to...I don't know, to do whatever will give all of us the chance to slip past him and get into the studio."

"I got this," Ayotunde said with a thumbs-up.

Hazel looked at Raven with a naughty grin. "You can let go of my hand now. I have to...you know."

"Oh, right, yeah," Raven said. When she looked away in embarrassment, she inadvertently caught a glimpse of Morgan, who did not appear pleased at the magnetism between Hazel and her.

Hazel seemed to study the door for a moment, then swirled her arm around, creating only a gust of wind strong enough to knock over a garbage can.

"Put a little more pepper on it," Morgan said with a nod of encouragement.

"I'm sorry," Hazel said, her mouth a half-moon of disappointment. "I guess I need more practice."

"There's no more practice, *mon cheri*," Morgan said sweetly. She then shouted, "Now blow that fucking door open."

Hazel recoiled from Morgan's menacing face and conjured a roaring wind that swept through the alley and blew the heavy door open.

When the security guard appeared and looked out, Ayotunde approached him, acting as if she was frazzled. "Excuse me, mister. Can you help me? My car has no service, and my phone broke down."

"Your what?" His face contorted in confusion, then he slumped down on the doorsill, fast asleep.

Raven and the others ran toward the door and had to step over his bulky body to get inside the building. "A for effort," Raven said to Ayotunde. She tried to move him by shutting the door, giving his head several whacks but to no avail. "Sarah?"

"Aye," Sarah said. She raised her hand and levitated him into the alley, letting him drop hard on the pavement.

"Good thing he has nothing in his head, or that would've been messy." Raven locked the door behind her, and all five of them headed down the hall toward the recording studio.

As they got closer, Raven felt as if her skin was on fire. She could smell and taste the presence of the hellhounds. Her side still burning from the pain of her last encounter with one, she hoped following Morgan into the abyss wouldn't result in a brutal and bloody ending for all of them.

Upon reaching the studio, Raven felt the toxic energy the party of hellhounds generated as they closed in on them. The adrenaline heated her veins as the years of training moved to her limbs, preparing to prove their worth.

Raven glanced at Hazel, who looked back with worry shadowing her eyes. She grabbed her without thinking and kissed her deeply, breathlessly. Hazel's fingers caressed Raven's face in what felt like a fevered effort to memorize as much as she could. Raven was aware that their kiss could only last a few seconds, but she was determined to make those few seconds resonate with her for the rest of her life. She wanted Hazel to know that despite all of the misspoken words, unclear intentions, and confusing dynamics, she was with her. When Hazel backed away and searched Raven's eyes, Raven hoped she saw what she'd intended her to see. She wouldn't get the chance to ask as eight large men turned the corner. She pushed Hazel toward the studio and pulled out her blades.

Raven braced herself for a fight unlike any she'd ever found herself in. The hellhounds were shedding their form in front of her eyes. Human skin stretched and shredded into animal skin. Hair exploded over the expanding bodies. Hands cracked and popped, transitioning into paws with claws that could tear her heart from her chest if the hounds were to outmaneuver them.

Raven looked at Morgan, who was forcing her hands together, a ball of white light expanding between them. She'd never seen anything like it before and was overwhelmed with a sense of astonishment and visceral fear. Morgan's eyes glowed blinding white as she levitated off the ground.

The first and either bravest or dumbest hellhound rushed toward them, followed in V-formation by his fellow hunters. Two went in the direction of Morgan while the other came for Raven. His coarse fur scratched her cheek, and she choked on his hot, foul breath as the hound attempted to devour her face. This time she was ready for the attack. She lifted her blades to both sides of his neck and held them in a crisscross fashion. Blood splattered her face, leaving her lips coated in copper-tasting liquid and her skin smelling like sulfur. The body fell to the ground and turned to ash.

Morgan had the other two hounds caught in an orb of white light. She was pushing, crushing the orb until it was nothing more than a marble in her hand. She let it fall through her fingers to the ground, and Raven watched in amazement as the small gem bounced off the walls and disappeared down the hallway.

A wave of relief washed through her. She allowed herself to believe that perhaps they would make it out of this alive, and better yet, in one piece. However, that sensation was short-lived as her knees buckled, and the air pushed out of her chest as if she was a deflating balloon. She looked down the hall to the burning red orbs hiding behind a black cloak.

"Blaise," Morgan said, sounding unimpressed.

As Blaise rushed Morgan, he roared with thunderous fury. Raven bent over and covered her ears against the pain riveting her brain. This was nothing like she'd ever experienced.

Morgan stopped him about two feet away, her hands up, and white light illuminating their proximity. She laughed and pushed him back farther. "Oh, Blaise, please tell me you had something better than this planned? Did you seriously spend the last several hundred years plotting your revenge just to rush me like some third-grader on the playground?"

Blaise struggled, and as he did, the grip on Raven lessened. "When I reach my full capacity, I will destroy you."

Morgan moved her hands downward, forcing him to his knees. "If I'd known you were so obsessed with me, we could've dated. You know how I love to be adored."

Five hellhounds seemed to radiate fury behind Blaise. She assumed they were waiting for the go-ahead to charge at Morgan and Raven. The stench of their hatred hung in the air like fog swallowing an entire city. Raven hoped they were all that remained for this battle.

Blaise shot Morgan an eerie smile and one of the hounds rushed and pounced on top of Raven. It snarled and growled, and spit like hot wax dripped onto her cheek. Raven struggled, but in her compromised state, she couldn't fight back as the hound wrapped its enormous teeth around her neck and held her there.

Blaise laughed, and the room shook with the energy. "Let me go, and I'll have the hound release your pet."

Anger flashed on Morgan's face as she looked between Raven and Blaise. "Do you honestly think I'd let you go free for a shadowhunter? There is nothing stopping me from annihilating you right now."

The white light allowed for glimpses of Blaise's scorched face. She wondered if perhaps Blaise had been the inspiration behind Freddy Krueger. His skin was twisted and raw. "That's the difference between you and me, Morgan; dark magic doesn't tie me to ridiculous notions like love and loyalty. They will be your downfall."

The hound bit down, and Raven's vision became clouded with spots. As she faded out of consciousness, she heard a loud pop. Her vision went black, and before she yielded to her fate, she hoped Hazel had been more successful and that she would forgive her for failing.

❖

The door shut behind them, and Hazel resisted the urge to go back into the large hallway when she heard the first ominous howl of the infamous hellhounds just beyond the door. Lucien, Tammi, and Dirk stood looking dumbfounded by their arrival.

When Lucien reached for something tucked into his waistband, Hazel shook her head. "Don't do that."

He continued his movement, and Sarah pointed in his direction. He winced as his wrist rolled over, pinning him to the desk.

Lucien croaked out words through the pain. "Sarah Hutchinson, you little bitch. I knew you were a witch."

Hazel laughed and put her hands on her hips. "That's a little too on the nose for you, isn't it, dark witch?"

Dirk rushed toward them from around the side of the desk, but Ayotunde stepped into his path. She raised her hand and spread her fingers in front of his face. He smiled like a child, started giggling like one, and sat on the floor, appearing to play with imaginary blocks.

Hazel looked at Tammi. "You wanna take your turn now, or do you want to listen?"

Tammi looked between the two men for a second and then decided to take a seat.

Hazel's fingertips shuddered with a surge of energy. She glanced back at the door, hearing Morgan and the sounds of growling intensify. She wanted to go and check on Raven, but Sarah put a hand on her shoulder, redirecting her attention to the people in front of them.

Hazel mustered up her most intimidating voice. "You three don't belong here."

Lucien pointed at Ayotunde and Sarah. "You're not exactly coming from a place devoid of hypocrisy. You think I don't know who these two women are? You should be ashamed of yourself, spending time with a slave and a dishonored woman."

When Hazel felt Sarah stiffen, the pang of defensiveness overtook her. "You're a pathetic excuse for a man, Lucien. You followed Sarah here from 1692, but you manifested yourself a decade earlier, when America was finally on the verge of positive change. But Blaise wasn't going to allow that change to hold. He knew an angry ne'er-do-well like you would never be capable of making a life for yourself here, so he sought you out, offering you false promises of protection and absolute power. And stupid you thought you'd get all of it without having to pay a price? The only dishonor in this room oozes from the pores of you three."

Finding her voice, Sarah held her head higher and stuck her chin out. "I shall enter the portal to depart to the day before I arrived here. And mark this, the second I do, I shall seek you out and end your despicable life." She took a step closer, and he cried out in pain as his arm twisted over farther. "Ridding this time of you and your hateful thoughts shall be my gift to the future."

Hazel watched the fear flicker across his face and wanted to make sure they were clear about their intentions. "Sarah and Ayotunde will end this where it all started, the hallowed ground of Salem." She walked closer and put her mouth next to his ear. "It will be as if you never existed at all; even Blaise won't remember your name."

He growled with anger and tried to get up, groaning when the position of his arm wouldn't allow it. "You'll never get the chance. It will be me that ends this, and Blaise will sing my praise from the rooftops of your fallen city."

Electricity crackled at Hazel's fingertips. She felt the energy building with each word he said. She wanted to trace a large H on his face, retribution for what Blaise had done to Raven. She'd leave her mark on him. She raised her hand, the desire to cause him pain growing stronger with each passing second. Then Morgan's voice appeared in her head as if she were standing next to her. *Get to the hotel.* The intrusion into her thoughts snapped her back to reality, and she pulled her hand back.

She looked between Ayotunde and Sarah. "Fate will give them what they have coming. Let's get out of here."

Sarah's narrowed eyelids and the way she glared at Lucien indicated that she wanted to say more. She was clearly trapped somewhere between wanting to inflict pain on this revolting man and following through with the plan. In the end, her greater angels won, and Sarah backed away from him.

Before they left, Hazel ran her hands in several circles, creating a windstorm in the small studio. Papers flew in every direction, the chair tipped over, and two ceramic lamps fell to the ground, shattering.

Ayotunde left Dirk where he sat playing with imaginary blocks as papers whipped across his face. Hazel winked at Sarah, wanting to convey that everything would be okay. They walked out the door and hurried to the car, needing to meet Raven and Morgan at the hotel.

As Hazel ran through the hallway, she prayed to the goddess that the blood she saw on the carpet belonged to anyone but Raven.

CHAPTER NINETEEN

Raven made her fifth lap around the hotel room, unable to settle down since they returned. The hellhound had rendered her unconscious just as Morgan had him swept into her orb. Her head throbbed from the exchange, but the adrenaline that raced through her system wasn't letting up.

Morgan sat on the large leather chair in the corner and sipped her scotch. "Stop pacing; you're making me dizzy. If you want something to do to pass the time, I can think of a few more entertaining options." She winked.

Raven continued, now chewing on her thumb. "We shouldn't have left them. They weren't ready to be kicked out of the nest."

Morgan ran a hand through her hair, snapped her fingers, and an invisible force thrust Raven into a seat. "You underestimate them. They're extremely capable women who were trained by the best mentors. I want to talk to you while we have a minute."

Raven picked up her glass of scotch, assuming she'd need the mind lubricant for whatever Morgan wanted to say. "I'm all ears." She took a sip and leaned forward, putting her elbows on her knees.

"This thing going on between you and Hazel." She put her hand up when Raven was about to protest. "Don't bother. Even if I wasn't the most powerful witch who ever lived, I'm not blind." She paused for Raven to bite back her retort. "What is your endgame?"

Raven took another sip of her drink. "My endgame?"

Morgan waved her hand in the air. "What do you hope will happen between you two? Before you answer, please remember that I know whenever someone lies to me."

Raven shook her head. "I don't know. I've never been in a situation like this before. I'm drawn to her, I think about her constantly, and I want to be near her all the time." She ran a hand over her face. "Christ, I sound like a teenager."

Morgan nodded. "Desperation isn't an attractive look on you, darling." She ran her hands down the tops of her legs, looking slightly distressed. "I can see her destiny, and Raven, you aren't in it."

Raven had been hit hundreds, if not thousands, of times in her life. She had come face-to-face with evil so old, its origins might never be discovered. She had felt the pits of Hell burning in the eyes of the damned and tasted the trappings of death more times than she could remember. She was also sure that none of that had ever frightened or hurt her more than Morgan's cutting words. Her stomach rolled, and she sat back, hoping the room would stop spinning.

Morgan looked as if she was going to say more, but before she had the chance, the door opened, and the three witches entered the room in a flurry. Hazel was in front of her in an instant. She ran her hands over Raven's face and body, clearly checking to verify that she was in one piece. Hazel's touch burned, but not like it had before with lust and tenderness. This time, the fire she felt as Hazel touched her was born in the truly unobtainable.

"Did everything go as planned?" Morgan asked.

Sarah and Ayotunde recounted the details, but Hazel never took her eyes off Raven. Raven willed Hazel's focus to be on something else, but she'd never have that power. She'd never be Hazel's equal and never be anything more than Morgan's shadowhunter. The complete picture that formed in Raven's mind nauseated her. She stood like stone, trying to protect herself from the anguish of an inevitable reality. She wanted to bolt but knew Hazel would chase her, and she couldn't deal with that, not yet.

"Hazel?" Morgan asked.

Hazel finally released her eyes from Raven. "Hmm?"

"Are you okay?" Morgan's tone didn't hold real concern—contempt maybe, but not concern.

Hazel shook her head, a blank expression clouding her face. "I wanted to hurt him. I almost did. I've never felt like that before. It scared the hell out of me."

A wicked smile split Morgan's face. "The powers within you compelled you to hurt Lucien?"

Hazel nodded.

"It's the white magic in you. It inherently wants to destroy the dark, and vice versa. It's a dirty little trick the goddess dreamt up, her version of balance."

"What's our next move?" Hazel said. "We've convinced them we're going to foil their plans at every turn, so Blaise isn't going to be very happy with us."

"And that's exactly what we wanted," Morgan said. "Our plan to get them back to the portal in Salem has been set in motion." She clapped, and flutes bubbling with champagne appeared in all of their hands. "We leave for Salem tomorrow. We have a week until All Hallows' Eve, and we need to prepare. Blaise will need to gather some reinforcements before him and his cronies make the journey. We'll have to get there, gather supplies, and do a few run-throughs before the big night." She clapped. "One of the reasons I needed to see Blaise in person today was to see what his primary source of energy is. Now that I know, I can beat him once and for all." She sipped her champagne. "Lucien, Dirk, and Tammi—without them, he will fall. Their power is stronger because they're related. Once we are able to get rid of them, it won't matter how many others he's drawing from. I'll be able to terminate his life force once and for all."

Ayotunde looked concerned. "What effect will that have on the other realms?"

Morgan shrugged. "I honestly don't know, but I can't let him wander around snagging other dum-dums who are willing to do his bidding." She smiled and rocked back and forth in her seat.

Raven's ears were hot, partially from Hazel's eyes and partially because she couldn't believe what she was hearing. "You don't know what will happen to the realms if you kill him?"

Morgan shrugged. "Nope. That's why I didn't to it a few thousand years ago. Oh my God, you guys have no idea; he's always been a total buzzkill. Always with the *there can be only one* and *I'm the most powerful*. Seriously, terrible at parties."

Raven stood and walked out of the room, needing space and some quiet. *And to be away from Hazel.* She couldn't bear the way her eyes seemed to claim possession of Raven. It was too much, it was all too much.

❖

Hazel knocked on the door to Raven's room and waited. She could sense Raven's unease and wanted nothing more than to make it stop. She hadn't been able to tap into Raven earlier with Morgan in the hallway. Still learning how to control and manifest her powers was both exciting and frustrating. She wasn't sure when she'd have another opportunity to get Raven alone, and she wanted to discuss what she'd found back in New Orleans while perusing her family grimoire. Raven might not feel like company, but this was important. She pressed the electric lock and felt the buzzing in her fingers until it opened. Raven looked up when she entered, but there was no look of surprise.

"Don't," Raven said.

"Don't what?"

"I can feel you trying to ease my feelings. Don't."

"Okay." Hazel took a seat at the desk across from her. She sat quietly for a moment, trying to gather her thoughts and choose her words carefully. "You know, everything has been such a whirlwind lately: you discovering Blaise, almost dying, and us coming here. It's like…" She shook her head. "Then there was our brief *encounter* and then tonight. Through it all, I haven't had the chance to really talk to you."

Raven rubbed her hands over her face. "There's nothing for us to talk about, Hazel. Please, let's not complicate this mission even further with speculation about things that will never be."

"Raven, there's something you need to know. Something I found." She stood and walked over, sitting next to her on the bed. "There's something in the grimoire, something that can save you."

Raven turned and looked at her. "Save me from what?" She put her hands in front of her. "From Morgan, from this life, from you? What are you trying to save me from today?"

Hazel searched Raven's eyes. Their vibrancy was fueled by anger, mistrust, and the loss of control. "From whichever you choose. But it should be your choice, Raven. The rest…it just doesn't matter." She took her hands. "Morgan hasn't told you the whole truth about the curse. The curse is contained in something called the Dare Stone. It's what ties you to Morgan, to this life, and if it's destroyed, you can have your life back."

Raven regarded her with skepticism and walked to the other side of the room. "What about my uncle?" she said as she looked out the window.

Hazel stayed where she was, wanting to give Raven her space. "As far as I can tell, it's your whole family line. If we can get it and break it, you'll be free."

Hazel thought of tapping into Raven now. She wanted to know what she was thinking, but she didn't. Some considerations deserved privacy. Raven deserved to wade through this information without her intrusion.

Raven crossed her arms. "Morgan knows about the stone?"

Hazel swallowed her laugh. "Raven, Morgan created the stone. It contains the details of the fate of the original Roanoke colony. Your cursed lineage was forged in their blood."

Raven turned toward her now, and Hazel clenched her fists to keep herself from going to her and wiping the tears away. "Where is the stone?"

"Morgan wears a piece of it around her neck. From what I read, it acts like a homing device. If we can get it, we can locate the rest."

Raven leaned against the wall and slid to the ground. She looked utterly defeated. "You're saying there's a way out that doesn't include my death?"

Hazel sat next to her and took her hand. She intertwined their fingers and kissed Raven's knuckles. "If that's what you want. I'll help you find it and destroy it, but only if that's what you want. I wanted to tell you earlier. In fact, I've wanted to tell you ever since I discovered it. But I didn't want it to be a distraction for you, and I didn't want to cause any unease between you and Morgan before dealing with Blaise. But now I think it may act as an inspiration for you, like the proverbial light at the end of the tunnel."

Raven watched her. She seemed to be searching for the truth in her words, and Hazel hoped she could feel it.

Hazel put Raven's hand against her face. "Whatever is happening between us, or doesn't end up happening, I want your future to be yours. I want you to choose it. You deserve that."

As Raven bit her lower lip, Hazel wanted nothing more than to cover her mouth with hers, but she remained rooted in her spot. The energy between them was different this time. It was laced with possibility and the hints of a potential future. But if anything happened right now, it needed to be Raven's decision.

Raven gently brushed a hand against Hazel's cheek. Hazel felt it trembling against her face and wanted so badly to soothe all her trepidation, but she did nothing. Her heart starting pounding in her ears as Raven's mouth moved closer to hers. Raven's breath against her face accented with hints of champagne, scotch, and Raven's unique scent awakened her body from head to toe. Her breathing stopped in anticipation, and she only hoped she wouldn't pass out before Raven made up her mind.

The kiss came so softly, it was like a whisper between their mouths. Hazel knew this moment would change everything between them. This kiss had the potential to change Hazel to her very core, and she could feel it doing just that. Raven's soft, warm lips moved gently against hers. Hazel's entire body reacted to the tenderness. She wanted to drink Raven in as slowly and completely as possible.

Raven's hand cascaded from her face down to her neck and pulled her more tightly against her. She felt her tongue in her mouth as Raven deepened the kiss. Hazel felt the weight of a lifetime of self-deprecating doubt bubble up through her body and ease out. Kissing Raven in this moment was the closest she'd ever come to understanding what the poets meant when they threw around words like *fate* and *destiny*. A soft moan escaped Raven as their mouths continued to explore each other, and Hazel felt her ears warm when the wonderful sound entered her psyche.

Raven stood and brought Hazel up along with her. She walked her over in front of the bed and sat her down. Hazel watched in amazement as the colors on Raven's body changed. Her normally perfect tanned complexion flushed red at her cheeks and down her neck as she ripped her shirt from her torso. Hazel marveled at the lines that made up Raven's structure. If she wasn't here, sitting in front of her, able to touch her, she would swear they were painted by an artist. Her curves were so soft, so welcoming, they begged to be caressed and appreciated. Her muscles were lean and firm, a perfect contrast to the exquisite curvature. Hazel reached for Raven, not only because she needed to feel her skin but also to ground herself to this moment. She needed to know it was real, to feel her senses come alive with the contact of her skin.

Hazel put a hand on Raven's waist, running her thumb over the expanse of her stomach. Her throat caught when she saw the goose bumps that erupted in the wake of her touch, realizing the effect she had. Raven leaned down and stripped Hazel's shirt off. In the past, Hazel would have felt exposed, shy, even embarrassed. That wasn't what she felt under Raven's gaze. She felt truly beautiful for the first time in her life as Raven's eyes traced over her. Her gaze seemed to consume every inch of her exposed skin like small kisses, intimate in a way Hazel had never experienced.

Hazel waited as long as she could; her body hummed with need. It was almost primitive, the urgency of desire and fervor. She craved Raven, felt the deprivation in every part of her body. When Hazel pulled Raven on top of her, the sense of relief and passion that flooded her senses when their skin touched was all-consuming.

Raven nipped and kissed her neck as she let her fingers push into the fleshy hollow of Raven's spine. Raven stopped to look at her, and for a split second, Hazel thought words like *can't and shouldn't* were going to fall from her lips. But concern was quickly replaced with a feverish kiss that was filled with intentions of *want* and *need.*

Hazel traced Raven's side and slipped her fingers below her waistband. She was rewarded with a shudder that traveled through Raven's body. Hazel undid the button and zipper on Raven's pants and slid the garments down her body. Raven traced kisses down her neck, stopping at her chest to tease the sensitive area. Hazel could feel her need growing with each caress of Raven's lips against her skin. She shoved her hands into Raven's short dark hair as her head moved lower.

Raven undid Hazel's pants and yanked them off her body. Her mouth traced along the area her clothing had just occupied, and Hazel almost cried out at the wonderful contradiction of the cool air and Raven's warmth that was seemingly trying to memorize every inch of her.

Raven worked her way farther down to Hazel's center, and when her warm tongue finally found its place on Hazel's sex, the sensation was so overwhelming, Hazel groaned in the exquisite abandon of Raven's touch. The noise that escaped her wasn't one Hazel had ever heard before. It conveyed pure sensuality and craving, and Hazel wanted more. Her senses started to ignite with anticipation as Raven moved her mouth around her center. She wanted this sensation to last forever, this closeness and sense of belonging she felt with Raven to go on for all of her days, but her ability to hang on was waning with each expert maneuver of Raven's tongue. Her rhythmic movements were becoming more focused, more intense. She was pushing Hazel closer to climax. Hazel felt as if she was swimming in a sea of euphoria when the first edge of the orgasm exploded through her body. Raven wrapped her hands around her legs and pushed deeper inside her. Hazel's body reacted in kind to Raven's attention, dispatching waves of bliss to every nerve ending in her body as she cried out her name.

She lay there for several seconds, allowing the tremors to subside. The experience hadn't been hurried, but it hadn't taken nearly as long as she wanted. Her body had betrayed her guttural desire for Raven. She needed more of her, all of her.

Hazel pulled Raven up alongside her and buried her face her in her neck. "You're amazing."

Raven kissed the top of her head and wrapped her arms around her. "I've never experienced anything like that."

Hazel climbed on top, straddling her waist. "We're just getting started. I have much more planned for you."

Raven grabbed the back of Hazel's head, pulling her down to her for another kiss. "What about tomorrow?"

Hazel slid her hand between Raven's legs and almost lost control of herself when Raven pushed back, accepting Hazel into her. "Tomorrow is whatever we decide it is."

Raven bit her lip and nodded as labored breathing started to shake her body. "I want this."

Hazel kissed her again as she pushed deeper. "Then it's yours."

CHAPTER TWENTY

The early morning sun spilled through the curtains and onto the bed where Raven and Hazel lay, still wrapped up in each other. They'd finally fallen asleep out of pure exhaustion a few hours before, and Raven couldn't remember a time when all-consuming fatigue felt so wonderful. Hazel had been everything she'd ever dreamed a sexual partner could be. She was passionate, sensual, attentive, and insatiable. Raven's muscles ached in the most incredible way possible, and all she wanted was to make this feeling, what they'd shared, last a lifetime.

A lifetime. Raven had never thought in those terms before, but now, lying here watching Hazel sleep, she didn't think she'd have the capacity to understand what that meant before last night. There was still so much to figure out...like the Dare Stone.

Part of her was angry at Morgan for having kept it a secret, but she wasn't surprised. For all Morgan's talk and attention, Raven was nothing more than a servant, a means to an end. Raven and her family had done Morgan's bidding for generations. Was Raven strong enough to finally break free? To halt the eternal cycle? She would've said no before last night. She would have said a lot of things before last night, but now she wasn't sure of anything she'd thought she knew.

A knock at the door jarred her back into her reality. "We need to go," Morgan said. Raven bristled at the void of any type of emotion in her voice.

Hazel reached for her hand and kissed the tops of her fingers. "It will be okay. We'll figure it out."

For the first time in her entire life, Raven believed that it just might be. She leaned over and kissed the side of Hazel's face, letting her lips linger of her soft cheek until her skin stretched in a smile.

"I'm going to get in the shower. I'll meet you in Morgan's room in thirty minutes." Raven pushed herself out of bed and headed to the bathroom.

Hazel collected her clothes from the floor. "You're buying me breakfast."

"Absolutely," Raven said as she turned on the water.

Twenty-five minutes later, Raven knocked on Morgan's door, which opened before she had the chance for her hand to stop moving. Ayotunde and Sarah were already there, sitting next to each other on the small couch in the large room.

"Morning," Raven said as she moved past. She tried not to look at Morgan, still unsure how she felt about the information she'd found out.

"Did you have a good night?" Morgan's tone was accusatory.

"I did." Raven didn't want to play these games with her, not today.

Hazel was next to her a moment later, a hand on her back. "Morning, everyone."

Morgan rolled her eyes as she stood. "Nice of you two to finally join us. We need to get going." Morgan motioned for the four of them to come closer.

"What's going on?" Hazel asked.

Morgan grabbed Raven's and Sarah's hands and motioned for the others to do the same. "I don't have the patience to drive, and I don't want to deal with the airport, so I'm going to send us to Salem."

"If you can do this, why do we ever bother with any other transportation?" Hazel asked, sounding annoyed.

Morgan opened one of her eyes. "Because it expends an extraordinary amount of energy, but I have no patience to be with you people any longer than necessary. Now be quiet and focus on your ugly little apartment."

The look on Hazel's face indicated that she was going to bite back, but Raven squeezed her hand, and instead, she closed her eyes as she was told. The air around them shook; Raven heard the lamp on the nightstand fall over, and the walls seemed to swim. There were bright lights, cold air, then hot air, more bright lights, then darkness.

Finally, the room seemed like it collapsed into itself only to open again in Hazel's living room.

Raven thought she might fall over. Her chest felt as if someone was stepping on it, her vision was blurry, and her ears were ringing. The other women were staring at her, trying to touch her; they were asking her questions, but the ringing was so loud she couldn't hear anything. Hazel stood over her, worried lines etched under eyes. Hazel put both hands on her shoulders and soothed. It took a few seconds, but the fuzz started to clear from Raven's mind. She blinked back tears and started coughing. The cough was so consuming, it shook her whole body with the ferocity of a heavy punch to the chest.

"Oh yes, the trip would be much harder on Raven; she isn't one of us," Morgan said.

Hazel turned on her. "What the fuck, Morgan?"

Morgan walked around the small space, seeming to inspect her new surroundings. "Oh, relax. She's fine."

Raven grasped Hazel's arm and nodded. "I'm okay."

Hazel moved her over to the couch and sat her down. "I'll get you some water."

Morgan sat next to Raven and patted her leg. "Don't cross me, Dare." She smiled, but it didn't reach her eyes.

Raven accepted the glass from Hazel, knowing it was already too late for that, and there was no turning back.

After hours of tossing and turning, Sarah got out of bed, threw on a pair of sweats, and headed toward the door of Hazel's apartment. With so much weighing so heavily on her mind, she knew further effort toward sleep would be in vain. She threw on a jacket from an antique coatrack, and as she was turning the doorknob, she felt a hand on her shoulder.

"What troubles you, Sarah?" Ayotunde whispered behind her.

"Sleep be not my luxury this night," Sarah replied. "I mean to explore the village to ease my beleaguered mind."

"'Tis too late to explore alone," Ayotunde said, wrapping herself in a sweater and following her out the door.

They walked together, holding hands in silence, Sarah inhaling the crisp night air, recalling when it was pure and untainted by any of the fabrications of the modern age. Although the village appeared nothing like the way she'd left it, an unmistakable vibration of familiarity pulsed through her with alarming intensity the more ground they covered. At times, she and Ayotunde needed to remind each other that otherwise ordinary farmers armed with muskets and makeshift badges weren't poised to leap at them from the shadows and whisk them back to the custody of the court.

"Sarah, we walk for miles. Will you tell me the nature of what troubles you?"

Sarah didn't answer her as she noticed a sign indicating they'd arrived at a place called Proctor's Ledge. She moved closer to Ayotunde as a chill engulfed her that had naught to do with weather. She rubbed the back of her arms as her body began to tremble. "This place…the stench of wickedness doth linger."

Ayotunde looked up at her. "Pray, Sarah. Speak plain."

"'Tis where the hangings commenced."

"You sense it?"

"Aye. This be where my friend, Bridget Bishop, drew her last breath on earth. I like not what it portend here."

"This be the hallowed ground Morgan speak of," Ayotunde said, pointing into the darkness. "The portal back be yonder."

Dread smacked Sarah's heart. She took both of Ayotunde's hands in hers. "I want not to go back. I fear for us, Ayotunde. A prodigious danger awaits us upon our return."

"The choice be not ours, Sarah. If we disobey Morgan, she be knowing it."

Sarah sighed and stepped away from her, knowing she was right. Even if they fled Salem and traveled far away, Morgan was the witch queen. She'd find them wherever they sought refuge. But she also knew what it would mean for her and Ayotunde when they returned. Even if they weren't hanged, they'd have to part, and Sarah would have to resume her life with Thomas. The thought of losing Ayotunde again was too much to bear.

"Sarah?" Ayotunde stretched her arms around Sarah's torso in the dark.

She draped her arms over Ayotunde's, and when Ayotunde rested her head against Sarah's back, she could no longer suppress her tears. She turned around, enveloped Ayotunde in her arms, and bawled into the unforgiving night.

After a moment, Ayotunde took Sarah's face in her hands. "Oh, my Sarah," she said, her own cheeks streaked with tears. "Don't you know nothing can break the spell of love between us? When we return, we pray, and we find a way back to each other."

"No!" Sarah broke free of Ayotunde's embrace and wiped her tears away in protest. "Prayer hath done nothing for us. I love you, Ayotunde, to the depths of my soul. Now that my heart hath felt the sweet burn of your love and my body, your heavenly touch, I'll not let you go, not so for the world and its cruelty to keep us apart."

"If we refuse, Blaise will grow strong and victorious and evil reign for all time. The fall of good in the world be upon us."

"Good hath no meaning to me if I must lose you for it."

"Sarah, that be not true. You be the most pious of women. Your heart be full of only good."

"Ayotunde, my love for you hath awakened a new woman. If I be forced to choose between piety and you, piety stands not a chance."

"Pray, speak such blasphemy no more, Sarah. We go to Miss Hazel."

"Aye," Sarah said, resigned to the fact that despite the depth of her passion for Ayotunde, the matter was indeed out of her hands. As the moon peeked out from behind the clouds, she embraced Ayotunde against her bosom and squeezed her tightly, searching the stars for some shred of hope.

As they walked back to Hazel's apartment, Sarah sensed a whirl of negative energy behind them. She glanced over her shoulder, but nothing trailed them, at least nothing her eyes could discern in the pre-dawn twilight. Without a word, she gripped Ayotunde's hand tighter and picked up their pace.

Ayotunde also looked back. "I feel it, too."

"We are yet a distance from Hazel's dwelling," Sarah said. "Let us keep onward. Perhaps whatever it be will not follow."

"I think whatever be pursuing us mean to accomplish what it set out to."

"Aye." Sarah looked over her shoulder but saw nothing taking form behind them.

As they broke into a jog, she pushed Ayotunde ahead of her to shield her from whatever danger was looming. As their pace progressed into a full sprint, so did the sound of extra footsteps on pavement behind them.

"Run, Sarah," Ayotunde shouted over her shoulder as she pulled farther ahead.

Although Sarah was trying harder to run, she was slowing. Something was drawing her back as though she were yoked to a bridle. "Keep going, Ayotunde," she shouted. "Don't stop."

She surrendered to the force and swung around to face her pursuers. Lucien McCoulter and Tammi Lee Sanderson stood before her, their legs planted apart and fists poised before their faces.

"Not such a badass without your witch queen protector, are you?" Lucien smirked and spat on the ground.

Tammi stepped forward. "Looks like you can't even count on your little house servant when shit gets real."

"Sarah?" Ayotunde called out from down the street.

"She's over here," Tammi replied. "About to meet her maker. Care to join her?"

"No, Ayotunde," Sarah shouted. "Turn away. Go back to Hazel's."

"Ooj. Brave Puritan woman," Lucien said as he moved closer. "You and your coven of amateurs are no match for Blaise. Any resistance you put up will only be in vain."

"You'll never succeed in defeating Blaise or us," Tammi said. "Blaise has empowered us to create an empire here, and that's exactly what we've done, and in a surprisingly short time. This pathetically weak country was ripe for it, and Blaise had the foresight to strike at precisely the right time."

Sarah stared at their menacing faces, unwavering in her defiance. "Many time in history society hath been ripe for evil, and many time evil hath been struck down. What prompt you to think it be different now?"

Lucien snorted. "A brave *and* educated Puritan woman. You certainly are ahead of your time."

"My father was a proper teacher. He hath raised no fool."

Tammi mimed sticking her finger down her throat. "What could be more nauseating than precolonial feminism?" She looked at Lucien. "Can we get this over with now?"

"Patience, my lovely daughter," he said as he circled Sarah. "Killing Sarah Hutchinson Cooper has been number one on my bucket list since 1690. I'd like to savor the exquisite flavor a little longer, if you don't mind."

Sarah swallowed her fear, praying Ayotunde had reached Hazel's apartment and was coming back with the lot of them. Although she'd been growing confident in her powers, the ominous vibes emanating from Lucien and Tammi seemed to be overpowering whatever strength and skill she'd been able to cultivate.

"Don't savor it too long, Father. That other one could be summoning Morgan le Fay right now."

A low grumble of laughter rolled up his throat. "Soon she'll be irrelevant, too. Blaise has almost reached his full potency, and our positions within his regime are all but secured." He paused to inhale the crisp early morning air and then walked up to Sarah's face. "Ah. I can almost smell the burnt embers of Morgan's realm as it smolders into oblivion."

Sarah's eyes remained fixed on Lucien's as her nose involuntarily crinkled at his acrid breath. "And if Blaise's realm were to triumph over Morgan's as you say, how is it you be so certain that you, too, shall profit?"

"Blaise's word, that's how." For a second, Lucien seemed somewhat less than convinced…but only for a second. "He's hand-selected me to orchestrate the plan that will topple Morgan le Fay and her white realm for once and all time. And I will not let him down. We're as close to victory as I am to your luscious mouth, Sarah Hutchinson." He licked his lips as he leered and moved to kiss her.

Sarah raised her hands, and Lucien lurched back with such force that he landed on his backside in the middle of the road several feet away.

"Enough of this foreplay, Father," Tammi shouted. "If you don't kill her, I will."

Lucien climbed to his feet and held up his hand to Tammi. "Silence, child. She is mine to destroy." He walked toward Sarah, holding out his arm, his hand upturned and fingers pointing at her. "You still haven't learned your lesson, have you?"

Sarah felt her throat constricting as Lucien's hand slowly closed in sync with his approach. She tried to impel him back, but her powers waned as he held her in his spell. She focused on a garbage can on the street corner, trying to hoist it and assail him with it, but she only managed to knock it over on its side.

"Harder, Daddy, harder," Tammi yelled. "She still has power. Choke her! Kill her!"

Sarah gurgled as she struggled to breathe, dropping to her knees in the middle of the street. She chopped at his arm with her fist as it hurtled toward her, but the energy behind it was unrelenting. His eyes seemed to flame when his hand clamped on her neck. Gritting his teeth, he squeezed even harder. "You will never defeat Blaise." He breathed heavily through clenched teeth as he worked at snuffing her out.

Sara's vision blurred as she fought to remain conscious, but his choke hold left her unable to imbibe enough air. After fading for what could've been a minute or a year, she awakened on the sidewalk to the contentious shouts of both Lucien and Tammi.

"Tammi, let go of me," he shouted as she held him in a headlock.

"I'm trying," she shouted as she and Lucien wrestled in the street. "She's making me restrain you, and I can't loosen my grip."

"Try harder," he growled, "or I'll…"

"Are you waking, my love?" Ayotunde asked Sarah as she maintained her sight and outstretched arm on the writhing mass that was Lucien and Tammi.

Sarah stood and rubbed her sore throat. "You did not do as I instructed you." She smiled at Ayotunde, her heart pounding as she watched that thrilling woman exercise complete control over their foes.

"Aye. And it be a good thing I didn't," she replied with a playful grin. "He be wringing your neck like a chicken's if I had."

Sarah looked down and couldn't help letting out a soft chuckle. "Now, what are we to do with this?" She pointed at Lucien and Tammi still tussling like rival siblings over a favored toy. "Daylight soon be upon us."

Ayotunde shrugged. "I could let them kill each other."

"Mmm," Sarah uttered as she pondered the option. "Methinks

Morgan may not approve. They must be in fit condition to return to sixteen and ninety-two."

"Aye. But I be sure to love watching that man draw his last breath. He do remind me of the slave trader what took me from my mother."

Sarah glanced in their direction with disdain, imagining the pleasure in smiting them both and leaving them there in the road for a vulture's morning feast. "Were he not a feckless drunkard when he was Samuel Cranwell, I might think it indeed possible it were him." She looked around the neighborhood, seeing buildings and trees more clearly in the orange sunrise. "Dawn be upon us, Ayotunde. Think on what to do with them."

Ayotunde stared at them and giggled as they continued wrestling. "They be lookin' weary from the struggle. I think they had enough." She whipped her arm back, and they parted, stumbling away from each other. Shaking their heads, they seemed dazed as they gathered themselves. Ayotunde wound up her right arm several times, then the left, and Lucien and Tammi punched each other in the face so hard, they fell to the curb, unconscious. She turned to Sarah with a tentative grin, then they linked hands and hopped up and down in their victory.

"Let us return before they wake." Sarah clutched Ayotunde by the hand, and they sprinted back to Hazel's apartment.

❖

Hazel stood at the window in her living room and glanced at the rising sun illuminating her neighborhood, hoping it would bring Sarah and Ayotunde home. What would've possessed them to go off by themselves in the middle of the night, knowing the dangers that lurked now that Lucien was aware of their presence and their plan? She stopped cold when something else occurred to her: What if Lucien and his two bad seeds were what had enticed them away in the first place? Just as she was about to wake Raven and Morgan in a panic, Sarah and Ayotunde walked in, their faces as effervescent as tourists back from a sightseeing adventure.

"Where the hell have you two been?" Hazel ran a hand through her messy hair as her heart thrummed against her chest. "Do you know how worried I was? And how hard it is to lie to a witch queen?"

"You lied for us?" Sarah said.

"Uh, yeah," Hazel said. "At which point, Morgan strung me up on my own coatrack until I told her the truth. Not that she needed me to. She knew exactly where you guys were with her innate witch GPS, but apparently, watching me make a fool of myself was her idea of entertainment."

"We spent time walking to clear our minds," Sarah said as she poured herself a cup of coffee. "Until the portal drew us thither."

"You went to the portal?" Hazel asked. "Sarah, what's going on?"

Sarah stared absently at her as she sipped her coffee. "What becomes of Ayotunde and me after we've lured Samuel and the others back through the portal?"

Hazel opened her mouth to speak, but she could think of nothing that would remotely pass for a satisfactory answer. She'd never even considered what it would mean for them, only the critical need to send the demons back to 1692 and the catastrophic consequences if they'd failed. She glanced back and forth between them, her heart sinking at the expressions of despair on their faces and her inability to reassure them.

"Then it is as I feared." Sarah walked to the couch and sat. Ayotunde followed and slipped her hand under Sarah's.

"No, no," Hazel said. "There has to be a way of making sure nothing bad happens to you afterward. Let me go talk to Morgan right now."

She trudged down the hall and after a light knock, walked into her own bedroom. Morgan was sitting up in bed against a pile of pillows with her arms folded across her chest, almost as if she'd been expecting her, her resting bitch face reaching new heights. "Good morning," Hazel sang in a sweet voice. "How did you sleep?"

"The best night's sleep in a thousand years," Morgan said as she stretched her arms in front of her. "You must tell me where you bought your mattress."

"Really?" Hazel said, pleased.

Morgan rolled her eyes in practically a complete revolution. "What's up with the Puritans?"

Hazel took the question as an invitation and rushed to sit on the foot of the bed. "Morgan, something terrible has come to my attention."

Morgan raised her arm and levitated Hazel off the bed and over to the accent chair next to it.

"Oh. Sorry," Hazel said.

"The problem, *s'il vous plait*, while I'm still interested."

"Do Sarah and Ayotunde actually have to go back to 1692 to send the demons back?"

"Naturally. They have to open the portal and then get Lucien and company to pass through it."

"Isn't there another way to achieve that?"

Morgan cocked an eyebrow. "What do you propose, opening the portal and dropping a banana peel on the ground in front it?"

Hazel chewed the inside of her lip in frustration. She couldn't decide what was more infuriating about Morgan, her condescension or her apathy toward Sarah and Ayotunde. "Well, do they have to stay there once they've lured them through?"

"Yes, they have to stay there." Morgan flung the covers off and rose from the bed, seeming as annoyed with Hazel as she was with her. "They don't belong here, Hazel. Need I remind you that it was their act of sheer recklessness that brought about this whole shit storm with Blaise in the first place?"

"No. You've already made that point abundantly clear. But you can't really blame them for doing whatever was within their power to save their own lives. I would've done the same thing if I was in their shoes."

Morgan looked pensive for a moment. "I suppose it is somewhat impressive of you mortals…this unrepentant drive *not* to die. That said, one simply does not leap across the time continuum willy-nilly and expect to be exempt from all repercussions." She raised her arms in a flourish and changed into her day clothing.

Hazel put her hands on the back of her head and released a gust of breath in an effort to calm down and present her case more effectively. "Morgan, when they go back, Sarah will be trapped in a loveless marriage, and poor Ayotunde…for God's sake, she's gotta return to a life of enslavement. How can you be okay with that?"

"Not okay, more like desensitized." Morgan examined her face in the mirror as she spoke. "I've witnessed you mortals do that and sometimes far worse to each other throughout the centuries, and you never learn from it. No matter what progress is made, there's always another crop of you eager to oppress and subjugate." She whirled around and offered an uncharacteristic stroke of comfort across Hazel's cheek. "However, I've also observed true revolutionaries. Remember, your aunt and Ayotunde are not returning the same women they were before they left. Who's to say they'll have to face the same ultimate fates? At any rate, they have to go back and fulfill their assigned destinies."

"But you're shipping them back to a time when women had zero rights, when people's fanatical devotion to religion and irrational fears made daily life a living hell for people like us. They should be allowed to stay here, especially in light of the chances they're willing to take to help us."

And as quickly as Morgan's soft side had surfaced, it plummeted to back to its cavernous recesses. "Oh, Raven," she called out without breaking her stare on Hazel. "Come get your girlfriend before she lives to regret working my last nerve before my first cup of nectar."

Hazel maintained her gaze, too. "I don't need a hero to rescue me. And neither does my aunt." She stormed out of her bedroom and met Raven in the hall.

"You're not doing anyone any favors pissing off Morgan." Raven smiled and kissed Hazel on the nose. "I admire your gumption, but you need to understand that any deviation from Morgan's plan will probably wreak even more havoc than Sarah and Ayotunde's original blunder. I know it goes against every fiber of your being, but can you just relax and go with the flow?"

Hazel followed closely as Raven headed into the kitchen. "Raven, do you know that Sarah and Ayotunde have to stay in 1692 after they lure Blaise's lackeys back?"

Raven poured a cup of coffee and sipped it black. "That's how it usually works."

Hazel leaned against the counter and sighed, slouching in defeat. "Hazel, they can't stay here. You know that."

She nodded. "I've also known a lot of other things that I thought to be true only a month ago that I now realize were just illusions."

"Look. I know it sucks that they have to finish out their predestined lives as Puritans, but that's the way it is."

"Raven? Hazel? Please join us in the parlor," Morgan said.

Hazel followed Raven into the living room, still stewing over the futility of her aunt's situation. What was the sense of having the power of enchantment if she couldn't even use it when she needed it most?

Morgan was perched on a throw pillow on the couch between Sarah and Ayotunde. "So, it appears our favorite rogue Puritans had an encounter with Lucien and Tammi on their early morning stroll."

Raven's head whipped toward them. "You guys went out on your own?"

"I already tore them new ones," Hazel said. "They won't be doing that again."

"Aye. Indeed not," Sarah said. "'Twas nearly my undoing."

Ayotunde touched her forearm. "But my Sarah fight like the bravest of warriors."

Sarah's face blossomed in a smile. "No, Ayotunde. Your actions be that of a great hero." She turned to Morgan, Hazel, and Raven. "It were she who be the bravest and saved my life when Lucien's hand was but moments from ripping me from this world."

"That's terrific," Morgan said, pursing her lips. She turned to Raven. "We know at least two of the stooges have arrived here in Salem, which I find rather unusual since Blaise usually opts for a full-on seek and destroy strategy."

Raven began to pace as she contemplated the latest development. "Either there's a calculated reason why only two of them accosted Sarah and Ayotunde, or Lucien had just foolishly underestimated their ability to defend themselves on their own."

"Blaise makes no miscalculations," Morgan said. "My guess is that it was an ill-conceived bid by Lucien to take initiative and prove himself indispensable to Blaise."

"We need to figure out where Dirk is hiding," Raven said.

"He can't be far off," Morgan said. "After Ayotunde cleaned the streets with them, they have to know that if they have any chance of taking out Sarah and Ayotunde, it'll require the three of them joining forces."

"Hey," Hazel said, clutching her phone. "I think I have an idea where Dirk will be later this afternoon. There's a big 'resistance' rally happening in Boston today." She showed Raven her phone. "One of Dirk's hate groups is undoubtedly going to be leading the counterprotest."

Raven scanned the phone and then looked up with a grave

expression. "We have to get there. Senator Harren is scheduled to attend, and I'm sure her people have no idea how much danger that puts her in."

Hazel's stomach tumbled into her slippers.

"Pray, what be the significance?" Sarah asked.

"She's the front-runner," Hazel said, "the only candidate who's polling even remotely close to being able to defeat the president next November."

Morgan stood and approached them. "Speaking of Blaise's lackeys, the president is Blaise's favorite one of all, his little golden boy, clueless, heartless, and more impressionable than overcooked jambalaya."

Hazel glanced anxiously between Morgan and Raven. "Are you seriously suggesting the master of evil installed the President of the United States and is currently in control of our country?"

Morgan shrugged. "It's not like this is the first time it's happened."

"I can't believe this," Hazel said, running a hand through her hair. "I mean how much more insane can things possibly get?"

"They're going to attempt an assassination, aren't they?" Raven said to Morgan.

"It's going to be more than attempt if Lucien and company aren't stopped."

"Ugh. I think I'm gonna puke," Hazel said and plopped down on the couch between Sarah and Ayotunde. "Be happy you have no concept of the implications of what they're saying."

"We sense the evil be upon us, Miss Hazel," Ayotunde said. "Yet we fear not to fight him by your side."

"It starts at one o'clock," Raven said. "We better make a plan and get ready to head out, stat."

"Shouldn't you be calling Senator Harren's office to warn her of the threat?" Hazel said.

"Why?" Morgan said. "So they can cancel her appearance at the rally and force Lucien, Tammi Lee, and Dirk back into hiding?"

Hazel sprang from the couch and approached them. "What if they succeed in assassinating her?"

"They're not going to," Morgan said. "That's the whole reason you're all here."

"How did we suddenly go from stuffing three goons back through a portal to foiling a murder plot?" Hazel said.

"Hazel, today's event is the culmination of everything Lucien, or Samwell Cranwell, has worked for since following Sarah through the portal and landing in 2008. If we fail to stop this assassination and this president wins a second term, our fate is sealed. Blaise will have attained full potency and be powerful enough to extinguish the white realm in its entirety. As for the fate of the mortals, evil will come full circle in its domination of the world. The whole of humanity will suffer the consequences until their species becomes so paralyzed by disease, violence, and despair, they'll eventually cease to exist."

"So, you're saying this mission's important," Hazel said in a deadpan. She started to giggle a little maniacally at the sheer terror of what they were about to face that afternoon.

"Hazel, are you okay?" Raven's forehead wrinkled with concern.

Morgan stepped between her and Raven, her face so close, Hazel felt the tingle of the ethereal vibrations of Morgan's essence. "She better be. Every single person is an integral part of this mission. Nobody is ancillary. Whatever you need to do to pull your hypersensitive self together, do it now because we're leaving in an hour and putting a stop to this madness once and for all." She brushed past them both, leaving them in awe as she disappeared into Hazel's bedroom.

Raven turned to Hazel. "She's quite a motivator, isn't she?"

Hazel wagged her hand in front of her own face, fearing she was about to hyperventilate. "Okay, okay," she mumbled. Then after a deep breath, she glanced at Raven, Sarah, and Ayotunde. "Well, if today's the day I meet my demise, I can't imagine any other group of women I'd rather be annihilated with." She raised the empowerment fist and walked toward the bathroom to perform the pregame ritual of retching her guts up she'd experienced during the state softball championship title series in high school.

After brushing her teeth, Hazel analyzed her reflection as she wiped her mouth with the hand towel. She suddenly felt ready for the fight...she had to be. Generations of Hutchinson women were depending on her.

She started at the light tap on the door. When she opened it, Raven was resting her head against the door frame, smiling.

"For what it's worth, there's nobody I'd rather be annihilated with either." She kissed Hazel's lips tenderly, slowly, and tantalizingly before walking toward the spare bedroom.

Hazel watched Raven saunter away until she reached the room, turned with another smile, and closed the door. She sighed and leaned her forehead against the door frame. Ironic that she'd never felt more invigorated with life than on the day on which her life was probably going to end.

CHAPTER TWENTY-ONE

Lucien tapped the cell phone against the car window and looked over at Tammi Lee. "I don't know why you look so worried. This will work."

Tammi stared out the window and shook her head. "I don't know. It feels like we just threw this together at the last minute. We didn't give ourselves long enough to prepare. If all of them are together, how are we supposed to beat them?"

"They won't all be together. That's why we've set up two different snipers. They'll have to split up. If we can even take out one of them, their coven will be broken, and they won't be able to access the portal."

Tammi turned and looked at him. "Sarah accessed it all by herself; what makes you think she can't do it again? Plus, we don't even know if they'll show up at this rally. This whole plan is a long shot."

Lucien patted her leg. "It's a good thing you're pretty because you aren't very bright." He smiled at her. "They know Dirk will be here, and they know what this blasted woman running for office means. They'll want to protect her. As far as Sarah opening the portal by herself, she didn't. We had a dozen women locked up, all praying for escape. They acted as a coven; they just didn't know it."

Tammi squinted at him, looking as if she was about to argue but changed her mind. "We should've sent demons; this could end badly for us, too."

Lucien shook his head. "Blaise has ordered us to handle it, so we will. Besides, demons are sloppy, and they draw too much attention."

Tammi choked on her laugh. "Sure, and seven witches battling in the streets will go unnoticed."

Lucien wrapped his hand around her neck and pulled her closer. "There will be no battle in the streets. If you have a problem with the way I do things, I suggest that you get out of the car, start walking, and don't ever look for me again."

She pushed him away. "When this fails, I hope for your sake neither Dirk nor I end up dead. Imagine how angry Blaise would be with you. You will have failed him."

"If you keep talking, I may just kill you myself." He glared at her. "Now get to your post and don't fuck this up."

She pushed open the door and disappeared into the building. Lucien cracked his knuckles and his neck, trying to relieve some of the building tension. He was feeling more unsettled than ever before. It was as if his nerve endings were on fire, and his anxiety was gnawing at his insides. He needed to end these witches and the white realm. It was more than a necessity at this point. It was an obsession.

He got out of the car and made his way down the street to a different building. *All we need is one.*

Raven rolled up to the curb on one of the side streets half a mile from the rally. She leaned her forearms against the steering wheel and stared at the tops of the buildings.

"Is there a problem?" Morgan asked from beside her.

"We can't cover the whole area. Do you have any witchy tricks up your sleeve to help us narrow down our perimeter?"

Morgan closed her eyes and turned her head in the direction the crowd was headed. "Too many voices mixed together, which I'm sure was by design. I can't distinguish specific ones from the crowd at this distance."

Hazel leaned forward between the two seats. "Let's be pragmatic. There will be security at this event, especially with the counterprotests. Only authorized people will be allowed in the buildings close to the park. We need to find the security guards who've been recently bewitched. Then we'll know where any snipers are. They wouldn't have bothered with fake identification to get a sniper inside when magic is much simpler."

Morgan stared down at Hazel with a questioning look. "How do we know for sure they'll use a sniper?"

Hazel shrugged. "It will cause the most chaos. Shots fired from somewhere overhead is the fastest and most efficient was to sow discourse. The authorities will scour the city looking for the shooter. It's much easier to create fear and confusion with that scenario than an up close and personal attack."

Raven nodded. "Fear is their most effective motivator. Some of us should get inside the crowd, just as a precaution."

"I wouldn't advise splitting up this time," Morgan said. "There are too many unknowns, which I'm afraid has also been by design."

"I worry not over a nincompoop like Dirk," Sarah said from her seat next to Ayotunde.

Ayotunde nodded. "Aye. We know what he be about now."

Morgan rolled her eyes. "Perfect. The fate of white magic could be in the hands of two Puritan women who don't even know how to properly anticipate an escalator. What could possibly go wrong?"

Raven moved her hand in a small circle around her face. "Do the thing where you change how we all look."

Morgan crossed her arms. "They'll be able to see your true self; they're witches."

"But we won't be caught on security cameras, and no one will be able to identify us outside the realm of magic. If things go sideways, we don't need the police looking for us, too. We have enough to deal with," Raven said.

Morgan sighed. "Fine. I see your point." She snapped her fingers.

Raven's body tingled, and a shiver ran up her spine. She looked in the mirror and saw a different face looking back, a very different face.

"Jesus, Morgan. I look just like Ruby Rose." Raven touched her chin and turned her face back and forth.

"That was definitely by design." Morgan wiggled her eyebrows lasciviously.

"How about something a little less conspicuous?" Hazel said. "If there are any lesbian protests groups in attendance, we'll have a riot of a different kind on our hands."

"She's right, Morgan," Raven said, sorry to see the look go.

"When did you become so boring?" Morgan snapped her fingers again.

Raven checked herself in the mirror. "Perfect." Her features were plain, simple, and normal, just what she needed.

Morgan turned, looked at the other three women, and snapped her fingers once more. Sarah and Ayotunde smiled at each other and giggled in the back seat. Raven let her eyes settle on Hazel, who now had a different face, but her eyes reflected the same enticing essence. The blue shimmered in the midafternoon sun, and Raven had to force herself to look away.

Morgan changed herself into a teenage girl. She popped the bubble gum now in her mouth and twirled her hair. "Raven and Hazel, check the buildings. I'm going to go with Ayotunde and Sarah, make sure they stay out of trouble." She popped her gum loudly and got out of the car.

Raven took Hazel's hand and led her down a side street. "I need you to close your eyes and concentrate. Tell me where we should head first."

Hazel looked up at the buildings surrounding them and shook out her shoulders. She stared directly in to Raven's eyes before closing hers. She tilted her head from side to side for several moments. When she opened her eyes, she pointed down the street. "I can't be sure, but I think we should head in that direction."

Raven nodded and entwined her fingers in Hazel's. "It's as good a place to start as any."

The chants grew louder from the counterprotestors starting to form a line around the staging area where Senator Harren would soon be speaking. Through the mind-numbing buzzing of voices, shouts of "white lives matter" drowned out the people proclaiming "love trumps hate."

Hazel gripped her hand tighter. "This is disturbing."

Raven led her up the steps of a building. "It's only going to get worse as Blaise grows more powerful. If what Morgan says is true and the president truly is a Blaise plant, we're all doomed."

Hazel looked at the guard standing outside the building and shook her head. "Not this one."

As they made their way to the next building, they could hear Dirk on a megaphone a few hundred feet away. "We need to start thinking about what comes after America. We need a period of ethnic cleansing to raise the white racial empire. The elites who've ignored you for so long know a tidal wave of white identity is coming. They know that once our words get out and our beliefs take hold, they won't be able to stop us. They've declared war on our race, our religion, and our way of life, and we're here to stand up and take our country back by any means necessary."

Raven's head throbbed with anger. "He's a vile human being."

"And look at how many people agree with him," Hazel said. The look of despair in her eyes morphed into anger. "We have to stop them."

Raven nodded. "We will."

Hazel looked up at the building and tilted her head to the side. "This is it."

Raven didn't turn to look, not wanting to draw attention. "We need to get past the guard."

With a quick swipe of Hazel's hand, a gust of wind blew the guard's hat off. When he turned to go after it, they hurried up the stairs behind him and made it into the building before he returned to his post.

They climbed the stairs carefully, pausing at each level to listen for any disturbances. Hazel tugged at Raven's shirt, stalling her progress. "One of them is here. I can feel it," she whispered.

Raven nodded and reached for her two blades before she put her hand on the door. "We have to be ready for anything." She laid her lips against Hazel's ear. "If you can feel them, they can feel you."

Raven pushed the door open with trepidation. She wasn't sure what she'd find on the other side, and not knowing was burning through her veins in the form of adrenaline. She looked on either side of the door before opening it fully. When she saw nothing, she pushed it all the way open and walked through.

The flash exploded in front of her eyes, throwing her backward into the wall. The force knocked one of the blades from her hand. She felt around the floor, trying to find it, still blinded from the painful light.

Raven heard Hazel step in front of her. "I wouldn't do that if I were you."

CHAPTER TWENTY-TWO

Tammi Lee's laugh erupted with fear and unease. "You may be able to stop me, but you'll never stop Blaise. He's more powerful than you could ever imagine."

Hazel noticed the man on the corner of the roof. He had his back to them and a gun perched in front of him, aiming down at the street. Tammi must have bewitched him because he didn't make any movement to see who'd just entered or who was behind him. His attention was fixated on the task in front of him.

Hazel tried to focus her energy. Her fingers crackled with anticipation, and her mind was racing with the different ways this could play out. "It's not too late, you know. You could leave all of this right now, come with us, and be safe."

Tammi looked confused for an instant and then smiled. "You want me to willingly go with the people who want to do me and my family harm? How stupid do you think I am?"

Hazel took a step closer and allowed the power to flow through her fingers. Stings of energy like mini lightning bolts launched from her fingertips and forced Tammi to her knees. "I want you to remember this moment. I want you to remember that I offered you a chance, a way out, and you decided not to take it."

Raven hurried to the man perched on the corner and made quick work of knocking him out and taking his weapon. Hazel watched, at first satisfied with their quick progress, but that quickly shifted to worry.

Hazel stepped closer to Tammi and increased the intensity of the electricity keeping her on her knees. "Where are the others?"

Tammi smiled, but Hazel could see the fear in her eyes. "I don't know what you're talking about."

The energy coursing through Hazel's body was unlike anything she'd ever experienced. A wave of fury ripped through her, and she pushed her hands forward, tossing Tammi backward several feet.

Hazel stood over her, letting the current feather over her body. "Where are they?"

Blood dripped from Tammi's nose, but she continued to smile sadistically. "What's wrong? Your witching powers lacking?"

Hazel had learned she could communicate with Morgan through telepathy, but it would take a significant amount of concentration, and she wasn't sure if she could hold Tammi in place at the same time.

Raven appeared beside her. "I'll hold her. See if you can communicate with the others." Raven got behind Tammi and put her blade against her throat.

Hazel let her focused energy on Tammi dissipate as she mentally tried to reach the others. Her mind hummed, but it was like reaching into the darkness. She'd only used this skill when Morgan had initiated the interaction; she had no idea how to do it on her own. She focused with more intensity, trying to let her natural abilities take root. Images flashed behind her eyelids, grainy pictures of a crowded area and a rooftop. An image of Lucien raising his fist up to strike. Then she seemed to be shoved out of the thought by a force she couldn't identify.

She hadn't realized she'd sat down until she opened her eyes and looked at her hands. Pebbles from the rooftop had made tiny dimples in her skin, and for a moment, she just stared at them.

Raven's voice pulled her out of her entrancement. "Hazel, are you okay?"

Hazel looked at Raven and felt the bile rise in the back of her throat. "I think something's gone wrong."

Raven stood, dragged Tammi up by the back of her shirt, and pushed her against the wall. "You're going to tell us everything, or I'm sending you to Hell."

Tammi pushed back against Raven. "You don't have the power to send me to Hell."

Raven put her blade under Tammi's throat. "Nothing prevents me from killing you, and I assure you, eternity for you won't be pleasant."

Tammi lifted her chin. "Go ahead and kill me; it won't matter anyway. There's no situation where you come out on top."

A fury ignited in Hazel, and her fingertips cracked with electricity as she placed them around Tammi's throat. "We're not going to kill you; death would be a mercy that you don't deserve. What I have in mind will be much worse." She looked at Raven. "We're taking her with us."

❖

Lucien watched as the two women from his time came out onto the rooftop. They compelled the sniper with a few words, ordering him to turn himself in to the police and tell them Dirk had set the whole thing in motion. That would definitely put a kink in his plan, but he wasn't worried about that now. There were other ways of dealing with Senator Harren. At the very least, this would gain Dirk more notoriety and possibly instill the idea of eliminating the senator into a few of their followers' minds. Right now, he needed to handle the two witches in front of him. He looked at the leather cuff in his hand.

He came around the corner and apprehended Ayotunde, slipping the cuff onto her wrist. "You're all mine now." When she struggled, he replied with a sinister laugh. "There's no point. This is a little gift from Blaise. It seizes your mystical energy and blocks it from leaving your body."

There was rage in Sarah's eyes. "Unhand her at once, you villain!"

He smiled at her as he pulled Ayotunde closer. "If I'd known how much you cared about this slave, I would've purchased her from your family back then."

Sarah raised her hands as if she was going to do something foolish.

"I'd think long and hard before you try something crazy." He kissed Ayotunde's cheek. "I'm in a rather good mood now, but that can change at a shift in the breeze. I don't want to kill her, but I will if you force my hand."

Ayotunde spat on the ground. "Do your best, and it still won't be enough."

He tightened his grip around her. "My, my, haven't we gotten emboldened out here in the modern era. Although, I have to say, I'd much prefer it if you behaved like you're still the chattel you were back in our day."

"And I much prefer you in my visions with a blade through your neck," Ayotunde said.

Rage bubbled in his throat. "Visions! You don't have the gift of premonition. Stop with your blasphemous lies."

Ayotunde smiled at him. "You white men, always thinking you know what be in our minds. If you could truly see, you'd know that your fate is one that ends in blood and madness."

"It's going to feel so good watching you wither as Blaise feeds off your energy," he said against her ear.

Sarah took a step forward. Longing and heartbreak pooled in her eyes. "Pray, Samuel. Don't hurt her. Take me instead."

Lucien was sure he'd never had this much fun. The feeling of power and dominance he was experiencing rarely presented itself in his former life, and it still eluded him at this potency in this one. He craved more.

He glared at Sarah. "You instead? For what? I have everything that matters to you right here. You're a vile, horrible woman. You brought all of this on yourself. You threatened me, my daughter, and our work here. Did you really think we were just going to let you go back and steal all of this from us?"

She reached for Ayotunde desperately. "I'll do whatever you want."

He produced a dagger from behind his back and put it against Ayotunde cheek, pushing it into her until she yelped. "It's too late. I'm going to relish watching the life drain from your eyes as I take hers."

"My goodness. You dark witches love your melodrama." The voice was so velvety and warm that Lucien wanted to curl up inside its essence.

He turned and saw Morgan, her hand on her hip, her beautiful hair obscuring her flawless skin and supple lips. He knew he was being enchanted, but he didn't care. He felt drawn to her, and all he wanted was to touch her skin, be near her.

"Why don't you save yourself a lot of hassle and let my friend go, honey?" Her lips curved upward in a seductive smile.

He fought the urge to do exactly as she asked, but he also wanted to give her whatever she desired. He'd forgotten all his plans, all his intentions; nothing mattered except to lay his hands on her divine body. He was just about to release Ayotunde when an overwhelming force sucked him into a vortex of disorienting darkness. Pain, heat, and rage gouged at the surface of his skin.

Then, as quickly as it had started it finished. He was lying on a cold hard floor at Blaise's feet in their underground lair.

His master fumed with ire. "You idiot! You almost ruined everything."

Lucien felt as if he were face-down in a scalding bathtub of shame. "I don't know what happened. I'm sorry."

"I warned you about her." Blaise wandered off in apparent frustration, then wheeled around on him. "Tell me something, Lucien. Have I chosen the wrong apprentice? Have I sorely misjudged your capability and level of commitment?"

Lucien turned over on his knees and hung his head. "No, my lord. You chose correctly. I'm as committed to you as ever."

Blaise picked up Ayotunde, who Lucien hadn't noticed, and tossed her into one of the cells that lined the wall. "The police are looking for Dirk, and the witches have Tammi."

Lucien's ears felt singed with anger. "You let them take Tammi?"

Blaise erupted. Fire spewed from his cloak, and Lucien felt the dense film of sulfur against his face. "I used my life force to rescue you! And now you've forced my hand. Your ridiculous plan to draw them out was poorly executed." He stared at Ayotunde through the bars. "Luckily for you, we have her. Morgan pretends that these creatures are expendable, but I know her better than that. Her affection for them is her weakness. They'll come for her, and that's when we'll kill them."

Lucien rubbed his aching temples. "And the portal? Tammi?"

Blaise looked up toward the ceiling. "It's right above us; we'll know when they're here. If we can get Tammi back, we will. If not, I'll replace her. The power won't be as great, but I'll make do."

CHAPTER TWENTY-THREE

Raven came out from the bedroom where Hazel was consoling Sarah and sat next to Morgan on the couch. Morgan sipped her bourbon and jiggled the ice in the glass as she stared pensively into space.

Tammi squirmed on the couch in front of them. "It doesn't matter how much you torture me; I'm not telling you anything."

Morgan took another sip. "Your moxie is impressive. I'll give you that." She waved her hand in front of her. "But, darling, I have no intention of torturing you. What do you think I am? A barbarian?"

Tammi stuck out her chin. "You'll do anything to stop Blaise."

Morgan smiled at her. "Tell me, dear. What do you know about Blaise?"

Tammi looked between Raven and Morgan. "I know he's the most powerful witch who ever lived. I know he controls levels of government that no other witch has ever been able to achieve. I know—"

Morgan put her hand up. "I'm going to stop you there. I am the most powerful witch who has ever lived, hence the whole living above ground thing and not sucking the life force out of other witches. Second, witches are not intended to interfere with the boring happenings of the common folk. We're here to keep the realms in balance. Blaise wants to control the mortals because he can't control the realms." She pointed to Tammi's hand. "Stop trying to signal your location. I put a cloaking spell on this apartment. This ain't my first rodeo, darlin'."

Raven noticed a small crack in Tammi's defenses as she looked toward the floor. "What do they want with Ayotunde?"

Tammi rolled her eyes. "Ayotunde doesn't mean anything to us."

Morgan sighed. "I have neither the desire nor the patience to play this game with you for the next several hours, so I'm going to tell you how this will go down. You're going to tell us everything we want to know, or I'm going to remove all your witchy powers, turn you into a person of color, and send you back to 1692. See how well you fare as an enslaved person." She put her hand up before Tammi could speak. "Before you tell me I can't, I assure you, I can. Before you tell me that Blaise could do worse to you, I assure you, he cannot. And before you tell me that you aren't afraid of me, let me be very clear: you should be." She waved, indicating that Tammi continue. "Now, what were you saying? And please, remember that I can tell when anyone is lying, and I'll only be giving you one chance."

Tammi massaged the palm of her hand with her thumb. "I don't know what they want with Ayotunde. It wasn't our plan to take her. Our plan was to kill one of you. It didn't really matter which one; we just needed to break apart the coven."

Raven stood, growing antsy. "Blaise needs you, though. He needs your familial bond to make himself more powerful. We can use Tammi to get Ayotunde back."

Tammi shrugged. "I'm not sure it matters much now. Dirk has corralled enough followers to give Blaise what he needs."

Raven felt a little dizzy. This was starting to spiral out of control. "Where is he?"

Tammi shook her head. "I don't know."

Morgan set her glass on the table. "She's telling the truth." She snapped her fingers, and Tammi slumped on the couch. "By the goddess, Blaise is insufferable."

Hazel walked in and looked among the three of them. "What the hell happened to her?" She pointed to Tammi.

Morgan waved her hand. "She's fine. I just put her to sleep. Her voice was annoying me."

"How's Sarah?" Raven asked.

Hazel ran her hand through her hair. She looked stressed and concerned. "About as you'd expect. She's worried sick, she's scared, and she's angry."

"Good," Morgan said as she poured herself another drink. "She's going to need all that energy to do what must be done."

"What is that exactly?" Hazel asked. "Do we have some sort of contingency plan that addresses a hostage situation?"

Morgan smiled. "The plan is the same as it's been all along. We're going to send the axis of evil back to their time, I'm going to destroy Blaise, and then you can go back to your life."

Raven put her hand on Hazel's shoulder when she saw her shoulders collapse at Morgan's words. "What about Sarah and Ayotunde?"

"Nothing has changed there either," Morgan said. "They have to go back, too. Blaise isn't going to hurt Ayotunde—at least I don't think he will. He wants to use her against me. If, I mean when, she's returned safely, she and Sarah will have to go." Morgan was matter-of-fact, but she didn't meet Raven's eyes. "You two should get some rest; big day tomorrow. I'll sit with Sarah."

Raven opened her mouth to speak, but Morgan swiftly disappeared.

Hazel sat on the bed in her guest room. She was feeling more emotions than she ever had before. She was scared, worried, nervous, anxious, and overwhelmed. All of these feelings were wrapped up in different possibilities, outcomes, but mostly, people. Morgan's words were sitting in her throat, a marble she couldn't swallow. *You can go back to your life.* But what life? A life where she didn't know her family history? A life where she only read about the possibility of the different realms? A life without Sarah? But mostly, a life without Raven. She'd told Raven she'd help her get away from Morgan. She'd told her about the Dare Stone, but they hadn't spoken about it since. Raven hadn't made it clear what she wanted, and that realization pushed down on her chest and squeezed.

"Are you okay?" Raven sat beside her, looking worried.

"I was just thinking about what Morgan said." Hazel wanted to be honest, knowing this might be their last opportunity for an open dialogue. "I don't know how I can go back to my old life, not now."

Raven nodded in understanding. "I can't imagine how overwhelming this must be for you."

Hazel took Raven's hand and kissed her knuckles. "What about you? Have you decided what to do about the Dare Stone?"

Raven looked as if she was going to clam up for a moment, but she took a deep breath and shook her head. "What will Morgan do without me? Who will help defend the realms?"

Hazel squeezed her hand. "Honey, Morgan existed for thousands of years before you, and she'll exist long after all of us are gone. What is it that you want?"

Raven freed her hand from Hazel's. "I don't know how to be anything but a shadowhunter. I've never been anything else."

Hazel's heart hurt from Raven's physical retreat, but she tried to keep her perspective. "Could you still be her shadowhunter without the curse? You could still work for her and have the entirety of your soul back. It could be on your terms, then, not someone else's."

"I don't know," Raven said. "Morgan rarely does or agrees to anything that isn't on her terms."

Hazel took her hand again. "I can't imagine you not being in my life. I know we've only known each other for a month, but with everything we've been through, it feels much longer."

Raven didn't pull away. "I don't know if I can be what you need."

Hazel cupped Raven's face, wanting to make sure she saw the truth in her eyes. "You already are."

Tears welled in Raven's eyes and rolled down her cheeks. "Can we just be together tonight and not worry about what may happen tomorrow? I know that's not what you want to hear right now, but it's all I can manage."

Hazel hugged her and pulled her down so they were lying next to one another. "Sure, we can stay like this for as long as you'd like."

Hazel held Raven as closely as possible, listening to her breathing settle and enjoying the way it felt to be wrapped in her arms. She tried to push away the foreboding sense that this might be the only time she had left with Raven like this. She wanted to be wrong. She wanted to know that they'd have countless more nights together, an unlimited number of days. But wishing was for children, people who'd managed to remain unscathed by all the cruel reality life had to offer. Hazel wasn't prone to childish dreams or the possibilities that hung somewhere between hope and love.

She let herself sink into Raven's warm, solid body. She was going to give herself this, the night, the moment, whatever Raven could give her.

CHAPTER TWENTY-FOUR

The glass Lucien threw at Dirk broke into a thousand pieces at his feet. "How could you be so foolish?"

Dirk crossed his arms and pushed out his chest. "It wasn't my idea to try to kill Harren before we disposed of the white witches; that's on you."

Lucien strode over and put his finger in his chest. "You have no idea what this is going to cost us."

Dirk pushed him away. "This is your fuckup. It's your fault they got away and your fault they got Tammi. What do we have to show for it, a slave?" He pointed at Ayotunde. "What the hell are we going to do with her?"

Lucien watched the small woman sitting in her cell, apparently deep in mediation. "Blaise has plans for her. He thinks we can use her to weaken their coven and lower Morgan's defenses."

Dirk threw his hands in the air. "He thinks? He *thinks* that will work? Perfect." He put his hands on his hips. "And if it doesn't? Then what? Sarah makes it back to 1692 and kills us before we even see it coming? Great plan, Dad."

Lucien scratched at his stubbly chin in thought. "Sarah will try to go through the portal tomorrow night. We'll have to get to her first."

Dirk kicked the desk in the corner. "That hasn't worked out all that well for us so far. No, I say we burn this whole damn town to the ground tonight. I'll incite a riot. People will take to the streets. There will be destruction, looting; we'll get her immersed in the chaos."

"You will do no such thing." Blaise's voice boomed through the small room. "Get your dog to heel, Lucien, or I'll do it for you."

Dirk glared at Blaise, anger flaring in his eyes. His chest heaved up and down, and his hands started to shake. Lucien knew his son's temper better than anyone. He knew it because he had watched it develop over time and even helped to hone certain aspects of it. He never wanted his son to be viewed as weak or helpless, descriptors that had been placed upon him through the years. He had taught Dirk to punch first, ask questions later, and he saw that fury now.

He wanted to push Dirk's hand away when he saw him grab the blade from the table. He wanted to yell for him to stop, to think about what he was doing. He wanted to jump in front of him, urge him back. But he didn't do any of those things; all he could do was watch as Dirk brandished the blade in Blaise's direction. His arm swung like a pendulum to strike, and Lucien watched as his only son fell to nothing but dust on the ground.

Lucien's legs gave out. He clawed at the dust that sifted through his fingers and clumped under his tears. He wanted to cry out in pain, but he had no air, no voice to express the injustice that racked his bones.

"Why?" he croaked.

"If you have to ask that, perhaps you deserve a similar fate to your useless offspring," Blaise said. "Your son met his demise because of a rash decision. Don't make the same mistake."

Lucien tried to stand, but the emotions were too overwhelming. He fell to the floor and continued to sob.

Blaise reached down and jerked him to his feet. "Now, get on Facebook and tell all his followers that Dirk has been killed by a black man. Tell them it was a random shooting in the street. Tell them you're holding a vigil in his honor at Salem Common tomorrow night. There will be enough anger and hate there for me to defeat Morgan."

"There's no body for me to prove it to them," Lucien said. "The police will investigate."

Blaise smiled, his teeth yellowed like an old dog's. "They won't need to see a body to believe you, and they want to believe you. They want a reason to fuel their hatred, their fear, their anger. You're going to give them something tangible. As far as the police are concerned, this will all be over long before we have to worry about them."

❖

Sarah stood in the corner of the living room, watching Tammi Lee glance around Hazel's apartment with a judgmental sneer. Although she was beautiful to the eye—golden blond hair and smooth, rosy skin—inside, she was a ghoul. How could a young woman with so much promise, with so many opportunities before her, choose such a bitter path? But then what else could one expect from the offspring of the foul Samuel Cranwell?

"What?" Tammi spat.

Sarah napped out of her meditation. "Hmm?"

"What are you staring at?"

She approached Tammi and sat on the arm of the sofa. "'Tis a heart-wrenching sight, thou art."

Tammi scoffed. "Please. I don't need your pity."

"'Tis not pity I offer. Resignation doth weigh heavy on my heart at the notion that a woman of such means could betray her sex in the manner in which thou hast."

"Uh, in English, *por favor*." Tammi shook her head in disgust.

"You were but a child in the early days of the new world. It were harsh, often hopeless times in which we toiled, but we believed in the promise of a better life, one in which we could live and worship freely once delivered from the oppression of our king."

"And I should care about this...why?"

Sarah bristled at her lack of concern. "The question be not why you should care. The question is why do you not?"

Tammi rolled her eyes.

"Since I have arrived here in this century, I have not yet ceased to marvel at all of the incredible changes the subsequent generations have created. Women have now a part in governing; they have gained independence from the rule of their fathers and husbands; they are free to choose whatever path in life their heart desires. While motor carriages and flushing chamber pots yet inspire awe in me, there be nothing that fills my heart with inspiration more than to live in a time when the female sex doth have a voice."

Tammi Lee struggled beneath Sarah's control, her eyes gray with contempt when she spoke. "My podcast downloads just hit the ten thousand mark last week. I have a voice, lady, and people are listening to it."

"Aye. Indeed they are. The prodigious crowds you and your father draw plainly show it. But think on what you use that voice for, child. Instead of empowering all people of this land with it, you use it to divide, to sow the seeds of strife and discontent among our modern-day brethren by casting judgment upon those who are different. You punish and demean those who follow their own paths just as the Church of England once did. You are no better than the oppressors our ancestors fled."

"You fool. Don't you see it? We're trying to save this great nation. Our way of life is threatened not only from outside invaders but also from within, from nonbelievers who want to erase God from our country. I'm using my voice to help prevent the destruction of our traditional values. You must remember what tradition and values are, Sarah. Or has your time spent here with these dykes warped that perception, too?"

Sarah sighed at the lost soul looking up at her. "If violence and oppression of the weak and corruption of God be your plan, then you hast triumphed most brilliantly." She shook her head and walked away.

"Sarah," Tammi called.

Sarah stopped before entering the kitchen and turned to her.

"They're not going to win."

"Who?"

"Your niece, the shadowhunter, that bitch queen. Blaise and Lucien have Ayotunde. Your coven is broken. They can't be defeated without her."

Sarah swallowed hard against this new grim suggestion. Was Tammi Lee right? Were Hazel and Raven not being forthright with her about these new events?

Tammi Lee craned her neck to look around the corner. "It's not too late, Sarah," she said softly. "You can join our side. You can be with Ayotunde again and not have to go back to 1692."

Sarah felt the shadow of trickery upon her. "How could it be that I shall not have to return? Madam le Fay be adamant about it."

"Who cares what that dusty old French baguette thinks? The realms are shifting, Sarah. Blaise is going to return any day now and begin the dawn of a new era. You won't have to go back because the old ways won't matter anymore once Blaise's reign comes to fruition."

The temptation Sarah felt must've shown on her face.

"Sarah, wouldn't you like to know you could be with Ayotunde forever here in the modern world?"

She held Tammi Lee's firm gaze as she fought a sudden battle with temptation. She knew full well what Tammi was suggesting, that the corruption of God she so scorned could be used to give her the thing her heart most desired. Her soul ached with sadness at the thought of losing Ayotunde again and likely for good. But could she forsake God? Each day of her life had been dedicated to following His word and striving with herself to please Him as a pious and humble servant. Her faith had offered little guarantee of an afterlife in paradise no matter how she dedicated herself to God. Now it seemed Tammi Lee Sanderson was offering her a guarantee of being with the person she loved to the depths of her soul for the remainder of her time here on earth. It was no longer clear what mattered more: the hope of eternal salvation or a brief but certain interlude of pleasure with Ayotunde in the physical world.

"It sounds good, doesn't it, Sarah? I can help you."

"How am I to believe thou speakest the truth? Moreover, how shall I trust that Blaise, the lord of the dark realm, would grant me favor?"

"Because you and Ayotunde are the only ones who can send us back. If you just walk away from Morgan le Fay's band of merry do-gooders, you and Ayotunde can go off somewhere like P-town or Key West or wherever the gays are doing their queer thing these days and live happily ever after."

Sarah licked her dry lips in shame as she contemplated accepting Tammi Lee's sinful offering. She got up and trudged to the window, trying to force down the desire to say "yes" as it lingered on her tongue. Her love for Ayotunde would surely be enough for her to live on...

"Hey, how about you release me from this couch potato spell, and we can talk more about it alone? My muscles are starting to atrophy."

Sarah turned from the window and padded toward the couch, her arm slowly rising to give Tammi Lee a little room to move.

"Sarah," Raven said, stunning Sarah out of her trance-like state. "What's going on here?"

"Oh, Goody Raven. You startled me."

"Why don't you come with me, Sarah?" She nodded to indicate Tammi Lee. "This one needs a time-out to think about how naughty she's been."

Sarah allowed Raven to usher her out of the room with a firm but gentle hand on her lower back. As she walked down the hall to Hazel's bedroom, she realized why Hazel had often looked at her with such adoration.

❖

Raven escorted Sarah into Hazel's bedroom for a strategy meeting about the candlelight vigil for Dirk Fowler that evening. He was dead, and Raven and Morgan anticipated the "vigil" turning into more of a riot than a memorial since it was reported that Dirk was killed by a black member of a radical-left protest group. A rather transparently convenient story, Raven thought, but the more powerful Lucien had become, the less effort he needed to expend on logic when it came to his flock. They'd long ago bought into his name and his message and were fully indoctrinated.

When Morgan invited them to make themselves comfy, Raven sat next to Hazel on her bed, and Sarah chose an antique rocking chair in the corner.

"I don't think I need to impress upon anyone how critical tonight is," Morgan said. "Oh, before we begin, who's got their eye on that ding-dong in the living room?"

Raven raised her hand. "I took care of it with zip ties." She then glanced at Sarah. "Not that we don't trust you, Sarah. It's just that Ayotunde's the one with the crack compelling skills."

Sarah offered a grateful smile. "None taken, Goody Raven."

"Okay, so now that Dirk is dead, I've been able to broker a deal with Lucien for a hostage exchange," Morgan said. "The vigil is taking place not far from the portal at Proctor's Ledge."

Hazel raised her hand like an eager student. "Why would they choose that location? It's the actual grounds where the witch hangings occurred."

"Yes, it does seem strange they would allow themselves to get so close to the portal, but Blaise's lair is below the hallowed ground. He can feed Lucien the most potent of powers from there."

"It may sound like it'll be a piece of cake for us," Raven added. "But if the execution of our plan goes awry, Lucien could end up sending Sarah and Ayotunde through the portal and sealing it for good. Then Blaise's coup will be complete, and the fate of humanity sealed."

Hazel shook her head in confusion. "How would Lucien be able to accomplish that with Morgan there? He can't overpower her."

"Unfortunately, he can," Morgan said. "Depending on how much energy this vigil-slash-riot stirs up, Blaise's renaissance may happen tonight. And if that should happen, it will become a contest of two: me against him."

"Good versus evil." Sarah rose from the rocking chair. "Madame le Fay, once we retrieve Ayotunde, she and Raven and Hazel and I shall not permit that to happen. We are your coven and shall be your protectors."

Morgan approached Sarah and gently stroked her cheek with the back of her fingers. "You're a sweet, good soul, Sarah. But I still cannot allow you to stay."

"I know it, Madame," Sarah said solemnly. "I offer to protect you not for favor but because it is what is right, what God would want of me, if I would be so bold as to presume His will. After all, you represent His realm, the white realm."

Raven's vision blurred from pooling tears. She cleared them with her index fingers when she heard a whimper from Hazel. She threw her arm around Hazel and drew her closer.

After a moment, Morgan cleared her throat, sounding surprisingly choked up. "I never said this would be easy. We're rescuing humanity from themselves, and that's no mission for sissies."

"I'm fine," Hazel said. "I'm fine." She plucked out a wad of tissues off her nightstand, and after blotting her face and blowing her nose, she assumed the composure of a war room strategist. "How's it going to go down?"

Raven was momentarily speechless as she smiled at Hazel's strength.

"Are you with us, Raven?" Morgan said.

"Oh yeah," Raven said, shaking off her momentary trance. "Once we get there, you're going to open the portal while Hazel and Sarah meet with Lucien to trade Ayotunde for Tammi Lee."

"Just us two?" Hazel shot Sarah a concerned look. "Where will you be?"

"I'll be standing near the portal," Raven said. "Prepared to contend with the variables, like a hellhound attack or if Lucien and Tammi Lee somehow elude Morgan's enchantment spell and try to escape. Tonight is literally our one and only chance to finish this."

"She's right," Morgan said. "Blaise has nearly reached his full potency. The hate-speech rallies are happening more frequently, and the attendance at each is higher than the one before. Membership in Neo-Nazi and Confederate groups continues growing in numbers, and the indifference toward them only grows stronger. Blaise has this country exactly where he wants it."

Raven nodded. "He's already succeeded in his plot to chip away at women's rights. With the onslaught of states outlawing abortion and the women who have them, the stage is set for another wave of females incarcerated in overcrowded prison cells like the one Sarah fled from. The hysteria has almost reached a fever pitch."

Sarah placed her hand over heart and gasped. "'Tis unfathomable that such a wave would once again return. I thought it but a dark stain in our history long over by now."

"Everyone thought that," Raven said. "That's how we ended up here again."

Morgan stuck up her palm in disgust. "Please. In the early nineteenth century, when I inspired the philosopher Santayana to write, 'When experience is not retained, as among savages, infancy is perpetual,' do you think you mortals took him seriously? Nope."

Raven looked at Hazel and Sarah. "Those who don't remember history's mistakes are doomed to repeat them."

They nodded and said, "Oh," in unison.

"Don't get me started," Morgan said. "I need to take a bubble before we save the world." She headed out the bedroom door and turned toward the bathroom. "Hazel, a glass of Prosecco, please?" Her voice trailed off down the hall. "No, just bring the bottle and a glass."

❖

Hazel tapped on the spare bedroom door and waited for Sarah to answer. She looked at Raven after a moment of no response. "You don't think she's done something foolish, like running off?"

Raven's lips pursed with concern, and then she knocked loudly. "Sarah?"

"Are you okay?" Hazel added.

"Aye." Her soft voice floated from behind the door.

"May we come in?"

"Aye. 'Tis not locked."

Hazel opened the door, and Raven followed her in. Sarah sat on Hazel's cushioned reading nook, staring blankly out the window. With her rigid posture and frozen, lifeless expression, Hazel thought she was looking at an old portrait in a history book.

"Do you mind if we join you?" Hazel said.

Sarah turned, allowing for them to sit on either side of her.

Hazel sat for a moment, compiling her thoughts. "I just want you to know that you're the strongest, most courageous woman I've ever met, and I'm proud to be your descendent."

"And I'm proud as hell just to know you," Raven said.

Sarah finally raised her head, offering each of them a smile as she clutched their hands.

Hazel peered over Sarah's head at Raven and shot her a look of helplessness. Her heart was breaking for Sarah, and she wanted so badly to say something of significance, something that would relieve even a modicum of her pain. But when Raven returned a similar hopeless glance, she realized the only meaningful thing they could offer Sarah was their silent support.

After a lengthy silence and a deep sigh, Sarah finally spoke. "Do you know what the name Ayotunde means?"

"No," Hazel said. Raven shook her head.

"It means 'joy has returned' in her mother's native tongue of Yoruba." Sarah placed her hand over her heart as she fought against a quivering lip. "Never hath a name befit a person so well."

Hazel cursed her teary eyes, not wanting her sadness to affect to Sarah.

"When I see her again in our prison cell, though she be in such a wretched state, my heart soared at the sparkle of her essence that still flicker in her eye. Even in that dank, stench-ridden jail, when I held her hand and touched my hand to her cheek, indeed, my joy hath returned."

Hazel sensed the authenticity and power of Sarah's sentiments as she'd often been bowled over by a similar feeling every time Raven returned to her.

"Never have I known the happiness that fills my heart since we travel here and profess our love for each other. Surely, the light of Heaven proper could feel no better if it chose to shine on us."

"I haven't given up trying to figure out a way for you and Ayotunde to stay here," Hazel said.

At that, Raven leaned back behind Sarah and shook her head as if telling her to stop making empty promises.

Sarah looked up at Hazel and smiled. "I be bound in a debt of gratitude to you for all eternity if were you able." She got up and drifted pensively across the room toward the dresser on which Hazel kept a collection of amulets and sage. "But I beguile myself not to believe it were a hope that would come to fruition."

Hazel got up and followed her. "Aunt Sarah, you can't give up hope. This mission isn't over yet. A lot can happen in the—"

"Hazel," Raven said curtly. She approached them with a stern countenance. "She can't stay. Look, I've already discussed this privately with Morgan. Do you know what will happen if Sarah doesn't return to 1692?"

"Yeah, she won't have to be tortured in a disease-ravaged prison until she's exonerated after six months in hell." Hazel felt herself getting flush with indignation. "And she won't have to lose the love of her life again. What's the big friggin' deal if she stays? According to my family's grimoire, she's not that significant in the grand scheme of things. So what if it causes a little hiccup in time? Doesn't her happiness matter to anyone around here?"

Raven scratched at the back of her head in apparent frustration and then blurted, "She has to go back, or you'll never be born."

Hazel and her aunt were stunned into silence as they glanced back and forth from each other to Raven. For a moment, Hazel wondered if Raven wasn't just making that up to make Sarah's sacrifice seem more valiant. But if it was true, then it momentously sucked to know that she was the real reason Sarah couldn't stay.

"How comes that?" Sarah finally asked.

"The way Morgan explained it to me, your sister Mary will go into an early labor with her sixth child, a girl. You'll be the only one at her home at the time and will assist her in a difficult birth. The child nearly dies as Mary drifts in and out of consciousness, but you, Sarah, save her life."

"And the baby girl lives to extend the line I'm born into," Hazel said and collapsed onto the bed.

"If Sarah isn't there when Mary goes into labor, the baby will die."

"And Hazel shall cease to exist," Sarah said quietly.

"I'm sorry," Raven said. Her eyes gleamed with empathy for both of them.

"Then the course I must follow be plain," Sarah said.

Hazel leapt up from the bed, her voice quivering as she spoke. "Aunt Sarah, how could I live with myself if I knew you lost Ayotunde again because of me?"

Sarah picked up her chin and smiled. "'Tis not because of you, my dearest niece. The workings of evil be set in motion long before your soul hath stepped upon the earth."

"But it's not fair," Hazel said in a whimper and walked into Sarah's open arms. Although they were about the same age, Hazel felt a deep nurturing in Sarah's embrace, one that resonated with their centuries-old matrilineal bond.

Raven cleared her throat. "I hate to break this up, but if we don't prepare for tonight, we all might as well dive through that portal."

Hazel dried her cheeks with her palm and smiled when Raven gave her a comforting caress on her back as they walked out of the room.

CHAPTER TWENTY-FIVE

That night, when they arrived at the staging area for Dirk's vigil, the gathering was small compared with most of Dirk's other insurrection ventures, maybe about a hundred or so people. With their somber faces illuminated by candles poked through circles of paper, they were quiet, as though waiting for someone to tell them what to do next, what to think or even feel.

Raven nodded toward Morgan. "This crowd is suspiciously small. Think Lucien has something extra up his sleeve?"

Morgan shook her head. "His power's clearly waning without Dirk and Tammi Lee. I'm sure this was the best he could do on short notice and in a blue state. We definitely have home field advantage for this one."

"It still feels weird to me. These people look like the walking dead. Why is it so quiet and peaceful?"

"Patience, my dear," Morgan said. "You don't think Lucien has some angry flunky standing by to get everyone fired up when he summons him? Goddess knows he's not that bright, but he knows how to foment social upheaval. He's making sure to press every emotional button on this herd before slapping the big fake outrage one."

Raven nodded, satisfied with Morgan's explanation. "So, let me ask you this..." She paused to select her phrasing. "Since Dirk is dead and we have Tammi Lee, can't we just have Sarah and Hazel stuff her down the portal, and then I can take out Lucien with my blades?"

Morgan laughed mirthlessly. "Oh, Raven. You know better than that. Risking the integrity of a mission to take the easy way out is so not sexy, and it's never been what you're about."

"I just figured that since Dirk's been dead for a day now and I haven't so much as noticed a change in temperature, let alone a major shift in the universe, it would be okay to expedite the matter."

Morgan rolled her eyes. "That's because Dirk Fowler was a waste of his mother's amniotic fluid. To this day, how such a collection of genetic shit ever survived those colonial-era New England winters still baffles me. He's one of the few mortals on this planet who truly has no purpose worth noting."

"Oh." Raven sighed and glanced over at Sarah and Hazel, who were huddled near the car chatting as they awaited the word to move.

"Hey." Morgan tugged Raven's arm and attention in her direction. "What's this really about?"

Raven shrugged. "Just a shot in the dark."

Morgan displayed an uncharacteristic expression of surprise. "You're fishing for a way to keep Sarah and Ayotunde here, aren't you?"

"No. I was just—"

"Holy *merde*," Morgan said. "Hazel has completely locked down your heart."

"What?" Raven wrinkled her eyebrows, trying to dismiss the accusation. "What are you talking about? That's ridiculous. I've been very clear. She knows we can never have anything."

"I thought you knew that, too."

"I do, Morgan. Believe me. Nobody knows it better than me." She stepped away when she heard the sadness in her own voice. She needed to shield herself from Morgan before she gave anything else away.

"If this life displeases you so much, you can always pull the Dare Stone and be free of me once and for all."

Unless Raven was hearing things, she detected a note of melancholy in Morgan's voice. Rather than becoming enraged and forcing her into violent capitulation right there, she was calm, eerily calm.

"And what happens to my uncle?"

Morgan shrugged. "He's an old man. He's already beaten the clock on the actuary table. You and Hazel, on the other hand, are young and have a lot of living yet to do."

Raven bit her lip at the response that was so typically Morgan. Everything had a catch to it; nothing would ever be a fifty-fifty split with her. It would always be eighty-twenty—if she was lucky.

"No matter how strongly I feel for Hazel, I'm also not about trading someone's life for my happiness. The world is full of enough of those kinds of people."

Morgan smirked. "You're getting soft. In Hazel's light, your heart is melting like an arctic glacier."

"Whatever." Raven shook her head in frustration.

"Raven," Hazel said in a loud whisper. She waved them over to the car.

"She must've gotten the text from Lucien about the exchange," Raven said. She and Morgan walked over.

"Did you notice the crowd?" Hazel asked. "It's gotten twice as large since we got here. Lucien and company can't have that many sycophants in this part of the country, can they?"

Raven shook her head as her stomach clenched in dread. "I'm certain they're counterprotesters. The only question is, are they real ones or another fake group supposedly there to incite the grieving followers?"

"It's more likely the latter," Morgan said. "Have you heard from Lucien?" she said to Hazel.

"Yes. He said Ayotunde was being difficult, so he was going to be a little late for the exchange, around nine p.m."

"That's a ruse," Morgan said. "We have to change our location."

"We have to keep an eye on this crowd, too," Raven said. "Lucien wants Sarah and Hazel in this spot because he's hatching a plan involving those counterprotesters."

"He wants the vigil to turn into a riot," Raven said, addressing Hazel and Sarah. "He must think that in all the chaos, he can grab Tammi and then execute the rest of the plan on the three of you."

Morgan looked at Raven. "He can't possibly be stupid enough to think you and I won't be lurking in the shadows in anticipation of that exact move."

"Maybe with what he has in mind, it doesn't matter," Raven said.

"We're changing the location of the swap," Morgan said. "We'll move it up the hill closer to the portal." She turned to Hazel. "Text Lucien back and tell him the police made you move for crowd control, and now you and Sarah will meet them a block from here."

"What if he insists we keep it here?" Hazel said.

"Then we'll know it's a trap," Raven said. "Come on. Let's get out of here."

❖

The world buzzed inside Hazel's head. She'd been able to feel the realms with greater power since she discovered she was a witch, but never with the fierceness she felt now. She always understood the severity of the situation they were heading into, but she didn't feel the full weight of it until now. There would be no real winners. If they succeeded, her aunt would be forced back into a loveless life with nothing to look forward to but small, stolen moments with the person she truly loved. If they failed, dark magic would swallow the world entirely. And neither scenario ended with a future where Raven was hers.

Raven placed a hand on her back. "What's wrong? You looked like you just saw a ghost."

It wasn't the right time, but it was the only time she had. If she didn't kiss her now, there might never be another opportunity. She put her hands on Raven's face and pulled her in. Raven seemed surprised at first but quickly gave into the kiss. Raven seemed to need this moment as much as her. Their mouths were hungry and the connection passionate. Hazel wasn't sure how she'd ever be able to give Raven up, to know she'd never feel like this about anyone ever again. It was so final, and the rest of her life stretched out in front of her. She realized, then, her fate would be the same as Sarah's. She'd never have the person her heart belonged to. She, too, would never get her happy ending. Raven wrapped her arms tighter around her, and Hazel wondered if she'd sent her thoughts into Raven's mind on accident. Tears welled in her eyes, and she gently pushed Raven away.

"I want you to know, it doesn't matter what you decide, I'll always be yours."

Raven kissed her forehead and then looked into her eyes. She seemed as if she was going to say something, but Lucien's voice cut through their poignant moment.

"If this was all I had to do to get you all in one place, I would've done it weeks ago." His hand was around Ayotunde's arm, squeezing with so much force, his fingertips were turning white.

Morgan stepped in front of them. "Why don't you just hand her over. I'll give you back your evil spawn here, and then the adults can talk."

Lucien shook his head. "It's not going to be that easy."

Morgan sighed heavily. "Listen, Lucy—"

"It's Lucien." He glared and jerked Ayotunde closer.

Morgan waved her hand, and then patted Tammi on the back. "Sure it is. Listen, give us back Ayotunde, and I will let you and Tammi here keep your powers."

Lucien continued to look down the street, clearly waiting for something.

Hazel's hands started to tingle as her heartrate picked up. "Something's not right."

Morgan closed her eyes for a moment, and when she opened them, they were a color green Hazel had never seen before. It was almost as if there were rays of light shining from behind them.

"Blaise," Morgan said, her eyes fixated on the park.

Raven brandished her blade and closed the distance between herself and Lucien. "Let her go, or this is it for you."

Lucien shrugged and released Ayotunde. "It's too late now anyway. None of you are getting out of here alive."

Morgan clutched the binding on Ayotunde's wrist, and it fell to the ground. Lucien grabbed Tammi and disappeared only to reappear about a hundred feet away, in the crowd.

"They can teleport?" Hazel hadn't realized she said it aloud until Morgan answered.

"No, they can't. They aren't powerful enough, but Blaise is." Morgan's voice no longer sounded like her own. Where there once was always a twinge of superiority and amusement, there was anger and vengeance.

Hazel wasn't completely sure what was happening. Lucien had handed over Ayotunde with no hesitation. She'd thought there would be an epic battle now, but all the commotion triangulated in the park.

Chants of hatred and vitriol thundered through the air. Hatred had a pulse, and it was beating alive and well in Salem tonight.

Ayotunde cried into Sarah's shoulder. "Everyone in the crowd thinks I put the bullet in Dirk. They callin' for my head."

Raven put her hand on Ayotunde's back as she addressed Morgan.

"We can't do this without her, but we can't get her any closer, or the mob will see her and tear her apart."

Hazel's heart felt as if it was pounding in her stomach. "Can't you give her a different face, like you did in Boston?"

Morgan shook her head. "It won't matter. Blaise and I will simply go back and forth, marking her and unmasking her. Besides, his power is growing by the second, and I need to preserve my energy."

Sarah stepped forward. "Send Ayotunde and me back now. We'll get rid of the Cranwells. It will be like they never came."

"The time continuum doesn't work like that." Morgan paced, uncharacteristically on edge. "Blaise has already used them to tap into his ultimate source of power, fear and hatred. I'm afraid I've underestimated how powerful he's become."

Hazel stepped forward, defiant. "No. We aren't just going to stand by and watch this happen. Sarah and Ayotunde, get Tammi Lee and Lucien back through the portal. Raven, Morgan, and I will handle Blaise."

Morgan shook her head. "You and I cannot defeat Blaise. We need the full coven, and even then, I'm not sure we can do it."

Hazel put her hands on Morgan's shoulders. "I'm a direct descendant of you, and so is Sarah. I know you haven't been challenged in like a million years, but I refuse to believe that you, the most powerful witch who's ever lived, can't defeat Blaise with our help. I don't care if he has a million people down there. We can do this together."

Morgan put her hand on Hazel's face. Her eyes were sincere and worried. "If I let the full force of my power flow through you, it may kill you. Or..."

"Or what?" Hazel asked impatiently.

"A fate worse than death," Morgan said gravely. "You may become immortal."

Hazel looked over at Raven. Her eyes held more fear and trepidation than anything Hazel had ever seen in another person. She forced herself to look away, not wanting the burden of Raven's thoughts on her decision.

"It doesn't matter. Blaise can't control the realms; humanity will never stand a chance." Hazel wanted to say more but there was nothing else *to* say. The finality of her statement was just that, a finality.

Morgan nodded. "Okay. As long as you understand the potential consequences, and you've made your choice."

"I have," Hazel said.

Sarah swept Hazel up in a hug. "My heart doth overflow with pride. I know you are most capable, my fair niece."

Hazel fought back the emotion rising from her aching heart. She was saying good-bye to her aunt, and although she wanted more time, there wasn't any left. "Take care of yourself, my dear aunt." She kissed her cheek. "I'm so sorry it has to be like this."

Sarah smiled at her, love filling her eyes. "Be not sorry for things out of your control. This be a duty to God, and I'm happy to play my part. I shall find strength in the knowledge that humanity will make such progress in the new world and that my family line will extend to someone as brave and honorable as you." She looked over at Ayotunde and reached for her hand. "My dearest Ayotunde, our story has only yet begun."

Raven said good-bye to Sarah and Ayotunde as Morgan focused on getting the portal open. The air shook, and light seemed to get sucked into a small hole and then expand into a glowing orb that floated two feet from the ground. It would have been beautiful if it didn't mean her aunt's departure.

Ayotunde was by her side a moment later. She lifted her hands in the air and closed her eyes. Hazel watched as Tammi Lee and Lucien pivoted in their direction.

Ayotunde smiled. "I rather enjoy the role of puppet master."

Blaise was still nowhere in sight as his minions walked closer. They were shrieking and shouting their disapproval, trying to resist the invisible force drawing them to the portal. Tears streamed down Tammi's cheeks, and Lucien's face had a sweaty gleam from the effort to rail against the unseen force.

Ayotunde compelled them to kneel in front of the portal. Their bodies were shaking in protest, trying to break free. When Lucien tried to call out, his mouth opened and closed like a netted fish gulping the air.

Morgan placed a hand on Lucien and instructed Hazel to put hers on Tammi. Then she joined her hand with Hazel's and chanted some words under her breath. A jolt of electricity tinged with pain and anger raced through Hazel's body. She coughed, and her head started to throb.

Morgan knelt in front of them. "You two brought this on yourselves." She put a hand under each of their chins, forcing them to look at her. "Hazel and I have stripped you of your powers. You will return to 1692 with no memory of what you've seen or experienced here. Your desire for evil will be replaced with an unquenchable thirst for charity. You will spend the remainder of your days making restitution for the pain you've caused by caring for the sickly and the downtrodden in your humble village." She snapped her fingers, and Tammi and Lucien collapsed in a heap on the ground.

"Alas. We must carry them, too?" Sarah put her hands on her hips and shook her head.

Raven rolled Lucien and Tammi forward, and they disappeared into the glowing orb. "I hope they land in someone's farm on an upturned pitchfork."

Sarah and Ayotunde turned to Hazel. She wanted to say more, to take her time saying good-bye, but a loud burst from somewhere behind them shook the ground.

Sarah embraced Hazel one last time and kissed her cheek. "Remember who you are and the lineage from where you come."

Hazel nodded and watched as Sarah and Ayotunde walked into the light together, holding hands.

CHAPTER TWENTY-SIX

Raven watched the crowd of protestors, their chants for justice becoming more feverish with each passing second. She searched the faces, looking for the cloaked figure responsible for siphoning their energy. She turned her attention to Morgan and Hazel whose faces were fixed on the same location.

Morgan raised her hand and pointed. "Blaise."

Raven didn't recognize the entity she was pointing to, but there was no mistaking his presence. He'd abandoned his dark cloak and sadistic form. He now stood at well over six feet with broad shoulders, blond hair, and the physique of an ancient Greek warrior.

"He's at his full power now," Morgan said so quietly that Raven wasn't sure if she meant for anyone to hear.

Hazel wrapped her fingers around Raven's forearm but spoke to Morgan. "You and Blaise look as if you could be siblings."

"I guess we are in a way," Morgan said. "We're made of the same forces. The same white light that drives my life force exists in him in equal measure. The only difference is his is dark magic." She looked over at Raven and Hazel. "I'm afraid this won't end as easily as we'd hoped. I was arrogant not to take him seriously when he first returned. I've gotten complacent, lazy over the years. You two are in far more danger than I'd originally thought, the entire world is."

Raven had never seen Morgan without her normal bravado; it was unnerving. "We're in this together."

Morgan gave her a weak smile. "I'd ask you to go, but I'm sure you wouldn't listen."

"I'm not going anywhere." Raven touched Morgan's arm, and for the first time in their relationship, Morgan flinched.

Hazel must have sensed the same insecurity. She gripped Morgan's shoulders and forced her to look at her. "You are Morgan le Fay, Queen of the Witches and the protector of this realm. There is no one more powerful than you. You've proven yourself over the centuries as he lurked in the shadowy underworld. You've kept the balance of the realms and have done your best to secure a bright future for humanity. Don't you dare falter now; it's not who you are."

Morgan raised her chin and gave Hazel a curt nod. "If my life force is extinguished today, my mantle will fall to you. Are you prepared to take on that role if necessary?"

Hazel glanced at Raven but only for a moment. "That won't happen, but yes, yes I am."

Raven knew then beyond any doubt that she loved Hazel. Not because of the power she could eventually possess, not because of her beauty or even the way Hazel made her feel when she was near. No. She loved Hazel because she was selfless, brave, and unwavering. Hazel's power came not just from her inherent powers but from her firm belief that evil must be pushed back into the darkness where it belonged.

Raven drew both her blades and looked at Blaise. There was little she'd be able to do that the two powerful witches could not, but she was determined to go down fighting. She rolled her shoulders and took a deep breath.

Raven looked over at Hazel one last time. "I love you," she said, then took off in Blaise's direction.

Hazel watched as Raven moved around the side of the crowd, clearly planning on approaching Blaise from behind. If Blaise saw her, he paid no attention, focused as he was on Morgan. As he walked toward them, the mob parted. They'd been rendered into a trancelike state. They gaped at him, awaiting further instruction from their trusted leader. Hazel felt crackling in her fingertips, her body reacting to what was coming.

Hazel and Morgan took several steps forward until they were face-to-face with Blaise. Hazel's body was humming as the power surged through her, a lightning rod ready to strike. Had she experienced this several weeks ago, she would have passed out from the overwhelming sensation. Now, she reveled in it, knowing the force building inside her was aching to defeat the monster who threatened the people she loved and the innocents she'd never met. Hazel had heard Raven's words before she took off toward the crowd. They'd been echoing in her ears for the last few minutes. They didn't frighten her as she thought they might have. They seemed rather to give her more purpose and more power. For all her apprehension and misgivings, Raven was hers.

Blaise was now only a few feet away. He smiled broadly, showing his transformed teeth, no longer dingy and discolored. His eyes glowed the same magnetic opaque white as Morgan's, a compelling transformation. Power and arrogance seeped out of him, nearly intoxicating Hazel by mere proximity. Hazel shook her head as if it would release whatever hold might have been spreading toward or over her.

"The day has finally come, Morgan." Blaise smiled and raked his eyes up and down Morgan's body. "I'm rather disappointed in you for assuming you'd seen the last of me. You're getting sloppy in your old age."

With hands on hips, Morgan took a half step closer, sporting a defiant grin. "I took pity on you last time we met. You have to admit, it wasn't your finest hour."

Blaise lifted his hand and caressed the side of Morgan's face. "You were always so beautiful, so radiant. We could have accomplished wonderful things together." He glanced at Hazel. "Hmm. She possesses more power than one would imagine from the look of her."

"She has my blood running through her veins," Morgan said. "You can't possibly think you'll be able to overpower us both."

Blaise stopped stroking Morgan's neck and glided his fingers around her throat. Morgan choked out a gurgling sound as he lifted her off the ground.

"You've underestimated their hatred," he growled into Morgan's face. "Weak people want to hate. They need to hate to survive the miserable lives they've been sentenced to endure as a result of their incompetence." He drew her closer still. "That's always been your problem, underestimating how tenuous the good really is in people. It's a mansion built on sand."

Hazel could tolerate Blaise's taunts no more. Impelled by instinct, she rammed her hands into his chest. Electricity erupted against his skin, and small funnels of smoke wafted out of his body from where her fingerprints remained. He released Morgan and stumbled several steps back to focus on Hazel. The magnificent blue now flashed with the flaming red she'd associated with him before. So intense, she was convinced it was the actual fire of Hell.

He squeezed his fingers into a ball. An invisible force gripped Hazel and lifted her off the ground. She thrashed against it, but her arms felt cemented to her sides, keeping her from using her hands.

As he thrust her higher, Raven ran in his direction. She had one shimmering blade raised and the other by her side. Hazel wanted to call out and tell her to stop, that he was too powerful, but her voice was trapped in her constricted throat.

Raven jumped through the air and plunged her blade into Blaise's neck. Hazel fell but hurried to her feet. Raven rolled away after she hit the ground and stood next to Morgan.

Blaise dislodged the blade from his neck and scrutinized. "Angel steel," he said in a strained voice. He crushed it between his hands, and it crumbled to dust.

He touched the wound in this neck and glanced at the black liquid coating his fingers. Rage again flared in his eyes, and he bolted in Raven's direction. Morgan stepped in front of Raven and crossed her forearms like a shield in front of her. When the two collided, their contact sparked an explosion of blinding blue light. Blaise tumbled back several feet but was grinning when he regained his footing.

He brought his hands above him. Hazel couldn't pull her eyes away from the tangles of electricity that crackled over his body, a sign he was siphoning energy from his followers. His chest heaved, and his body started to glow with a red aura.

Morgan lurched toward him, encircled with her own aura of luminous ice blue, but Blaise pitched to the left. Electricity flared through Hazel again as she hurried to Morgan's side where their powers blended with exponential force. She felt as if her body might explode as the intensity of their commingled power coursed through her. When Morgan and Hazel joined hands, they created a massive ball of quivering light. Morgan hurled it in Blaise's direction, but he vanquished their attack with red glowing hands.

He guffawed. "Face it, Morgan. I'm the superior entity, and this will not end well for you and your gaggle of witch wannabes." He brought his hands together, and a red ball of fire formed between his palms.

Hazel prepared to deflect the attack, but he wheeled around and heaved the flaming weapon at Raven. She used her remaining blade to shield herself, and when it hit, the ball evaporated into the metal.

"Bet you didn't know I carry demon steel, too," she said as she charged again.

Hazel rushed to assist with the next blow, willing all her power to rocket him backward as Raven sliced into his side. He stumbled. Morgan seized the opportunity to hit him again with more bolts of white light, knocking him onto his back.

Raven dove toward him, but he was quicker with his counter. She flew through the air and crashed into a distant tree.

Hazel channeled her fury into action, standing side by side with Morgan. They assailed Blaise in unison, their collective power searing through Hazel's fingertips as it blasted toward him. He held his hands up to block their energy but fell to his knees and scrambled over the ground to flee.

They gained more ground, ushering him back with increasing strength and speed. Finally, when they were within a foot of him, Morgan raised her hand to deliver the final blow. Hazel smiled with satisfaction as she anticipated his departure back to hell.

But Blaise thrust his waning dark magic against theirs in a powerful, raw, and terrifying display. Hazel backpedaled as the aromas of sulfur and freshly cut grass mingled in the air. Blaise groaned as he drove toward them harder, his skin and eyes glowing redder with fire. The muscles in Hazel's upper torso felt as if they were tearing as she swallowed an anguished yelp. Her entire body was breaking down, but there was nothing she could do to stop it. Her desire to rid the world of this monster was more important than her life.

She could see the world in its entirety: past, present, and future. All came together as one in her mind. She could hear the shrill cries of the women whose lives were stolen from them on these grounds centuries ago. Their souls cried out to her, urging her to find the strength to carry on. She sensed the full weight of their futile determination to resist the ideological nightmare that had infested their village and from which there had been no earthly escape.

A surge of energy exploded from her hands and slammed Blaise back to the ground. She leapt on top of him and pressed her hand on his chest where his heart should've been. Morgan clamped her hand on his head and held on. They worked in unison to strip the energy from his body. It passed through Hazel, the dark energy thick as lava, bubbling with all the attributes that wrought pain and despair in the world. The anger, hatred, fear, mistrust, and resentment eviscerated her as it worked its way through her body. And then, it was gone.

Fully expecting to collapse, Hazel didn't understand how her body was still working. She stooped beside Raven without remembering how she got there. She touched her cold, pale face, hoping she wasn't too late. Gliding her hands over Raven's body, she was intent on identifying the issue so she could heal her.

Morgan knelt next to her and took Hazel's hand. She hadn't realized tears were soaking her cheeks until Morgan placed a hand on her face and tried to quiet her.

"Bring her back," Hazel choked through sobs. "Please. Bring her back to me right now."

Morgan placed Hazel's hand over Raven's heart. She felt the same level of energy as before, when they were seizing Blaise's life force. But this time, instead of anger and fear, love and tenderness radiated from her feet up through her entire body, and into Raven. She watched in awe as the color slowly returned to Raven's cheeks, and after a few more seconds, she detected a heartbeat under her palm.

Raven rolled over coughing. "What the hell just happened?"

Hazel fell on top of her, not thinking about Raven's other injuries. She cradled Raven's head and said through her tears, "Don't you ever leave me again, Raven Dare. Do you hear me?"

Raven wrapped her arms around her and hugged her tightly. "It's not so easy getting rid of a shadowhunter. Just ask Blaise."

Hazel kissed her softly, tears still falling. "I love you, too."

CHAPTER TWENTY-SEVEN

Raven let her head fall against the couch. Her aching body and thrumming in her head were welcome reminders that she was still alive. Hazel and Morgan had made quick work of replacing the memories of the "vigil" with something more pleasant. They'd also removed the feelings of helplessness, anger, and rage. It wouldn't solve all the world's problems, but it was a step in the right direction.

Hazel tapped her shoulder with a glass of vodka. "I thought you might need this."

Raven took a sip. The alcohol warmed her chest and made her lips tingle. "Thank you."

Hazel sat on the couch next to her. She put a hand on Raven's face, and her eyes filled with tears. "I almost lost you today."

"But you didn't," Raven said. "Try to focus on that." She didn't know how to erase the memory of her dying from Hazel's memory. Although she'd wished it, that power wasn't in her wheelhouse.

Morgan sat on the couch across from them. She raised her glass in their direction. "To us."

Hazel and Raven raised their glasses as well, acknowledging all they'd accomplished.

"What now?" Hazel asked as she sunk into the crook of Raven's side.

Morgan let out a long breath. "There will be another; there must be balance in the realms. This time, I hope to find them early to help guide them. I don't want to be dealing with another Blaise any time soon."

Hazel sighed. "I can't imagine going through all that again. I'm glad I'll be long gone."

Morgan paused, placing her glass down on the table. "Oh honey, you'll still be here."

Hazel snorted. "Doubtful."

"I know you felt it; you must know what you've become."

Raven stiffened, and she felt Hazel do the same.

"What are you saying?" Hazel asked as she sat forward.

Morgan, normally boisterous, took on a calm tone. "You're immortal now."

Hazel shook her head, looked at Raven, and then back at Morgan. "No. It can't be."

Morgan picked up her glass again and looked into the amber liquid. "I'm afraid it's true. I warned you this may happen."

Hazel clapped her hand over her mouth. "But I'll have to watch everyone I love die. I'll never grow old? I'll never be able to grow old with Raven?"

The words shouldn't have warmed Raven's chest, but they did. The idea that Hazel wanted to spend her life with her was overwhelming in the best possible way. They hadn't had a chance to discuss their future, but Raven knew she wanted Hazel in it. Knowing Hazel felt the same was a gift greater than she'd ever expected to receive.

Morgan sighed. "That's not necessarily true. There is a way to make Raven immortal as well."

Raven sat forward. "What do you mean?"

"A potion exists in the farthest hills of the realms, but it's guarded by the ancients. If they deem you worthy, they can give it to you."

Raven curled her fingers around Hazel's hand. "What do I need to do?"

Morgan laughed. "We just saved the world. Think this can wait for the morning?" She fingered the chain around her neck, then removed it and placed it on the table. "I wasn't sure what to get you. What does one get for two people who helped saved the realm?" She snorted. "You'd be surprised what the internet suggested." She flicked a tear from her eye. "Take it."

Raven reached forward and picked up the necklace. In the center was a broken piece of stone. "Is this?"

"It's what binds you to me, a piece of the Dare Stone. My gift to you is your freedom."

Raven felt tears well in her eyes. "Morgan, I—"

Morgan cut her off. "Don't make a big deal about it. It's what you've wanted and worked for your entire life. Your uncle will be brought out of his stasis unharmed and be free to live out his days however he chooses, just like you."

Raven smiled. "You never let me finish." She placed the chain around her neck. "Thank you for this amazing gift. I..." She paused to search for the proper words but came up short. "How do you thank someone for the gift of freedom?"

"Good luck trying," Morgan said with a chuckle and sipped her drink.

"I think I've already found a way." Raven smiled knowingly at Hazel.

Morgan looked puzzled. "How?"

"I want to keep working for you...willingly."

"I don't understand. You're finally free to go and do whatever you please."

Raven nodded. "I understand, and I choose to stay and work with you. It's my choice now. I know I can go if I feel the need to, but my place is with you, Morgan, helping to keep the balance."

Morgan's face flushed. "Hazel, how do you feel about that?"

Hazel clasped Raven's hand. "All I wanted was for her to be able to make the choice herself. She's done that. Besides, I'll be staying with you, too. I still have a lot to learn, and we have a potion to find."

Morgan choked back a sob. "We'll be like a real family? I never thought...I never thought it would be possible for me."

Hazel smiled. "Someone will have to take over for you someday. I may as well learn from the best."

Morgan chuckled. "Don't get too ambitious, honey. I'm not going anywhere anytime soon."

Hazel made her way over and hugged Morgan from behind. "Good. I'm just starting to like you."

Raven let her fingers play over the necklace, the symbol of her life, her freedom, and the trust she shared with Morgan. When she looked at Hazel, she was overcome with a gratitude she'd never thought she'd experience. She could've never imagined this was where her life would take her. Not knowing which gods to thank for her fortune, she thanked them all.

For the first time in her life, she settled into a peace she never dared to believe she deserved.

❖

Hazel lifted the shirt over Raven's head and kissed her way down her neck, finally settling on her chest. Her lips grazed the stone on the necklace. "How does it feel? To be free?" she asked, twirling it in her fingers.

Raven smiled against Hazel's cheek as she placed dozens of kisses along her face and neck. "Wonderful. I never imagined I could have this life. I never thought being in love was something I deserved, let alone something I'd be allowed. I never imagined having a forever with anyone."

Hazel felt her cheeks flush. "Say it again."

Raven smiled and kissed her. "Which part?"

"All of it." Hazel wrapped her arms around Raven's neck and pulled her closer. "Tell me you love me."

Raven tantalized her with kisses, drawing out their connection until Hazel whimpered. "I love you."

Hazel traced her hand down Raven's six-pack abs. "Forever."

Raven's body shuddered. "Forever."

Hazel continued to explore Raven, letting the word repeat in her mind. *Forever* meant something different for them than it did for other couples. Forever really was obtainable, and Hazel would make sure it came true. There was no version of life, no existence she could imagine without Raven by her side.

Tomorrow they would start on their journey to forever, but tonight, she would brand Raven with her body, her love, her devotion, her everything.

EPILOGUE

Sarah sat on the side of her sister Mary's bed as she labored into her sixth hour, about to birth her third child. As Sarah blotted the sweat from Mary's forehead with a damp cloth, Ayotunde returned to the room with a mug of fresh water.

"This child be a fighter," Mary said, huffing to catch her breath.

"Praise be to God that you are, too, my sister," Sarah said.

"I will get the tincture of chamomile and lavender from my bag," Ayotunde said. "She need the help."

Mary let out a guttural groan. "Oh, heavens. The child be on its way."

Sarah leapt off the bed and peeked under the blanket. "Ayotunde," she shouted. "'Tis too late for your remedy. Come quick."

Mary's moan was now a full-on scream. Ayotunde ran back to help hold the blanket and join Sarah in assisting the birth.

"Push, Mary," Sarah said. "The child is crowning."

Mary let out an awful yelp as the head broke through her skin, and blood trickled onto the bed.

"Miss Sarah," Ayotunde said near her ear. "I know of yet another way to assist."

Sarah shook her head, wary of the potential consequences of Ayotunde's offer. "It is almost there," she said to Mary. "You must push harder."

"I haven't the strength. Please. A Rest."

Ayotunde dabbed Mary's head with a compress.

"I see a shoulder," Sarah said. "Another good, strong push will birth the child."

As Mary lay writhing, gasping, Sarah and Ayotunde exchanged looks of grave concern.

Unable to bear her sister's agony any longer, Sarah gave Ayotunde a nod. When Ayotunde lifted her hand off Mary's compress, Sarah positioned herself with both hands firmly under the infant's head. After a quick flourish of Ayotunde's arm, the rest of the baby slid out almost as though it were fired from a musket.

Sarah swept up the baby, cleared its mouth, and gave it a swift slap on its backside. When the roar of the infant's cry filled the room, she smiled at her sister. "God giveth you your girl, Mary. And she be a hearty one."

Mary whimpered with joy as she struggled up on her elbows to glimpse her daughter. Sarah wrapped the child in a clean cloth and laid her on her sister's chest. Mary wept as she kissed her infant daughter's head.

Sarah led Ayotunde aside and whispered, "She is the one from which Hazel shall come forth."

Ayotunde returned Sarah's smile. "We will watch over this child and make sure of it."

"Aye. And each other," she added as she studied Ayotunde's beautiful, smiling face. She turned to her sister, still fawning over the baby. "I'll summon Jacob and the boys."

Sarah and Ayotunde left Mary and her family to their privacy. As they prepared to head home, Sarah unwound the horse's bridle and led him to the water trough. Ayotunde gathered a few apples from the ground under a tree and fed the horse before they began the journey back to their homestead.

When Sarah and Ayotunde had returned to Salem Village through the portal, they'd arrived in the same place from which they'd originally fled but precisely one year later. By then, the witch hysteria and ensuing legal trials had been over for months, the final one occurring in May of 1693. When they'd awoken together on the straw-lined floor, the cell, still fetid and covered in filth, was empty.

They walked freely out of the jail into the early summer sunlight and made their way on foot to the homestead Sarah shared with her husband, Thomas.

They discovered it abandoned and overgrown. What little

livestock they'd owned were gone, either wondered off or stolen during the height of the hysteria. Sarah had instructed Ayotunde to stay behind as she ventured into town to inquire about her husband, assuming he'd found another wife in Sarah's long absence. But Thomas had not replaced her with another woman—he'd met an untimely demise after receiving a blow to the head trying to fight for Sarah's release from jail.

Once the shock had subsided, Sarah leaned against a fence post in town and wept for Thomas, a good man who had given her everything he was capable of. With no male heirs, the modest acreage he'd owned reverted to Sarah. And since Sarah's brother had owned Ayotunde, he'd allowed her to stay with Sarah to "help her around the homestead."

Thus, Sarah and Ayotunde lived together in relative peace and happiness. Since they'd given up going to church, they only dealt with town folk at the market to sell vegetables, eggs, cheeses, and other foodstuffs they made together on the farm. But they weren't always alone; many of the town's misfits who hadn't felt they'd belonged among Salem's wealthy or blindly devout had befriended them and would visit their home during the warmer seasons.

Many years later, when Ayotunde, in her sixties, took ill during a particularly harsh winter, Sarah made peace with the doctor's prediction that the end of their earthly journey together was nigh.

"My love," Sarah whispered as she cradled Ayotunde's limp hand. "Thank you for bringing such joy into my bleak, dank world here in Salem Village. You reside in my heart forever, and I know not how I will go on without you."

Sarah's deep sadness escaped down her cheeks, the droplets splashing on the back of Ayotunde's hand.

Ayotunde pried open her eyes, and with a rattle in her chest, she said, "Our separation be not long, my Sarah. Do you remember New Orleans many years agone?"

"Aye." Sarah smiled, remembering well the delight that had filled her when Ayotunde had come walking around Marie Laveau's tomb.

"'Twas a binding spell, Sarah. Even death cannot separate us. Our souls be bound together for eternity."

"Pray, let it be so," Sarah said and kissed her lover's forehead.

"You will see, my love." Ayotunde's voice grew small and quiet.

"It is so." With a last deep gasp of breath, her head fell deep into the pillow as the life departed her body.

It was not long after Ayotunde had been laid to rest that Sarah, in her despondency, lay down in their bed, closed her eyes, and succumbed to a heart that refused to beat more.

About the Authors

JEAN COPELAND is an-award winning author from Connecticut. Her novel *The Revelation of Beatrice Darby* won an Alice B Readers Lavender Certificate and a Goldie award for debut author. Her second novel, *The Second Wave*, received a Rainbow Awards honorable mention.

When not writing novels or teaching English at an alternative high school, Jean enjoys blogging, chatting it up with women on *The Weekly Wine Down* podcast, and visiting local breweries. Women's and LGBTQ rights as well as shelter animal adoption are causes dear to her. Look for her contemporary romance, *One Woman's Treasure*, coming July 2020.

JACKIE D was born and raised in the San Francisco, East Bay Area of California. She lives with her wife, son, and their numerous furry companions. She earned a bachelor's degree in recreation administration and a dual master's degree in management and public administration. She is a Navy veteran and served in Operation Iraqi Freedom as a flight deck director, onboard the USS *Abraham Lincoln*. She spends her free time with her wife, friends, family, and their incredibly needy dogs. She enjoys playing golf but is resigned to the fact she would equally enjoy any sport where drinking beer is encouraged during game play. Her first book, *Infiltration*, was a finalist for a Lambda Literary Award, and *Lucy's Chance* won a Goldie in 2018.

Books Available From Bold Strokes Books

Flight to the Horizon by Julie Tizard. Airline captain Kerri Sullivan and flight attendant Janine Case struggle to survive an emergency water landing and overcome dark secrets to give love a chance to fly. (978-1-63555-331-4)

In Helen's Hands by Nanisi Barrett D'Arnuk. As her mistress, Helen pushes Mickey to her sensual limits, delivering the pleasure only a BDSM lifestyle can provide her. (978-1-63555-639-1)

Jamis Bachman, Ghost Hunter by Jen Jensen. In Sage Creek, Utah, a poltergeist stirs to life and past secrets emerge.(978-1-63555-605-6)

Moon Shadow by Suzie Clarke. Add betrayal, season with survival, then serve revenge smokin' hot with a sharp knife. (978-1-63555-584-4)

Spellbound by Jean Copeland and Jackie D. When the supernatural worlds of good and evil face off, love might be what saves them all. (978-1-63555-564-6)

Temptation by Kris Bryant. Can experienced nanny Cassie Miller deny her growing attraction and keep her relationship with her boss professional? Or will they sidestep propriety and give in to temptation? (978-1-63555-508-0)

The Inheritance by Ali Vali. Family ties bring Tucker Delacroix and Willow Vernon together, but they could also tear them, and any chance they have at love, apart. (978-1-63555-303-1)

Thief of the Heart by MJ Williamz. Kit Hanson makes a living seducing rich women in casinos and relieving them of the expensive jewelry most won't even miss. But her streak ends when she meets beautiful FBI agent Savannah Brown. (978-1-63555-572-1)

Face Off by PJ Trebelhorn. Hockey player Savannah Wells rarely spends more than a night with any one woman, but when photographer Madison Scott buys the house next door, she's forced to rethink what she expects out of life. (978-1-63555-480-9)

Hot Ice by Aurora Rey, Elle Spencer, and Erin Zak. Can falling in love melt the hearts of the iciest ice queens? Join Aurora Rey, Elle Spencer, and Erin Zak to find out! A contemporary romance novella collection. (978-1-63555-513-4)

Line of Duty by VK Powell. Dr. Dylan Carlyle's professional and personal life is turned upside down when a tragic event at Fairview Station pits her against ambitious, handsome police officer Finley Masters. ((978-1-63555-486-1)

London Undone by Nan Higgins. London Craft reinvents her life after reading a childhood letter to her future self and, in doing so, finds the love she truly wants. (978-1-63555-562-2)

Lunar Eclipse by Gun Brooke. Moon De Cruz lives alone on an uninhabited planet after being shipwrecked in space. Her life changes forever when Captain Beaux Lestarion's arrival threatens the planet and Moon's freedom. (978-1-63555-460-1)

One Small Step by MA Binfield. In this contemporary romance, Iris and Cam discover the meaning of taking chances and following your heart, even if it means getting hurt. (978-1-63555-596-7)

Shadows of a Dream by Nicole Disney. Rainn has the talent to take her rock band all the way, but falling in love is a powerful distraction, and her new girlfriend's meth addiction might just take them both down. 978-1-63555-598-1)

Someone to Love by Jenny Frame. When Davina Trent is given an unexpected family, can she let nanny Wendy Darling teach her to open her heart to the children and to Wendy? (978-1-63555-468-7)

Uncharted by Robyn Nyx. As Rayne Marcellus and Chase Stinsen track the legendary Golden Trinity, they must learn to put their differences aside and depend on one another to survive. (978-1-63555-325-3)

Where We Are by Annie McDonald. A sensual account of two women who discover a way to walk on the same path together with the help of an Indigenous tale, a Canadian art movement, and the mysterious appearance of dimes. (978-1-63555-581-3)

A Moment in Time by Lisa Moreau. A longstanding family feud separates two women who unexpectedly fall in love at an antique clock shop in a small Louisiana town. (978-1-63555-419-9)

Aspen in Moonlight by Kelly Wacker. When art historian Melissa Warren meets Sula Johansen, director of a local bear conservancy, she discovers that love can come in unexpected and unusual forms. (978-1-63555-470-0)

Back to September by Melissa Brayden. Small bookshop owner Hannah Shepard and famous romance novelist Parker Bristow maneuver the landscape of their two very different worlds to find out if love can win out in the end. (978-1-63555-576-9)

Changing Course by Brey Willows. When the woman of her dreams falls from the sky, intergalactic space captain Jessa Arbelle had better be ready to catch her. (978-1-63555-335-2)

Cost of Honor by Radclyffe. First Daughter Blair Powell and Homeland Security Director Cameron Roberts face adversity when their enemies stop at nothing to prevent President Andrew Powell's reelection. Book 11 in the Honor series. (978-1-63555-582-0)

Fearless by Tina Michele. Determined to overcome her debilitating fear through exposure therapy, Laura Carter all but fails before she's even begun until dolphin trainer Jillian Marshall dedicates herself to helping Laura defeat the nightmares of her past. (978-1-63555-495-3)

Not Dead Enough by J.M. Redmann. In the tenth book of the Micky Knight mystery series, a woman who may or may not be dead drags Micky into a messy con game. (978-1-63555-543-1)

Not Since You by Fiona Riley. When Charlotte boards her honeymoon cruise single and comes face-to-face with Lexi, the high school love she left behind, she questions every decision she has ever made. (978-1-63555-474-8)

Tennessee Whiskey by Donna K. Ford. After losing her job, Dane Foster starts spiraling out of control. She wants to put her life on pause and ask for a redo, a chance for something that matters. Emma Reynolds is that chance. (978-1-63555-556-1)